ANTHONY TROLLOPE

AYALA'S ANGEL

VOLUME 3

Elibron Classics
www.elibron.com

Elibron Classics series.

ISBN 1-4021-6915-9 (paperback)
ISBN 1-4021-2974-2 (hardcover)

This Elibron Classics Replica Edition is an unabridged facsimile of the edition published in 1881 by Bernhard Tauchnitz, Leipzig.

COLLECTION
OF
BRITISH AUTHORS

TAUCHNITZ EDITION.

VOL. 2003.

AYALA'S ANGEL BY ANTHONY TROLLOPE.

IN THREE VOLUMES.

VOL. III.

AYALA'S ANGEL

BY

ANTHONY TROLLOPE,

AUTHOR OF

"DOCTOR THORNE," "THE PRIME MINISTER," "ORLEY FARM,"

ETC. ETC.

COPYRIGHT EDITION.

IN THREE VOLUMES.

VOL. III.

LEIPZIG

BERNHARD TAUCHNITZ

1881.

CONTENTS

OF VOLUME III.

			Page
CHAPTER	I.	In the Haymarket	7
—	II.	There is something of the Angel about him	20
—	III.	Ayala goes again to Stalham	33
—	IV.	Captain Batsby at Merle Park	47
—	V.	The Journey to Ostend	61
—	VI.	The new Frock	75
—	VII.	Gobblegoose Wood on Sunday	89
—	VIII.	"No!"	103
—	IX.	"I call it Folly"	116
—	X.	How Lucy's Affairs arranged themselves	128
—	XI.	Tom's last Attempt	141
—	XII.	In the Castle there lived a Knight	154
—	XIII.	Gobblegoose Wood again	167
—	XIV.	Captain Batsby in Lombard Street	181
—	XV.	Mr. Traffick in Lombard Street	195
—	XVI.	Tregothnan	209
—	XVII.	Aunt Rosina	223

			Page
CHAPTER	XVIII.	Tom Tringle goes upon his Travels . .	237
—	XIX.	How very much he loved Her	250
—	XX.	Ayala again in London	264
—	XXI.	Ayala's Marriage	278

AYALA'S ANGEL.

CHAPTER I.

IN THE HAYMARKET.

It was now the beginning of February. As Tom and his uncle had walked from Somerset House the streets were dry and the weather fine; but, as Mr. Dosett had remarked, the wind was changing a little out of the east and threatened rain. When Tom left the house it was already falling. It was then past six, and the night was very dark. He had walked there with a top coat and umbrella, but he had forgotten both as he banged the door after him in his passion; and, though he remembered them as he hurried down the steps, he would not turn and knock at the door and ask for them. He was in that humour which converts outward bodily sufferings almost into a relief. When a man has been thoroughly ill-used in greater matters it is almost a consolation to him to feel that he has been turned out into the street to get wet through without his dinner,—even though he may have turned himself out.

He walked on foot, and as he walked became damp and dirty, till he was soon wet through. As soon as he reached Lancaster Gate he went into the park, and under the doubtful glimmer of the lamps trudged on through the mud and slush, not regarding his path, hardly thinking of the present moment in the full appreciation of his real misery. What should he do with himself? What else was there now left to him? He had tried everything and had failed. As he endeavoured to count himself up, as it were, and tell himself whether he were worthy of a happier fate than had been awarded to him, he was very humble,—humble, though so indignant! He knew himself to be a poor creature in comparison with Jonathan Stubbs. Though he could not have been Stubbs had he given his heart for it, though it was absolutely beyond him to assume one of those tricks of bearing, one of those manly, winning ways, which in his eyes was so excellent in the other man, still he saw them and acknowledged them, and told himself that they would be all powerful with such a girl as Ayala. Though he trusted to his charms and his rings, he knew that his charms and his rings were abominable, as compared with that outside look and natural garniture which belonged to Stubbs, as though of right,—as though it had been born with him. Not exactly in those words, but with a full inward sense of the words, he told himself that Colonel Stubbs was a gentleman,—whereas he acknowledged himself to be a cad. How could he have hoped that Ayala should accept such a one, merely because he would have a good house of his own and a carriage? As he thought of all this, he hardly knew which he hated most,—himself or Jonathan Stubbs.

He went down to the family house in Queen's Gate, which was closed and dark,—having come there with no special purpose, but having found himself there, as though by accident, in the neighbourhood. Then he knocked at the door, which, after a great undoing of chains, was opened by an old woman, who with her son had the custody of the house when the family were out of town. Sir Thomas in these days had rooms of his own in Lombard Street in which he loved to dwell, and would dine at a city club, never leaving the precincts of the city throughout the week. The old woman was an old servant, and her son was a porter at the office. "Mr. Tom! Be that you? Why you are as wet as a mop!" He was wet as any mop, and much dirtier than a mop should be. There was no fire except in the kitchen, and there he was taken. He asked for a great coat, but there was no such thing in the house, as the young man had not yet come home. Nor was there any food that could be offered him, or anything to drink; as the cellar was locked up, and the old woman was on board wages. But he sat crouching over the fire, watching the steam as it came up from his damp boots and trousers. "And ain't you had no dinner, Mr. Tom?" said the old woman. Tom only shook his head. "And ain't you going to have none?" The poor wretch again shook his head. "That's bad, Mr. Tom." Then she looked up into his face. "There is something wrong I know, Mr. Tom. I hears that from Jem. Of course he hears what they do be saying in Lombard Street."

"What is it they say, Mrs. Tapp?"

"Well;—that you ain't there as you used to be. Things is awk'ard, and Sir Thomas, they say, isn't best pleased. But of course it isn't no affair of mine, Mr. Tom."

"Do they know why?" he asked.

"They do say it's some'at about a young lady."

"Yes; by heavens!" said Tom, jumping up out of his chair. "Oh, Mrs. Tapp, you can't tell the condition I'm in. A young lady indeed! D—— the fellow!"

"Don't 'ee now, Mr. Tom."

"D—— the fellow! But there's no good in my standing here cursing. I'll go off again. You needn't say that I've been here, Mrs. Tapp?"

"But you won't go out into the rain, Mr. Tom?"

"Rain,—what matters the rain?" Then he started again, disregarding all her prayers, and went off eastward on foot, disdaining the use of a cab because he had settled in his mind on no place to which he would go.

Yes; they knew all about it, down to the very porters at the office. Everyone had heard of his love for Ayala; and everyone had heard also that Ayala had scorned him. Not a man or woman connected by ever so slight a tie to the establishment was unaware that he had been sent away from his seat because of Ayala! All this might have been borne easily had there been any hope;

but now he was forced to tell himself that there was none. He saw no end to his misery,—no possibility of escape. Where was he to go in this moment of his misery for any shred of comfort? The solitude of his lodgings was dreadful to him; nor had he heart enough left to him to seek companionship at his club.

At about ten o'clock he found himself, as it were, by accident, close to Mr. Bolivia's establishment. He was thoroughly wet through, jaded, wretched, and in want of sustenance. He turned in, and found the place deserted. The diners had gone away, and the hour had not come at which men in quest of later refreshment were wont to make their appearance. But there were still one or two gas-lights burning; and he threw himself wearily into a little box or partition nearest to the fire. Here Signor Bolivia himself came to him, asking in commiserating accents what had brought him thither in so wretched a plight. "I have left my coat and umbrella behind," said Tom, trying to pluck up a little spirit,—"and my dinner too."

"No dinner, Mr. Tringle; and you wet through like that! What shall I get you, Mr. Tringle?" But Tom declared that he would have no dinner. He was off his appetite altogether, he said. He would have a bottle of champagne and a devilled biscuit. Mr. Walker, who, as we are aware, put himself forward to the world generally as Signor Bolivia, felt for the moment a throb of pity, which overcame in his heart the innkeeper's natural desire to make the most he could of his customer. "Better have a mutton chop and a little drop of brandy-and-water hot."

"I ain't up to it, Bolivia," said the young man. "I couldn't swallow it if I had it. Give us the bottle of champagne and the devilled biscuit." Then Mr. Walker,—for Bolivia was in truth Walker,—fetched the wine and ordered the biscuit; and poor Tom was again brought back to the miserable remedy to which he had before applied himself in his misfortune. There he remained for about an hour, during a part of which he slept; but before he left the house he finished the wine. As he got up to take his departure Mr. Walker scanned his gait and bearing, having a friendly feeling for the young man, and not wishing him to fall again into the hands of the police. But Tom walked forth apparently as sober as a judge, and as melancholy as a hangman. As far as Mr. Walker could see the liquor had made no impression on him. "If I were you, Mr. Tringle," said the keeper of the eating-house, "I'd go home at once, because you are so mortal wet."

"All right," said Tom, going out into the pouring rain.

It was then something after eleven, and Tom instead of taking the friendly advice which had been offered to him, walked, as fast as he could, round Leicester Square; and as he walked the fumes of the wine mounted into his head. But he was not drunk,—not as yet so drunk as to misbehave himself openly. He did not make his way round the square without being addressed, but he simply shook off from him those who spoke to him. His mind was still intent upon Ayala. But now he was revengeful rather than despondent. The liquor had filled him once again with a desire to do something. If he could destroy himself and the Colonel by one and the same blow, how fitting a punishment would that be for Ayala! But how was he to do it? He would throw himself down from the top of the Duke of York's column, but that would be nothing unless he could force the Colonel to take the jump with him! He had called the man out and he wouldn't come! Now, with the alcohol in his brain, he again thought that the man was a coward for not coming. Had not such a meeting been from time immemorial the resource of gentlemen injured as he now was injured? The Colonel would not come when called, —but could he not get at him so as to strike him? If he could do the man a real injury he would not care what amount of punishment he might be called upon to bear.

He hurried at last out of the square into Coventry Street and down the Haymarket. His lodgings were in Duke Street, turning out of Piccadilly,—but he could not bring himself to go home to his bed. He was unutterably wretched, but yet he kept himself going with some idea of doing something, or of fixing some purpose. He certainly was tipsy now, but not so drunk as to be unable to keep himself on his legs. He gloried in the wet, shouting inwardly to himself that he in his misery was superior to all accidents of the weather. Then he stood for awhile watching the people as they came out of the Haymarket Theatre. He was at this time a sorry sight to be seen. His hat was jammed on to his head and had been almost smashed in the jamming. His coat reeking wet through was fastened by one button across his chest. His two hands were thrust into his pockets, and the bottle of champagne was visible in his face. He was such a one,—to look at,—that no woman would have liked to touch or any man to address. In this guise he stood there amidst the crowd, foremost among those who were watching the ladies as they got into their vehicles. "And she might be as good as the best of them, and I might be here to hand her into her own carriage,"—said he to himself,—"if it were not for that intruder!"

At that moment the intruder was there before him, and on his arm was a lady whom he was taking across to a carriage, at the door of which a servant in livery was standing. They were followed closely by a pretty young girl who was picking her steps after them alone. These were Lady Albury and Nina, whom Colonel Stubbs had escorted to the play.

"You will be down by the twentieth?" said the elder lady.

"Punctual as the day comes," said the Colonel.

"And mind you have Ayala with you," said the younger.

"If Lady Albury can manage it with her aunt of course I will wait upon her," said the Colonel. Then the door of the carriage was shut, and the Colonel was left to look for a cab. He had on an overcoat and an opera hat, but otherwise was dressed as for dinner. On one side a link-boy was offering him assistance, and on another a policeman tendering him some service. He was one of those who by their outward appearance always extort respect from those around them.

As long as the ladies had been there,—during the two minutes which had been occupied while they got into the carriage,—Tom had been restrained by their presence. He had been restrained by their presence even though he had heard Ayala's name and had understood the commission given to the man whom he hated. Had Colonel Stubbs luckily followed the ladies into the carriage Tom, in his fury, would have taken himself off to his bed. But now,—there was his enemy within a yard of him! Here was the opportunity the lack of which seemed, a few moments since, to be so grievous to him! He took two steps out from the row in which he stood and struck his rival high on his breast with his fist. He had aimed at the Colonel's face but in his eagerness had missed his mark. "There," said he, "there! You would not fight me, and now you have got it." Stubbs staggered, and would have fallen but for the policeman. Tom, though no hero, was a strong young man, and had contrived to give his blow with all his force. The Colonel did not at first see from whom the outrage had come, but at once claimed the policeman's help.

"We've got him, Sir;—we've got him," said the policeman.

"You've got me," said Tom, "but I've had my revenge." Then, though two policemen and one waterman were now holding him, he stretched himself up to his full height and glared at his enemy in the face.

"It's the chap who gave that hawful blow to Thompson in the bow'ls!" said one of the policemen, who by this time had both Tom's arms locked behind his own.

Then the Colonel knew who had struck him. "I know him," said the Colonel to the policeman. "It is a matter of no consequence."

"So do we, Sir. He's Thomas Tringle, junior."

"He's a friend of mine," said the Colonel. "You must let him come with me."

"A friend, is he?" said an amateur attendant. The policeman, who had remembered the cruel onslaught made on his comrade, looked very grave, and still held Tom tight by the arms. "A very hugly sort of friend," said the amateur. Tom only stretched himself still higher, but remained speechless.

"Tringle," said the Colonel, "this was very foolish, you know,—a most absurd thing to do! Come with me, and we will talk it all over."

"He must come along with us to the watch-house just at present," said the policeman. "And you, Sir, if you can, had better please to come with us. It ain't far across to Vine Street, but of course you can have a cab if you like it." This was ended by two policemen walking off with Tom between them, and by the Colonel following in a cab, after having administered divers shillings to the amateur attendants. Though the journey in the cab did not occupy above five minutes, it sufficed to enable him to determine what step he should take when he found himself before the night officers of the watch.

When he found himself in the presence of the night officer he had considerable difficulty in carrying out his purpose. That Tom should be locked up for the night, and be brought before the police magistrate next morning to answer for the outrage he had committed, seemed to the officers to be a matter of course. It was long before the Colonel could persuade the officer that this little matter between him and Mr. Tringle was a private affair, of which he at least wished to take no further notice. "No doubt," he said, "he had received a blow on his chest, but it had not hurt him in the least."

"'E 'it the gen'leman with all his might and main," said the policeman.

"It is quite a private affair," said the Colonel. "My name is Colonel Stubbs; here is my card. Sir —— is a particular friend of mine." Here he named a pundit of the peace, very high in the estimation of all policemen. "If you will let the gentleman come away with me I will be responsible for him to-morrow, if it should be necessary to take any further step in the matter." This he said very eagerly, and with all the authority which he knew how to use. Tom, in the meantime, stood perfectly motionless, with his arms folded akimbo on his breast, wet through, muddy, still tipsy, a sight miserable to behold.

The card and the Colonel's own name, and the name of the pundit of the peace together, had their effect, and after a while Tom was dismissed in the Colonel's care. The conclusion of the evening's affair was, for the moment, one which Tom found very hard to bear. It would have been better for him to have been dragged off to a cell, and there to have been left to his miserable solitude. But as he went down through the narrow ways leading from the police-office out into the main street he felt that he was altogether debarred from making any further attack upon his protector. He could not strike him again, as he might have done had he escaped from the police by his own resources. His own enemy had saved him from durance, and he could not, therefore, turn again upon his enemy.

"In heaven's name, my dear fellow," said the Colonel, "what good do you expect to get by that? You have hit me a blow when you knew that I was unprepared, and, therefore, unarmed. Was that manly?" To this Tom made no reply. "I suppose you have been drinking?" And Stubbs, as he asked this question, looked into his companion's face. "I see you have been drinking. What a fool you are making of yourself!"

"It is that girl," said Tom.

"Does that seem to you to be right? Can you do yourself any good by that? Will she be more likely to listen to you when she hears that you have got drunk, and have assaulted me in the street? Have I done you any harm?"

"She says that you are better than me," replied Tom.

"If she does, is that my doing? Come, old fellow, try to be a man. Try to think of this thing rightly. If you can win the girl you love, win her; but, if you cannot, do not be such an ass as to suppose that she is to love no one because she will not love you. It is a thing which a man must bear if it comes in his way. As far as Miss Dormer is concerned, I am in the same condition as you. But do you think that I should attack you in the street if she began to favour you to-morrow?"

"I wish she would; and then I shouldn't care what you did."

"I should think you a happy fellow, certainly; and for a time I might avoid you, because your happiness would remind me of my own disappointment; but I should not come behind your back and strike you! Now, tell me where you live, and I will see you home." Then Tom told him where he lived, and in a few minutes the Colonel had left him within his own hall door.

CHAPTER II.

THERE IS SOMETHING OF THE ANGEL ABOUT HIM.

THE little accident which was recorded at the close of the last chapter occurred on a Tuesday night. On the following afternoon Tom Tringle, again very much out of spirits, returned to Merle Park. There was now nothing further for him to do in London. He had had his last chance with Ayala, and the last chance had certainly done him no good. Fortune, whether kindly or unkindly, had given him an opportunity of revenging himself upon the Colonel; he had taken advantage of the opportunity, but did not find himself much relieved by what he had done. His rival's conduct had caused him to be thoroughly ashamed of himself. It had at any rate taken from him all further hope of revenge. So that now there was nothing for him but to take himself back to Merle Park. On the Wednesday he heard nothing further of the matter; but on the Thursday Sir Thomas came down from London, and, showing to poor Tom a paragraph in one of the morning papers, asked whether he knew anything of the circumstance to which reference was made. The paragraph was as follows:—

"That very bellicose young City knight who at Christmas time got into trouble by thrashing a policeman within an inch of his life in the streets, and who was then incarcerated on account of his performance, again exhibited his prowess on Tuesday night by attacking Colonel ——, an officer than whom none in the army is more popular,—under the portico of the Haymarket theatre. We abstain from mentioning the officer's name,—which is, however, known to us. The City knight again fell into the hands of the police and was taken to the watch-house. But Colonel ——, who knew something of his family, accompanied him, and begged his assailant off. The officer on duty was most unwilling to let the culprit go; but the Colonel used all his influence and was successful. This may be all very well between the generous Colonel and the valiant knight. But if the young man has any friends they had better look to him. A gentleman with such a desire for the glories of battle must be restrained if he cannot control his propensities when wandering about the streets of the metropolis."

"Yes," said Tom,—who scorned to tell a lie in any matter concerning Ayala. "It was me. I struck Colonel Stubbs, and he got me off at the police office."

"And you're proud of what you've done?"

"No, Sir, I'm not. I'm not proud of anything. Whatever I do or whatever I say seems to go against me."

"He didn't go against you as you call it."

"I wish he had with all my heart. I didn't ask him to get me off. I struck him because I hated him; and whatever might have happened I would sooner have borne it than be like this."

"You would sooner have been locked up again in prison?"

"I would sooner anything than be as I am."

"I tell you what it is, Tom," said the father. "If you remain here any longer with this bee in your bonnet you will be locked up in a lunatic asylum, and I shall not be able to get you out again. You must go abroad." To this Tom made no immediate answer. Lamentable as was his position, he still was unwilling to leave London while Ayala was living there. Were he to consent to go away for any lengthened period, by doing so he would seem to abandon his own claim. Hope he knew there was none; but yet, even yet, he regarded himself as one of Ayala's suitors. "Do you think it well," continued the father, "that you should remain in London while such paragraphs as these are being written about you?"

"I am not in London now," said Tom.

"No, you are not in London while you are at Merle Park,—of course. And you will not go up to London without my leave. Do you understand that?" Here Tom again was silent. "If you do," continued his father, "you shall not be received down here again, nor at Queen's Gate, nor will the cheques for your allowance be honoured any longer at the bank. In fact if you do not obey me I will throw you off altogether. This absurdity about your love has been carried on long enough." And so it came to be understood in the family that Tom was to be kept in mild durance at Merle Park till everything should have been arranged for his extended tour about the world. To this Tom himself gave no positive assent, but is was understood that when the time came he would yield to his father's commands.

It had thus come to pass that the affray at the door of the Haymarket became known to so much of the world at large as interested itself in the affairs either of Colonel Stubbs or of the Tringles. Other paragraphs were written in which the two heroes of the evening were designated as Colonel J—— S—— and as T—— T——, junior, of the firm of T—— and T——, in the City. All who pleased could read these initials, and thus the world was aware that our Colonel had received a blow, and had resented the affront only by rescuing his assailant from the hands of the police. A word was said at first which seemed to imply that the Colonel had not exhibited all the spirit which might have been expected from him. Having been struck should he not have thrashed the man who struck him;—or at any rate have left the ruffian in the hands of the policemen for proper punishment? But many days had not passed over before the Colonel's conduct had been viewed in a different light, and men and women were declaring that he had done a manly and a gallant thing. The affair had in this way become sufficiently well known to justify the allusion made to it in the following letter from Lady Albury to Ayala;—

"Stalham, Tuesday, 11th February, 18—.

"MY DEAR AYALA,

"It is quite indispensable for the happiness of everybody, particularly that of myself and Sir Harry, that you should come down here on the twentieth. Nina will be here on her farewell visit before her return to her mother. Of course you have heard that it is all arranged between her and Lord George Bideford, and this will be the last opportunity which any of us will have of seeing her once again before her martyrdom. The world is to be told that he is to follow her to Rome, where they are to be married,—no doubt by the Pope himself under the dome of St. Peter's. But my belief is that Lord George is going to travel with her all the way. If he is the man I take him to be he will do so, but of course it would be very improper.

"You, however, must of course come and say pretty things to your friend; and, as you cannot go to Rome to see her married, you must throw your old shoe after her when she takes her departure from Stalham. I have written a line to your aunt to press my request for this visit. This she will no doubt show to you, and you, if you please, can show her mine in return.

"And now, my dear, I must explain to you one or two other arrangements. A certain gentleman will *certainly* not be here. It was not my fault that a certain gentleman went to Kingsbury Crescent. The certain gentleman is, as you are aware, a great friend of ours, and was entitled to explain himself if it so seemed good to him; but the certain gentleman was not favoured in that enterprise by the Stalham interest. At any rate, the certain gentleman will not be at Stalham on this occasion. So much for the certain gentleman.

"Colonel Stubbs will be here, and, as he will be coming down on the twentieth, would be glad to travel by the same train, so that he may look after your ticket and your luggage, and be your slave for the occasion. He will leave the Paddington Station by the 4 P.M. train if that will suit you.

"We all think that he behaved beautifully in that little affair at the Haymarket theatre. I should not mention it only that everybody has heard of it. Almost any other man would have struck the poor fellow again; but he is one of the very few who always know what to do at the moment without taking time to think of it.

"Mind you come like a good girl.—Your affectionate friend,

"ROSALINE ALBURY."

It was in this way that Ayala heard what had taken place between her cousin Tom and Colonel Stubbs. Some hint of a fracas between the two men had reached her ears; but now she asked various questions of her aunt, and at last elicited the truth. Tom had attacked her other lover in the street,—had attacked Colonel Stubbs because of his injured love, and had grossly misbehaved himself. As a consequence he would have been locked up by the police had not the Colonel himself interfered on his behalf. This to Ayala seemed to be conduct worthy almost of an Angel of Light.

Then the question of the proposed visit was discussed,—first with her aunt, and then with herself. Mrs. Dosett was quite willing that her niece should go to Stalham. To Mrs. Dosett's thinking, a further journey to Stalham would mean an engagement with Colonel Stubbs. When she had read Lady Albury's letter she was quite sure that that had been Lady Albury's meaning. Captain Batsby was not to receive the Stalham interest;—but that interest was to be used on the part of Colonel Stubbs. She had not the slightest objection. It was clear to her that Ayala would have to be married before long. It was out of the question that one man after another should fall in love with her violently, and that nothing should come of it. Mrs. Dosett had become quite despondent about Tom. There was an amount of dislike which it would be impossible to overcome. And as for Captain Batsby there could be no chance for a man whom the young lady could not be induced even to see. But the other lover, whom the lady would not admit that she loved,—as to whom she had declared that she could never love him,—was held in very high favour. "I do think it was so noble not to hit Tom again," she had said. Therefore, as Colonel Stubbs had a sufficient income, there could be no reason why Ayala should not go again to Stalham. So it was that Mrs. Dosett argued with herself, and such was the judgment which she expressed to Ayala.

But there were difficulties. Ayala's little stock

of cash was all gone. She could not go to Stalham without money, and that money must come out of her Uncle Reginald's pocket. She could not go to Stalham without some expenditure, which, as she well knew, it would be hard for him to bear. And then there was that terrible question of her clothes! When that suggestion had been made of a further transfer of the nieces a cheque had come from Sir Thomas. "If Ayala comes to us she will want a few things," Sir Thomas had said in a note to Mrs. Dosett. But Mr. Dosett had chosen that the cheque should be sent back when it was decided that the further transfer should not take place. The cheque had been sent back, and there had been an end of it. There must be a morning dress, and there must be another hat, and there must be boots. So much Mrs. Dosett acknowledged. Let them do what they might with the old things, Mrs. Dosett acknowledged that so much as that would at least be necessary. "We will both go to work," Mrs. Dosett said, "and we will ask your uncle what he can do for us." I think she felt that she had received some recompense when Ayala kissed her.

It was after this that Ayala discussed the matter with herself. She had longed to go once again to Stalham,—"dear Stalham," as she called it to herself. And as she thought of the place she told herself that she loved it because Lady Albury had been so kind to her, and because of Nina, and because of the hunting, and because of the general pleasantness and luxury of the big comfortable house. And yes; there was something to be said, too, of the pleasantness of Colonel Stubbs. Till he had made love to her he had been, perhaps, of all these fine new friends the pleasantest. How joyous his voice had sounded to her! How fraught with gratification to her had been his bright ugly face! How well he had known how to talk to her, and to make her talk, so that everything had been easy with her! How thoroughly she remembered all his drollery on that first night at the party in London,—and all his keen sayings at the theatre;—and the way he had insisted that she should hunt! She thought of little confidences she had had with him, almost as though he had been her brother! And then he had destroyed it all by becoming her lover!

Was he to be her lover still; and if so would it be right that she should go again to Stalham, knowing that she would meet him there? Would it be right that she should consent to travel with him,—under his special escort? Were she to do so would she not be forced to do more,—if he should again ask her? It was so probable that he would not ask her again! It was so strange that such a one should have asked her!

But if he did ask her? Certainly he was not like that Angel of Light whom she had never seen, but of whom the picture in her imagination was as clearly drawn as though she were in his presence daily. No;—there was a wave of hair and a shape of brow, and a peculiarity of the eye, with a nose and mouth cut as sharp as chisel could cut them out of marble, all of which graced the Angel but none of which belonged to the Colonel. Nor were these the chief of the graces which made the Angel so glorious to her. There was a depth of poetry about him, deep and clear, pellucid as a lake among grassy banks, which make all things of the world mean when compared to it. The Angel of Light lived on the essence of all that was beautiful, altogether unalloyed by the grossness of the earth. That such a one should come in her way! Oh, no; she did not look for it! But, having formed such an image of an angel for herself, would it be possible that she should have anything less divine, less beautiful, less angelic?

Yes; there was something of the Angel about him; even about him, Colonel Jonathan Stubbs. But he was so clearly an Angel of the earth, whereas the other one, though living upon the earth, would be of the air, and of the sky, of the clouds, and of the heaven, celestial. Such a one she knew she had never seen. She partly dreamed that she was dreaming. But if so had not her dream spoilt her for all else? Oh, yes; indeed he was good, this red-haired ugly Stubbs. How well had he behaved to Tom! How kind he had been to herself! How thoughtful of her he was! If it were not a question of downright love, of giving herself up to him, body and soul, as it were—how pleasant would it be to dwell with him! For herself she would confess that she loved earthly things,—such as jumping over the brook with Larry Twentyman before her to show her the way. But for her love, it was necessary that there should be an Angel of Light. Had she not read that angels had come from heaven and taken in marriage the daughters of men?

But was it right that she should go to Stalham, seeing that there were two such reasons against it? She could not go without costing her uncle money, which he could ill afford; and if she did go would she—would she not confess that she had abandoned her objection to the Colonel's suit. She, too, understood something of that which had made itself so plain to her aunt. "Your uncle thinks it is right that you should go," her aunt said to her in the drawing-room that evening; "and we will set to work to-morrow and do the best that we can to make you smart."

Her uncle was sitting in the room at the time, and Ayala felt herself compelled to go to him and kiss him, and thank him for all his kindness. "I am so sorry to cost you so much money, Uncle Reginald," she said.

"It will not be very much, my dear," he answered. "It is hard that young people should not have some amusement. I only hope they will make you happy at Stalham."

"They always make people happy at Stalham," said Ayala, energetically.

"And now, Ayala," said her aunt, "you can write your letter to Lady Albury before we go out to-morrow. Give her my compliments, and tell her that as you are writing I need not trouble her."

Ayala, when she was alone in her bedroom, felt almost horrified as she reflected that in this manner the question had been settled for her. It had been impossible for her to reject her uncle's liberal offer when it had been made. She could not find the courage at that moment to say that she had thought better of it all, and would decline the visit. Before she was well aware of what she was doing she had assented, and had thus, as it were, thrown over all the creations of her dream. And yet, as she declared herself, not even Lady Albury could make her marry this man, merely because she was at her house. She thought that, if she could only avoid that first journey with Colonel Stubbs in the railway, still she might hold her own. But, were she to travel with him of her own accord, would it not be felt that she would be wilfully throwing herself in his way? Then she made a little plan for herself, which she attempted to carry out when writing her letter to Lady Albury on the following morning. What was the nature of her plan, and how she effected it, will be seen in the letter which she wrote;—

"Kingsbury Crescent, Thursday.

"Dear Lady Albury,

"It is so very good of you to ask me again, and I shall be so happy to visit Stalham once more! I should have been very sorry not to see dear Nina before her return to Italy. I have written to congratulate her of course, and have told her what a happy girl I think she is. Though I have not seen Lord George I take all that from her description. As she is going to be his wife immediately, I don't at all see why he should not go back with her to

Rome. As for being married by the Pope, I don't think he ever does anything so useful as that. I believe he sits all day and has his toe kissed. That is what they told me at Rome.

"I am very glad of what you tell me about the certain gentleman, because I don't think I could have been happy at Stalham if he had been there. It surprised me so much that I could not think that he meant it in earnest. We never hardly spoke to each other when we were in the house together.

"Perhaps, if you don't mind, and I shan't be in the way,"—here she began to display the little plan which she had made for her own protection,—"I will come down by an earlier train than you mention. There is one at 2.15, and then I need not be in the dark all the way. You need not say anything about this to Colonel Stubbs, because I do not at all mind travelling by myself.—Yours affectionately,

"AYALA."

This was her little plan. But she was very innocent when she thought that Lady Albury would be blind to such a scheme as that. She got three words from Lady Albury, saying that the 2.15 train would do very well, and that the carriage would be at the station to meet her. Lady Albury did not also say in her note that she had communicated with Colonel Stubbs on the subject, and informed him that he must come up from Aldershot earlier than he intended in order that he might adapt himself to Ayala's whims. "Foolish little child," said Lady Albury to herself! "As if that would make any difference!" It was clear to Lady Albury that Ayala must surrender now that she was coming to Stalham a second time, knowing that the Colonel would be there.

CHAPTER III.

AYALA GOES AGAIN TO STALHAM.

THE correspondence between Lady Albury and Colonel Stubbs was close and frequent, the friendship between them being very close. Ayala had sometimes asked herself why Lady Albury should have been so kind and affectionate to her, and had failed to find any sufficient answer. She had been asked to Stalham at first,—so far as she knew,—because she had been intimate at Rome with the Marchesa Baldoni. Hence had apparently risen Lady Albury's great friendship, which had seemed even to herself to be strange. But in truth the Marchesa had had very little to do with it,—nor had Lady Albury become attached to Ayala for Ayala's own sake. To Lady Albury Colonel Stubbs was,—as she declared to herself very often,—"her own real brother." She had married a man very rich, well known in the world, whom she loved very well; and she was not a woman who in such a position would allow herself to love another man. That there might certainly be no danger of this kind she was continually impressing on her friend the expediency of marriage,—if only he could find some one good enough to marry. Then the Colonel had found Ayala. Lady Albury at the beginning of all this was not inclined to think that Ayala was good enough. Judging at first from what she heard and then from what she saw, she had not been very favourable to Ayala. But when her friend had insisted,—had declared that his happiness depended on it,—had shown by various signs that he certainly would carry out his intentions, if not at Stalham then elsewhere, Lady Albury had yielded herself to him, and had become Ayala's great friend. If it was written in the book that Ayala was to become Mrs. Stubbs then it would certainly be necessary that she and Ayala should be friends. And she herself had such confidence in Jonathan Stubbs as a man of power, that she did not doubt of his success in any matter to which he might choose to devote himself. The wonder had been that Ayala should have rejected the chance when it had come in her way. The girl had been foolish, allowing herself to be influenced by the man's red hair and ill-sounding name,—not knowing a real pearl when she saw it. So Lady Albury had thought,—having only been partially right in so thinking,—not having gone to the depth of Ayala's power of dreaming. She was very confident, however, that the girl, when once again at Stalham, would yield herself easily; and therefore she went to work, doing all that she could to smoothen love's road for her friend Jonathan. Her woman's mind had seen all those difficulties about clothes, and would have sent what was needful herself had she not feared to offend both the Dosetts and Ayala. Therefore she prepared a present which she could give to the girl at Stalham without offence. If it was to be the girl's high fate to become Mrs. Jonathan Stubbs, it would be proper that she should be adorned and decked, and made beautiful among others of her class,—as would become the wife of such a hero.

Of all that passed between her and Ayala word was sent down to Aldershot. "The stupid little wretch will throw you out, I know," wrote Lady Albury, "by making you start two hours before you have done your work. But you must let your work do itself for this occasion. There is nothing like a little journey together to make people understand each other."

The Colonel was clearly determined to have the little journey together. Whatever might be the present military duties at Aldershot, the duties of love were for the nonce in the Colonel's mind more imperative. Though his Royal Highness had been coming that afternoon to inspect all the troops, still he would have resolved so to have arranged matters as to travel down with Ayala to Stalham. But not only was he determined to do this, but he found it necessary also to arrange a previous meeting with Lady Albury before that important twentieth of the month. This he did by making his friend believe that her presence in London for a few hours would be necessary for various reasons. She came up as he desired, and there he met her at her hotel in

Jermyn Street. On his arrival here he felt that he was almost making a fool of himself by the extent of his anxiety. In his nervousness about this little girl he was almost as insane as poor Tom Tringle, who, when she despised his love, was altogether unable to control himself. "If I cannot persuade her at last, I shall be knocking somebody over the head, as he did." It was thus he was talking to himself as he got out of the cab at the door of the hotel.

"And now, Jonathan," said Lady Albury, "what can there possibly be to justify you in giving me all this trouble?"

"You know you had to come up about that cook's character."

"I know that I have given that as a reason to Sir Harry; but I know also that I should have gone without a cook for a twelvemonth had you not summoned me."

"The truth is I could not get down to Stalham and back without losing an additional day, which I cannot possibly spare. With you it does not very much matter how many days you spare."

"Nor how much money I spend, nor how much labour I take, so that I obey all the commands of Colonel Jonathan Stubbs! What on earth is there that I can say or do for you more?"

"There are one or two things," said he, "that I want you to understand. In the first place, I am quite in earnest about this."

"Don't I know that you're in earnest?"

"But perhaps you do not understand the full

extent of my earnestness. If she were to refuse me ultimately I should go away."

"Go away! Go where?"

"Oh; that I have not at all thought of;—probably to India, as I might manage to get a regiment there. But in truth it would matter very little."

"You are talking like a goose."

"That is very likely, because in this matter I think and feel like a goose. It is not a great thing in a man to be turned out of his course by some undefined feeling which he has as to a young woman. But the thing has occurred before now, and will occur again, in my case, if I am thrown over."

"What on earth is there about the girl?" asked Lady Albury. "There is that precious brother-in-law of ours going to hang himself incontinently because she will not look at him. And that unfortunate friend of yours, Tom Tringle, is, if possible, worse than Ben Batsby or yourself."

"If two other gentlemen are in the same condition it only makes it the less singular that I should be the third. At any rate, I am the third."

"You do not mean to liken yourself to them?"

"Indeed I do. As to our connection with Miss Dormer, I can see no difference. We are all in love with her, and she has refused us all. It matters little whether a man's ugliness or his rings or his natural stupidity may have brought about this result."

"You are very modest, Jonathan."

"I always was, only you never could see it. I am modest in this matter; but not for that reason the less persistent in doing the best I can for myself. My object now in seeing you is to let you understand that it is—well, not life and death, because she will not suffice either to kill me or to keep me alive,—but one of those matters which, in a man's career, are almost as important to him as life and death. She was very decided in her refusal."

"So is every girl when a first offer is made to her. How is any girl so to arrange her thoughts at a moment's notice as to accept a man off-hand?"

"Girls do do so."

"Very rarely, I think; and when they do they are hardly worth having," said Lady Albury, laying down the law on the matter with great precision. "If a girl accept a man all at once when she has had, as it were, no preparation for such a proposal, she must always surely be in a state of great readiness for matrimonial projects. When there has been a prolonged period of spooning then of course it is quite a different thing. The whole thing has in fact been arranged before the important word has been spoken."

"What a professor in the art you are!" said he.

"The odd thing is, that such a one as you should be so ignorant. Can't you understand that she would not come to Stalham if her mind were made up against you? I said nothing of you as a lover, but I took care to let her know that you were coming. You are very ready to put yourself in the same boat with poor Ben Batsby or that other unfortunate wretch. Would she, do you think, have consented to come had she known that Ben would have been there, or your friend Tom Tringle?"

There was much more of it, but the upshot was, —as the Colonel had intended that it should be,— that Lady Albury was made to understand that Ayala's good-will was essential to his happiness. "Of course I will do my best," she said, as he parted from her. "Though I am not quite as much in love with her myself as you are, yet I will do my best." Then when she was left alone, and was prosecuting her inquiries about the new cook, and travelling back in the afternoon to Stalham, she again considered how wonderful a thing it was such a girl as Ayala, so small, apparently so unimportant, so childish in her manner, with so little to say for herself, should become a person of such terrible importance.

The twentieth came, and at ten minutes before two Ayala was at the Paddington Railway Station. The train, which was to start at 2.15, had been chosen by herself so that she might avoid the Colonel, and there she was, with her aunt, waiting for it. Mrs. Dosett had thought it to be her duty to see her off, and had come with her in the cab. There were the two boxes laden with her wardrobe, such as it was. Both she and her aunt had worked hard; for though,—as she had declared to herself, —there was no special reason for it, still she had wished to look her best. As she saw the boxes put into the van, and had told herself how much shabbier they were than the boxes of other young ladies who went visiting to such houses as Stalham, she rejoiced that Colonel Stubbs was not there to see them. And she considered whether it was possible that Colonel Stubbs should recognise a dress which she had worn at Stalham before, which was now to appear in a quite altered shape. She wondered also whether it would be possible that Colonel Stubbs should know how poor she was. As she was thinking of all this there was Colonel Stubbs on the platform.

She had never doubted but that little plan would be efficacious. Nor had her aunt doubted,—who had seen through the plan, though not a word had been spoken between them on the subject. Mrs. Dosett had considered it to be impossible that a Colonel engaged on duties of importance at Aldershot should run away from them to wait upon a child like Ayala,—even though he had professed himself to be in love with the child. She had never seen the Colonel, and on this occasion did not expect to see him. But there he was, all suddenly, shaking hands with Ayala.

"My aunt, Mrs. Dosett," whispered Ayala. Then the Colonel began to talk to the elder lady as though the younger lady were a person of very much less importance. Yes; he had run up from Aldershot a little earlier than he had intended. There had been nothing particular to keep him down at Aldershot. It had always been his intention to go to Stalham on this day, and was glad of the accident which was bringing Miss Dormer there just at the same time. He spent a good deal of his time at Stalham because Sir Harry and he, who were in truth cousins, were as intimate as brothers. He always lived at Stalham when he could get away from duty and was not in London. Stalham was a very nice place certainly; one of the most comfortable houses he knew in England. So he went on till he almost made Mrs. Dosett believe, and did make Ayala believe, that his visit to Stalham had nothing to do with herself. And yet Mrs. Dosett knew that the offer had been made. Ayala bethought herself that she did not care so much for the re-manufactured frock after all, nor yet for the shabby appearance of the boxes. The real Angel of Light would not care for her frock nor for her boxes; and certainly would not be indifferent after the fashion of,—of,—! Then she began to reflect that she was making a fool of herself.

She was put into the carriage, Mr. Dosett having luckily decided against the use of the second class. Going to such a house as Stalham Ayala ought, said Mr. Dosett, to go as any other lady would. Had it been himself or his wife it would have been very different; but for Ayala, on such an occasion as this, he would be extravagant. Ayala was therefore put into her seat while the Colonel stood at the door outside, still talking to Mrs. Dosett. "I don't think she will be let to come away at the end of a week," said the Colonel. "Sir Harry doesn't like people to come away very soon." Ayala heard this, and thought that she remembered that Sir Harry himself was very indifferent as to the coming and going of the visitors. "They go up to London about the end of March," said the Colonel, "and if Miss Dormer were to return about a week before it would do very well."

"Oh, no," said Ayala, putting her head out of the window; "I couldn't think of staying so long as that." Then the last final bustle was made by the guard; the Colonel got in, the door was shut, and Mrs. Dosett, standing on the platform, nodded her head for the last time.

There were only four persons in the carriage. In the opposite corner there were two old persons, probably a husband and wife, who had been very careful as to a foot-warming apparatus, and were muffled up very closely in woollen and furs. "If you don't mind shutting the door, Sir," said the old gentleman, rather testily, "because my wife has a pain in her face." The door absolutely was shut when the words were spoken, but the Colonel made some sign of closing all the apertures. But there was a ventilator above, which the old lady spied. "If you don't mind shutting that hole up there, Sir, because my husband is very bad with neuralgia." The Colonel at once got up and found that the ventilator was fast closed, so as not to admit a breath of air. "There are draughts come in everywhere," said the old gentleman. "The Company ought to be prosecuted." "I believe the more people they kill the better they like it," said the old lady. Then the Colonel looked at Ayala with a very grave face, with no hint at a smile, with a face which must have gratified even the old lady and gentleman.

But Ayala understood the face, and could not refrain from a little laugh. She laughed only with her eyes,—but the Colonel saw it.

"The weather has been very severe all day," said the Colonel, in a severe voice.

Ayala protested that she had not found it cold at all. "Then, Miss, I think you must be made of granite," said the old lady. "I hope you'll remember that other people are not so fortunate." Ayala again smiled, and the Colonel made another effort as though to prevent any possible breath of air from making its way into the interior of the vehicle.

There was silence among them for some minutes, and then Ayala was quite surprised by the tone in which her friend addressed her. "What an ill-natured girl you must be," said he, "to have put me to such a terrible amount of trouble all on purpose."

"I didn't," said Ayala.

"Yes, you did. Why wouldn't you come down by the four o'clock train as I told you? Now I've left everything undone, and I shouldn't wonder if I get into such a row at the Horse Guards that I shall never hear the end of it. And now you are not a bit grateful."

"Yes, I am grateful; but I didn't want you to come at all," she said.

"Of course I should come. I didn't think you were so perverse."

"I'm not perverse, Colonel Stubbs."

"When young persons are perverse, it is my opinion they oughtn't to be encouraged," said the old lady from her corner.

"My dear, you know nothing about it," said the old gentleman.

"Yes, I do," said the old lady. "I know all about it. Whatever she does a young lady ought not to be perverse. I do hate perversity. I am sure that hole up there must be open, Sir, for the wind does come in so powerful." Colonel Stubbs again jumped up and poked at the ventilator.

In the meantime Ayala was laughing so violently that she could with difficulty prevent herself from making a noise, which, she feared, would bring down increased wrath upon her from the old lady. That feigned scolding from the Colonel at once brought back upon her the feeling of sudden and pleasant intimacy which she had felt when he had first come and ordered her to dance with him at the ball in London. It was once again with her as though she knew this man almost more intimately, and certainly more pleasantly, than any of her other acquaintances. Whatever he said she could answer him now, and pretend to scold him, and have her joke with him as though no offer had ever been made. She could have told him now all the story of that turned dress, if that subject had come naturally to her, or have laughed with him at her own old boxes, and confided to him any other of the troubles of her poverty, as if they were jokes which she could share at any rate with him. Then he spoke again. "I do abominate a perverse young woman," he said. Upon this Ayala could no longer constrain herself, but burst into loud laughter.

After a while the two old people became quite

familiar, and there arose a contest, in which the lady took part with the Colonel, and the old man protected Ayala. The Colonel spoke as though he were quite in earnest, and went on to declare that the young ladies of the present time were allowed far too much licence. "They never have their own bread to earn," he said, "and they ought to make themselves agreeable to other people who have more to do."

"I quite agree with you, Sir," said the old lady. "They should run about and be handy. I like to see a girl that can jump about the house and make herself useful."

"Young ladies ought to be young ladies," said the old man, putting his mouth for a moment up out of his comforter.

"And can't a young lady be useful and yet be a young lady?" said the Colonel.

"It is her special province to be ornamental," said the old gentleman. "I like to see young ladies ornamental. I don't think young ladies ought to be scolded, even if they are a little fractious."

"I quite agree with you, Sir," said Ayala. And so the fight went on with sundry breaks and changes in the matter under discussion till the station for Stalham had been reached. The old gentleman, indeed, seemed to lose his voice before the journey was half over, but the lady persevered, so that she and the Colonel became such fast friends that she insisted on shaking hands with him when he left the carriage.

"How could you be so wicked as to go on hoaxing her like that?" said Ayala, as soon as they were on the platform.

"There was no hoax at all. I was quite in earnest. Was not every word true that I said? Now come and get into the carriage quickly, or you will be as bad as the old gentleman himself."

Ayala did get into the carriage quickly, where she found Nina.

The two girls were full of conversation as they went to Stalham; but through it all Ayala could not refrain from thinking how the Jonathan Stubbs of to-day had been exactly like that Jonathan Stubbs she had first known,—and how very unlike a lover.

CHAPTER IV.

CAPTAIN BATSBY AT MERLE PARK.

When Ayala went to Stalham Captain Batsby went to Merle Park. They had both been invited by Lady Tringle, and when the letter was written to Ayala she was assured that Tom should not be there. At that time Tom's last encounter with the police had not as yet become known to the Tringles, and the necessity of keeping Tom at the house in the country was not manifest. The idea had been that Captain Batsby should have an opportunity of explaining himself to Ayala. The Captain came; but, as to Ayala, Mrs. Dosett sent word to say that she had been invited to stay some days just at that time with her friend Lady Albury at Stalham.

What to do with Captain Batsby had been felt to be a difficulty by Lady Albury. It was his habit to come to Stalham some time in March and there finish the hunting season. It might be hoped that Ayala's little affair might be arranged early in March, and then, whether he came or whether he did not, it would be the same to Ayala. But the Captain himself would be grievously irate when he should hear the trick which would have been played upon him. Lady Albury had already desired him not to come till after the first week in

March, having fabricated an excuse. She had been bound to keep the coast clear both for Ayala's sake and the Colonel's; but she knew that when her trick should be discovered there would be unmeasured wrath. "Why the deuce don't you let the two men come, and then the best man may win!" said Sir Harry, who did not doubt but that, in such a case, the Colonel would prove to be the best man. Here too there was another difficulty. When Lady Albury attempted to explain that Ayala would not come unless she were told that she would not meet the Captain, Sir Harry declared that there should be no such favour. "Who the deuce is this little girl," he asked, "that everybody should be knocked about in this way for her?" Lady Albury was able to pacify the husband, but she feared that any pacifying of the Captain would be impossible. There would be a family quarrel;—but even that must be endured for the Colonel's sake.

In the meantime the Captain was kept in absolute ignorance of Ayala's movements, and went down to Merle Park hoping to meet her there. He must have been very much in love, for Merle Park was by no means a spot well adapted for hunting. Hounds there were in the neighbourhood, but he turned up his nose at the offer when Sir Thomas suggested that he might bring down a hunter. Captain Batsby, when he went on hunting exhibitions, never stirred without five horses, and always confined his operations to six or seven favoured counties. But Ayala just at present was more to him than hunting, and therefore, though it was now the end of February, he went to Merle Park.

"It was all Sir Thomas's doing." It was thus that Lady Tringle endeavoured to console herself when discussing the matter with her daughters. The Honourable Septimus Traffick had now gone up to London, and was inhabiting a single room in the neighbourhood of the House. Augusta was still at Merle Park, much to the disgust of her father. He did not like to tell her to be gone; and would indeed have been glad enough of her presence had it not been embittered by the feeling that he was being "done." But there she remained, and in discussing the affairs of the Captain with her mother and Gertrude was altogether averse to the suggested marriage for Ayala. To her thinking Ayala was not entitled to a husband at all. Augusta had never given way in the affair of Tom;—had declared her conviction that Stubbs had never been in earnest; and was of opinion that Captain Batsby would be much better off at Merle Park without Ayala than he would have been in that young lady's presence. When he arrived nothing was said to him at once about Ayala. Gertrude, who recovered from the great sickness occasioned by Mr. Houston's misconduct, though the recovery was intended only to be temporary, made herself as pleasant as possible. Captain Batsby was made welcome, and remained three days before he sought an opportunity of asking a question about Ayala.

During this time he found Gertrude to be a very agreeable companion, but he made Mrs. Traffick his first confidant. "Well, you know, Captain Batsby, to tell you the truth, we are not very fond of our cousin."

"Sir Thomas told me she was to be here."

"So we know. My father is perhaps a little mistaken about Ayala."

"Was she not asked?" demanded Captain Batsby, beginning to think that he had been betrayed.

"Oh, yes; she was asked. She has been asked very often, because she is mamma's niece, and did live with us once for a short time. But she did not come. In fact she won't go anywhere, unless——"

"Unless what?"

"You know Colonel Stubbs?"

"Jonathan Stubbs. Oh dear, yes; very intimately. He is a sort of connection of mine. He is my half-brother's second cousin by the father's side."

"Oh indeed! Does that make him very near?"

"Not at all. I don't like him, if you mean that. He always takes everything upon himself down at Stalham."

"What we hear is that Ayala is always running after him."

"Ayala running after Jonathan?"

"Haven't you heard of that?" asked Mrs. Traffick. "Why;—she is at Stalham with the Alburys this moment, and I do not doubt that Colonel Stubbs is there also. She would not have gone had she not been sure of meeting him."

This disturbed the Captain so violently that for

two or three hours he kept himself apart, not knowing what to do with himself or where to betake himself. Could this be true about Jonathan Stubbs? There had been moments of deep jealousy down at Stalham; but then he had recovered from that, having assured himself that he was wrong. It had been Larry Twentyman and not Jonathan Stubbs who had led the two girls over the brook,—into which Stubbs had simply fallen, making himself an object of pity. But now again the Captain believed it all. It was on this account, then, that his half-sister-in-law, Rosaline, had desired him to stay away from Stalham for the present! He knew well how high in favour with Lady Albury was that traitor Stubbs; how it was by her favour that Stubbs, who was no more than a second cousin, was allowed to do just what he pleased in the stables, while Sir Harry himself, the master of the hounds, confined himself to the kennel! He was determined at first to leave Merle Park and start instantly for Stalham, and had sent for his servant to begin the packing of his things; but as he thought of it more maturely he considered that his arrival at Stalham would be very painful to himself as well as to others. For the others he did not much care, but he saw clearly that the pain to himself would be very disagreeable. No one at Stalham would be glad to see him. Sir Harry would be disturbed, and the other three persons with whom he was concerned,—Lady Albury, Stubbs, and Ayala,—would be banded together in hostility against him. What chance would he have under such circumstances? Therefore he determined that he would stay at Merle Park yet a little longer.

And, after all, was Ayala worth the trouble which he had proposed to take for her? How much had he offered her, how scornfully had his offer been received, and how little had she to give him in return! And now he had been told that she was always running after Jonathan Stubbs! Could it be worth his while to run after a girl who was always running after Jonathan Stubbs? Was he not much higher in the world than Jonathan Stubbs, seeing that he had, at any rate, double Stubbs's income? Stubbs was a red-haired, ugly, impudent fellow, who made his way wherever he went simply by "cheek"! Upon reflection, he found that it would be quite beneath him to run after any girl who could so demean herself as to run after Jonathan Stubbs. Therefore he came down to dinner on that evening with all his smiles, and said not a word about Ayala to Sir Thomas, who had just returned from London.

"Is he very much provoked?" Sir Thomas asked his wife that evening.

"Provoked about what?"

"He was expressly told that he would meet Ayala here."

"He seems to be making himself very comfortable, and hasn't said a word to me about Ayala. I am sick of Ayala. Poor Tom is going to be really ill." Then Sir Thomas frowned, and said nothing more on that occasion.

Tom was certainly in an uncomfortable position,

and never left his bed till after noon. Then he would mope about the place, moping even worse than he did before, and would spend the evening all alone in the housekeeper's room, with a pipe in his mouth, which he seemed hardly able to take the trouble to keep alight. There were three or four other guests in the house, including two Honourable Miss Traffick's, and a couple of young men out of the City, whom Lady Tringle hoped might act as antidotes to Houston and Hamel. But with none of them would Tom associate. With Captain Batsby he did form some little intimacy; driven to it, no doubt, by a community of interest. "I believe you were acquainted with my cousin, Miss Dormer, at Stalham?" asked Tom. At the moment the two were sitting over the fire in the housekeeper's room, and Captain Batsby was smoking a cigar, while Tom was sucking an empty pipe.

"Oh, yes," said Captain Batsby, pricking up his ears, "I saw a good deal of her."

"A wonderful creature!" ejaculated Tom.

"Yes, indeed!"

"For a real romantic style of beauty, I don't suppose that the world ever saw her like before. Did you?"

"Are you one among your cousin's admirers?" demanded the Captain.

"Am I?" asked Tom, surprised that there should be anybody who had not as yet heard his tragic story. "Am I one of her admirers? Why,—rather! Haven't you heard about me and Stubbs?"

"No, indeed."

"I thought that everybody had heard that. I challenged him, you know."

"To fight a duel?"

"Yes; to fight a duel. I sent my friend Faddle down with a letter to Stalham, but it was of no use. Why should a man fight a duel when he has got such a girl as Ayala to love him?"

"That is quite true, then?"

"I fear so! I fear so! Oh, yes; it is too true. Then you know;"—and as he came to this portion of his story he jumped up from his chair and frowned fiercely;—"then, you know, I met him under the portico of the Haymarket, and struck him."

"Oh,—was that you?"

"Indeed it was."

"And he did not do anything to you?"

"He behaved like a hero," said Tom. "I do think that he behaved like a hero,—though of course I hate him." The bitterness of expression was here very great. "He wouldn't let them lock me up. Though, in the matter of that, I should have been best pleased if they would have locked me up for ever, and kept me from the sight of the world. Admire that girl, Captain Batsby! I don't think that I ever heard of a man who loved a girl as I love her. I do not hesitate to say that I continue to walk the world,—in the way of not committing suicide, I mean,—simply because there is still a possibility while she has not as yet stood at the hymeneal altar with another man. I would have shot Stubbs willingly, though I knew I was to be tried for it at the Old Bailey,—and hung! I would have done it willingly,—willingly; or any other man." After that Captain Batsby thought it might be prudent not to say anything especial as to his own love.

And how foolish would it be for a man like himself, with a good fortune of his own, to marry any girl who had not a sixpence! The Captain was led into this vain thought by the great civility displayed to him by the ladies of the house. With Lucy, whom he knew to be Ayala's sister, he had not prospered very well. It came to his ears that she was out of favour with her aunt, and he therefore meddled with her but little. The Tringle ladies, however, were very kind to him,—so kind that he was tempted to think less than ever of one who had been so little courteous to him as Ayala. Mrs. Traffick was of course a married woman, and it amounted to nothing. But Gertrude——! All the world knew that Septimus Traffick without a shilling of his own had become the happy possessor of a very large sum of money. He, Batsby, had more to recommend him than Traffick! Why should not he also become a happy possessor? He went away for a week's hunting into Northamptonshire, and then, at Lady Tringle's request, came back to Merle Park.

At this time Miss Tringle had quite recovered her health. She had dropped all immediate speech as to Mr. Houston. Had she not been provoked, she would have allowed all that to drop into oblivion. But a married sister may take liberties.

"You are well rid of him, I think," said Augusta. Gertrude heaved a deep sigh. She did not wish to acknowledge herself to be rid of him until another string were well fitted to her bow. "After all, a man with nothing to do in the world, with no profession, no occupation, with no money——"

"Mr. Traffick had not got very much money of his own."

"He has a seat in Parliament, which is very much more than fortune, and will undoubtedly be in power when his party comes in. And he is a man of birth. But Frank Houston had nothing to recommend him."

"Birth!" said Gertrude, turning up her nose.

"The Queen, who is the fountain of honour, made his father a nobleman, and that constitutes birth." This the married sister said with stern severity of manner, and perfect reliance on the constitutional privileges of her Sovereign.

"I don't know that we need talk about it," said Gertrude.

"Not at all. Mr. Houston has behaved very badly, and I suppose there is an end of him as far as this house is concerned. Captain Batsby seems to me to be a very nice young man, and I suppose he has got money. A man should certainly have got money,—or an occupation."

"He has got both," said Gertrude, which, however, was not true, as Captain Batsby had left the service.

* * * * *

"Have you forgotten my cousin so soon?" Gertrude asked one day, as she was walking with the happy Captain in the park. The Captain, no doubt, had been saying soft things to her.

"Do you throw that in my teeth as an offence?"

"Inconstancy in men is generally considered as an offence," said Gertrude. What it might be in women she did not just then declare.

"After all I have heard of your cousin since I have been here, I should hardly have thought that it would be reckoned so in this case."

"You have heard nothing against her from me."

"I am told that she has treated your brother very badly."

"Poor Tom!"

"And that she is flirting with a man I particularly dislike."

"I suppose she does make herself rather peculiar with that Colonel Stubbs."

"And, after all, only think how little I saw of her! She is pretty."

"So some people think. I never saw it myself," said Gertrude. "We always thought her a mass of affectation. We had to turn her out of the house once you know. She was living here, and then it was that her sister had to come in her place. It is not their fault that they have got nothing;—poor girls! They are mamma's nieces, and so papa always has one of them." After that forgiveness was accorded to the Captain on account of his fickle conduct, and Gertrude consented to accept of his services in the guise of a lover. That this was so Mrs. Traffick was well aware. Nor was Lady Tringle very much in the dark. Frank Houston was to be considered as good as gone, and if so it would be well that her daughter should have another string. She was tired of the troubles of the girls around her, and thought that as Captain Batsby was supposed to have an income he would do as a son-in-law. But she had not hitherto been consulted by the young people, who felt among themselves that there still might be a difficulty. The difficulty lay with Sir Thomas. Sir Thomas had brought Captain Batsby there to Merle Park as Ayala's lover, and as he had been very little at home was unaware of the changes which had taken place. And then Gertrude was still supposed to be engaged to Mr. Houston, although this lover had been so violently rejected by himself. The ladies felt that, as he was made of sterner stuff than they, so would it be more difficult to reconcile him to the alterations which were now proposed in the family arrangements. Who was to bell the cat? "Let him go to papa in the usual way, and ask his leave," said Mrs. Traffick.

"I did suggest that," said Gertrude, "but he seems not to like to do it quite yet."

"Is he such a coward as that?"

"I do not know that he is more a coward than anybody else. I remember when Septimus was quite afraid to go near papa. But then Benjamin has got money of his own, which does make a difference."

"It's quite untrue saying that Septimus was ever afraid of papa. Of course he knows his position as a Member of Parliament too well for that. I suppose the truth is, it's about Ayala."

"It is a little odd about Ayala," said Gertrude, resuming her confidential tone. "It is so hard to make papa understand about these kind of things. I declare I believe he thinks that I never ought to speak to another man because of that scoundrel Frank Houston."

All this was in truth so strange to Sir Thomas that he could not understand any of the existing perplexities. Why did Captain Batsby remain as a guest at Merle Park? He had no special dislike to the man, and when Lady Tringle had told him that she had asked the Captain to prolong his visit he had made no objection. But why should the man remain there, knowing as he did now that there was no chance of Ayala's coming to Merle Park? At last, on a certain Saturday evening, he did make inquiry on the subject. "What on earth is that man staying here for?" he said to his wife.

"I think he likes the place."

"Perhaps he likes the place as well as Septimus Traffick, and means to live here always!" Such allusions as these were constant with Sir Thomas, and were always received by Lady Tringle with dismay and grief. "When does he mean to go away?" asked Sir Thomas, gruffly.

Lady Tringle had felt that the time had come in which some word should be said as to the Captain's intentions; but she feared to say it. She dreaded to make the clear explanation to her husband. "Perhaps," said she, "he is becoming fond of some of the young ladies."

"Young ladies! What young ladies? Do you mean Lucy?"

"Oh dear no!" said Lady Tringle.

"Then what the deuce do you mean? He came here after Ayala, because I wanted to have all that nonsense settled about Tom. Ayala is not here, nor likely to be here; and I don't know why he should stay here philandering away his time. I hate men in a country-house who are thorough idlers. You had better take an opportunity of letting him know that he has been here long enough."

All this was repeated by Lady Tringle to Mrs. Traffick, and by Mrs. Traffick to Gertrude. Then they felt that this was no time for Captain Batsby to produce himself to Sir Thomas as a suitor for his youngest daughter.

CHAPTER V.

THE JOURNEY TO OSTEND.

"No doubt it will be very hard to make papa understand." This was said by Gertrude to her new lover a few days after that order had been given that the lover should be sent away from Merle Park. The purport of the order in all its severity had not been conveyed to Captain Batsby. The ladies had felt,—Gertrude had felt very strongly,—that were he informed that the master of the house demanded his absence he would take himself off at once. But still something had to be said,—and something done. Captain Batsby was, just at present, in a matrimonial frame of mind. He had come to Merle Park to look for a wife, and, as he had missed one, was, in his present mood, inclined to take another. But there was no knowing how long this might last. Augusta had hinted that "something must be done, either with papa's consent or without it." Then there had come the conversation in which Gertrude acknowledged the existing difficulty. "Papa, too, probably, would not consent quite at once."

"He must think it very odd that I am staying here," said the Captain.

"Of course it is odd. If you could go to him and tell him everything!" But the Captain, looking at the matter all round, thought that he could not go to Sir Thomas and tell him anything. Then she began gently to introduce the respectable clergyman at Ostend. It was not necessary that she should refer at length to the circumstances under which she had studied the subject, but she gave Captain Batsby to understand that it was one as to which she had picked up a good deal of information.

But the money! "If Sir Thomas were made really angry, the consequences would be disastrous," said the Captain. But Gertrude was of a different way of thinking. Her father was, no doubt, a man who could be very imperious, and would insist upon having his own way as long as his own way was profitable to him. But he was a man who always forgave.

"If you mean about the money," said Gertrude, "I am quite sure that it would all come right." He did mean about the money, and was evidently uneasy in his mind when the suggested step was made manifest to him. Gertrude was astonished to see how long and melancholy his face could become. "Papa was never unkind about money in his life," said Gertrude. "He could not endure to have any of us poor."

On the next Saturday Sir Thomas again came down, and still found his guest at Merle Park. We are now a little in advance of our special story, which is, or ought to be, devoted to Ayala. But, with the affairs of so many lovers and their loves, it is almost impossible to make the chronicle run at equal periods throughout. It was now more than three weeks since Ayala went to Stalham, and Lady Albury had written to the Captain confessing something of her sin, and begging to be forgiven. This she had done in her anxiety to keep the Captain away. He had not answered his sister-in-law's letter, but, in his present frame of mind, was not at all anxious to finish up the hunting-season at Stalham. Sir Thomas, on his arrival, was very full of Tom's projected tour. He had arranged everything,—except in regard to Tom's own assent. He had written to New York, and had received back a reply from his correspondent assuring him that Tom should be made most heartily welcome. It might be that Tom's fighting propensities had not been made known to the people of New York. Sir Thomas had taken a berth on board of one of the Cunard boats, and had even gone so far as to ask the Captain to come down for a day or two to Merle Park. He was so much employed with Tom that he could hardly afford time and consideration to Captain Batsby and his affairs. Nevertheless he did ask a question, and received an answer with which he seemed to be satisfied. "What on earth is that man staying here for?" he said to his wife.

"He is going on Friday," replied Lady Tringle, doubtingly;—almost as though she thought that she would be subjected to further anger because of this delay. But Sir Thomas dropped the subject, and passed on to some matter affecting Tom's outfit. Lady Tringle was very glad to change the subject, and promised that everything should be supplied befitting the hottest and coldest climates on the earth's surface.

"She sails on the nineteenth of April," said Sir Thomas to his son.

"I don't think I could go as soon as that, Sir," replied Tom, whining.

"Why not? There are more than three weeks yet, and your mother will have everything ready for you. What on earth is there to hinder you?"

"I don't think I could go—not on the nineteenth of April."

"Well then, you must. I have taken your place, and Firkin expects you at New York. They'll do everything for you there, and you'll find quite a new life. I should have thought you'd have been delighted to get away from your wretched condition here."

"It is wretched," said Tom; "but I'd rather not go quite so soon."

"Why not?"

"Well, then——"

"What is it, Tom? It makes me unhappy when I see you such a fool."

"I am a fool! I know I am a fool!"

"Then make a new start of it. Cut and run, and begin the world again. You're young enough to forget all this."

"So I would, only——"

"Only what?"

"I suppose she is engaged to that man Stubbs! If I knew it for certain then I would go. If I went before, I should only come back as soon as I got to New York. If they were once married and it were all done with I think I could make a new start."

In answer to this his father told him that he must go on the nineteenth of April, whether Ayala were engaged or disengaged, married or unmarried; —that his outfit would be bought, his cabin would be ready, circular notes for his use would be prepared, and everything would be arranged to make his prolonged tour as comfortable as possible; but that if he did not start on that day all the Tringle houses would be closed against him, and he would be turned penniless out into the world. "You'll have to learn that I'm in earnest," said Sir Thomas, as he turned his back and walked away. Tom took himself off to reflect whether it would not be a grand thing to be turned penniless out into the world,—and all for love!

By the early train on Monday Sir Thomas returned to London, having taken little or no heed of Captain Batsby during his late visit to the country. Even at Merle Park Captain Batsby's presence was less important than it would otherwise have been to Lady Tringle and Mrs. Traffick, because of the serious nature of Sir Thomas's decision as to his son. Lady Tringle perhaps suspected something. Mrs. Traffick, no doubt, had her own ideas as to her sister's position; but nothing was said and nothing was done. Both on the Wednesday and on the Thursday Lady Tringle went up to town to give the required orders on Tom's behalf. On the Thursday her elder daughter accompanied her, and returned with her in the evening. On their arrival they learnt that neither Captain Batsby nor Miss Gertrude had been seen since ten o'clock; that almost immediately after Lady Tringle's departure in the morning Captain Batsby had caused all his luggage to be sent into Hastings; and that it had since appeared that a considerable number of Miss Gertrude's things were missing. There could be no doubt that she had caused them to be packed up with the Captain's luggage. "They have gone to Ostend, mamma," said Augusta. "I was sure of it, because I've heard Gertrude say that people can always get themselves married at Ostend. There is a clergyman there on purpose to do it."

It was at this time past seven o'clock, and Lady Tringle when she heard the news was so astounded that she did not at first know how to act. It was not possible for her to reach Dover that night before the night-boat for Ostend should have started,—even could she have done any good by going there. Tom was in such a condition that she hardly dared to trust him; but it was settled at last that she should telegraph at once to Sir Thomas, in Lombard Street, and that Tom should travel up to London by the night train.

On the following morning Lady Tringle received a letter from Gertrude, posted by that young lady at Dover as she passed through on her road to Ostend. It was as follows;—

"Dear Mamma,

"You will be surprised on your return from London to find that we have gone. After much thinking about it we determined it would be best, because we had quite made up our mind *not to be kept separated.* Ben was so eager about it that I was obliged to yield. We were afraid that if we asked papa at once he would not have given his consent. Pray give him my most dutiful love, and tell him that I am sure he will never have occasion to be ashamed of his son-in-law. I don't suppose he knows, but it is the fact that Captain Batsby has about three thousand a year of his own. It is very different from having nothing, like that wretch Frank Houston, or, for that matter, Mr. Traffick. Ben was quite in a position to ask papa, but things had happened which made us both feel that papa would not like it just at present. We mean to be married at Ostend, and then will come back as soon as you and papa say that you will receive us. In the meantime I wish you would send some of my clothes after me. Of course I had to come away with very little luggage, because I was obliged to have my things mixed up with Ben's. I did not dare to have my boxes brought down by the servants. Could you send me the green silk in which I went to church the last two Sundays, and my pink gauze, and the grey poplin? Please send two or three flannel petticoats, as I could not put them among his things, and as many cuffs and collars as you can cram in. I suppose I can get boots at Ostend, but I should like to have the hat with the little brown feather. There is my silk jacket with the fur trimming; I should like to have that. I suppose I shall have to be married without any regular dress, but I am sure papa will make up my trousseau to me afterwards. I lent a little lace fichu to Augusta; tell her that I shall so like to have it.

"Give papa my best love, and Augusta, and poor Tom, and accept the same from your affectionate daughter,

"GERTRUDE."

"I suppose I must not add the other name yet."

Sir Thomas did not receive the telegram till eleven o'clock, when he returned from dinner, and could do nothing that night. On the next morning he was disturbed soon after five o'clock by Tom, who had come on the same errand. "Idiots!" exclaimed Sir Thomas, "What on earth can they have gone to Ostend for? And what can you do by coming up?"

"My mother thought that I might follow them to Ostend."

"They wouldn't care for you. No one will care for you until you have got rid of all this folly. I must go. Idiots! Who is to marry them at Ostend? If they are fools enough to want to be married, why shouldn't they get married in England?"

"I suppose they thought you wouldn't consent."

"Of course I shan't consent. But why should I consent a bit more because they have gone to Ostend? I don't suppose anybody ever had such a set of fools about him as I have." This would have been hard upon Tom had it not been that he had got beyond the feeling of any hardness from contempt or contumely. As he once said of himself, all sense of other injury had been washed out of him by Ayala's unkindness.

On that very day Sir Thomas started for Ostend, and reached the place about two o'clock. Captain Batsby and Gertrude had arrived only during the previous night, and Gertrude, as she had been very sick, was still in bed. Captain Batsby was not in bed. Captain Batsby had been engaged since an early hour in the morning looking for that respectable clergyman of the Church of England of whose immediate services he stood in need. By the time that Sir Thomas had reached Ostend he had found that no such clergyman was known in the place. There was a regular English clergyman who would be very happy to marry him,—and to accept the usual fees,—after the due performance of certain preliminaries as ordained by the law, and as usual at Ostend. The lady, no doubt, could be married at Ostend, after such preliminaries,—as she might have been married also in England. All this was communicated by the Captain to Gertrude,—who was still very unwell,—at her bedroom door. Her conduct during this trying time was quite beyond reproach,—and also his,—as Captain Batsby afterwards took an opportunity of assuring her father.

"What on earth, Sir, is the meaning of all this?" said Sir Thomas, encountering the man who was not his son-in-law in the sitting-room of the hotel.

"I have just run away with your daughter, Sir Thomas. That is the simple truth."

"And I have got the trouble of taking her back again."

"I have behaved like a gentleman through it all, Sir Thomas," said the Captain, thus defending his own character and the lady's.

"You have behaved like a fool. What on earth am I to think of it, Sir? You were asked down to my house because you gave me to understand that you proposed to ask my niece, Miss Dormer, to be your wife; and now you have run away with my daughter. Is that behaviour like a gentleman?"

"I must explain myself?"

"Well, Sir?" Captain Batsby found the explanation very difficult; and hummed and hawed a great deal. "Do you mean to say that it was a lie from beginning to end about Miss Dormer?" Great liberties of speech are allowed to gentlemen whose daughters have been run away with, and whose hospitality has been outraged.

"Oh dear no. What I said then was quite true. It was my intention. But—but—." The perspiration broke out upon the unhappy man's brow as the great immediate trouble of his situation became clear to him. "There was no lie,—no lie at all. I beg to assure you, Sir Thomas, that I am not a man to tell a lie."

"How has it all been, then?"

"When I found how very superior a person your daughter was!"

"It isn't a month since she was engaged to somebody else," said the angry father, forgetting all propriety in his indignation.

"Gertrude?" demanded Captain Batsby.

"You are two fools. So you gave up my niece?"

"Oh dear yes, altogether. She didn't come to Merle Park, you know. How was I to say anything to her when you did'nt have her there?"

"Why didn't you go away then, instead of remaining under a false pretence? Or why, at any rate, didn't you tell me the truth?"

"And what would you have me to do now?" asked Captain Batsby.

"Go to the d——," said Sir Thomas, as he left the room, and went to his daughter's chamber.

Gertrude had heard that her father was in the house, and endeavoured to hurry herself into her clothes while the interview was going on between him and her father. But she was not yet perfectly arrayed when her father burst into her room. "Oh, papa," she said, going down on her knees, "you do mean to forgive us?"

"I mean to do nothing of the kind. I mean to carry you home and have you locked up."

"But we may be married!"

"Not with my leave. Why didn't you come and ask if you wanted to get yourselves married? Why didn't you tell me?"

"We were ashamed."

"What has become of Mr. Houston, whom you loved so dearly?"

"Oh, papa!"

"And the Captain was so much attached to Ayala!"

"Oh, papa!"

"Get up, you stupid girl. Why is it that my children are so much more foolish than other people's? I don't suppose you care for the man in the least."

"I do, I do. I love him with all my heart."

"And as for him,—how can he care for you when it is but the other day he was in love with your cousin?"

"Oh, papa!"

"What he wants is my money, of course."

"He has got plenty of money, papa."

"I can understand him, fool as he is. There is something for him to get. He won't get it, but he might think it possible. As for you, I cannot understand you at all. What do you expect? It can't be for love of a hatchet-faced fellow like that, whom you had never seen a fortnight ago."

"It is more than a month ago, papa."

"Frank Houston was, at any rate, a manly-looking fellow."

"He was a scoundrel," said Gertrude, now standing up for the first time.

"A good-looking fellow was Frank Houston; that at least may be said for him," continued the father, determined to exasperate his daughter to the utmost. "I had half a mind to give way about him, because he was a manly, outspoken fellow, though he was such an idle dog. If you'd gone off with him, I could have understood it;—and perhaps forgiven it," he added.

"He was a scoundrel!" screamed Gertrude, remembering her ineffectual attempts to make her former lover perform this same journey.

"But this fellow! I cannot bring myself to believe that you really care for him."

"He has a good income of his own, while Houston was little better than a beggar."

"I'm glad of that," said Sir Thomas, "because there will be something for you to live upon. I can assure you that Captain Batsby will never get a shilling of my money. Now, you had better finish dressing yourself, and come down and eat your dinner with me if you've got any appetite. You will have to go back to Dover by the boat to-night."

"May Ben dine with us?" asked Gertrude, timidly.

"Ben may go to the d——. At any rate he had better not show himself to me again," said Sir Thomas.

The lovers, however, did get an opportunity of exchanging a few words, during which it was settled between them that as the young lady must undoubtedly obey her father's behests, and return to Dover that night, it would be well for Captain Batsby to remain behind at Ostend. Indeed, he spoke of making a little tour as far as Brussels, in order that he might throw off the melancholy feelings which had been engendered. "You will come to me again, Ben," she said. Upon this he looked very grave. "You do not mean to say that after all this you will desert me?"

"He has insulted me so horribly!"

"What does that signify? Of course he is angry. If you could only hear how he has insulted me."

"He says that you were in love with somebody else not a month since."

"So were you, Ben, for the matter of that." He did, however, before they parted, make her a solemn promise that their engagement should remain an established fact, in spite both of father and mother.

Gertrude, who had now recovered the effects of her sea-sickness,—which, however, she would have to encounter again so very quickly,—contrived to eat a hearty dinner with her father. There, howt ever, arose a little trouble. How should she contrive to pack up the clothes which she had brough- with her, and which had till lately been mixed with the Captain's garments. She did, however, at last succeed in persuading the chamber-maid to furnish her with a carpet-bag, with which in her custody she arrived safely on the following day at Merle Park.

CHAPTER VI.

THE NEW FROCK.

AYALA'S arrival at Stalham was full of delight to her. There was Nina with all her new-fledged hopes and her perfect assurance in the absolute superiority of Lord George Bideford to any other man either alive or dead. Ayala was quite willing to allow this assurance to pass current, as her Angel of Light was as yet neither alive nor dead. But she was quite certain,—wholly certain,—that when the Angel should come forth he would be superior to Lord George. The first outpouring of all this took place in the carriage as Nina and Ayala were driven from the station to the house, while the Colonel went home alone in a dog-cart. It had been arranged that nothing should be said to Ayala about the Colonel, and in the carriage the Colonel's name was not mentioned. But when they were all in the hall at Stalham, taking off their cloaks and depositing their wraps, standing in front of the large fire, Colonel Stubbs was there. Lady Albury was present also, welcoming her guests, and Sir Harry, who had already come home from hunting, with one or two other men in red coats and top breeches, and a small bevy of ladies who were staying in the house. Lady Albury was anxious to know how her friend had sped with Ayala, but at such a moment no question could be asked. But Ayala's spirits were so high that Lady Albury was at a loss to understand whether the whole thing had been settled by Jonathan with success,—or whether, on the other hand, Ayala was so happy because she had not been troubled by a word of love.

"He has behaved so badly, Lady Albury," said Ayala.

"What;—Stubbs?" asked Sir Harry, not quite understanding all the ins and outs of the matter.

"Yes, Sir Harry. There was an old lady and an old gentleman. They were very funny and he would laugh at them."

"I deny it," said the Colonel.

"Why shouldn't he laugh at them if they were funny?" asked Lady Albury.

"He knew it would make me laugh out loud. I couldn't help myself, but he could be as grave as a judge all the time. So he went till the old woman scolded me dreadfully."

"But the old man took your part," said the Colonel.

"Yes;—he did. He said that I was ornamental."

"A decent and truth-speaking old gentleman," said one of the sportsmen in top-boots.

"Quite so;—but then the old lady said that I was perverse, and Colonel Stubbs took her part. If you had been there, Lady Albury, you would have thought that he had been in earnest."

"So I was," said the Colonel.

All this was very pleasant to Ayala. It was a return to the old joyousness when she had first discovered the delight of having such a friend as Colonel Stubbs. Had he flattered her, paid her compliments, been soft and delicate to her,—as a lover might have been,—she would have been troubled in spirit and heavy at heart. But now it seemed as though all that love-making had been an episode which had passed away, and that the old pleasant friendship still remained. As yet, while they were standing there in the hall, there had come no moment for her to feel whether there was anything to regret in this. But certainly there had been comfort in it. She had been able to appear before all her Stalham friends, in the presence even of the man himself, without any of that consciousness which would have oppressed her had he come there simply as her acknowledged lover, and had she come there conscious before all the guests that it was so.

Then they sat for a while drinking tea and eating buttered toast in the drawing-room. A supply of buttered toast fully to gratify the wants of three or four men just home from hunting has never yet been created by the resources of any establishment. But the greater marvel is that the buttered toast has never the slightest effect on the dinner which is to follow in an hour or two. During this period the conversation turned chiefly upon hunting,—which is of all subjects the most imperious. It never occurs to a hunting-man to suppose that either a lady, or a bishop, or a political economist, can be indifferent to hunting. There is something beyond millinery,—beyond the interests of the church,—beyond the price of wheat,—in that great question whether the hounds did or did not change their fox in Gobblegoose Wood. On the present occasion Sir Harry was quite sure that the hounds did carry their fox through Gobblegoose Wood, whereas Captain Glomax, who had formerly been master of the pack which now obeyed Sir Harry, was perfectly certain that they had got upon another animal, who went away from Gobblegoose as fresh as paint. He pretended even to ridicule Sir Harry for supposing that any fox could have run at that pace up Buddlecombe Hill who had travelled all the way from Stickborough Gorse. To this Sir Harry replied resentfully that the Captain did not know what were the running powers of a dog-fox in March. Then he told various stories of what had been done in this way at this special period of the year. Glomax, however, declared that he knew as much of a fox as any man in England, and that he would eat both the foxes, and the wood, and Sir Harry, and, finally, himself, if the animal which had run up Buddlecombe Hill was the same which they brought with them from Stickborough Gorse into Gobblegoose Wood. So the battle raged, and the ladies no doubt were much interested;—as would have been the bishop had he been there, or the political economist.

After this Ayala was taken up into her room, and left to sit there by herself for a while till Lady Albury should send her maid. "My dear," said Lady Albury, "there is something on the bed which I expect you to wear to-night. I shall be broken-hearted if it doesn't fit you. The frock is a present from Sir Harry; the scarf comes from me. Don't say a word about it. Sir Harry always likes to make presents to young ladies." Then she hurried out of the room while Ayala was still thanking her. Lady Albury had at first intended to say something about the Colonel as they were sitting together over Ayala's fire, but she had made up her mind against this as soon as she saw their manner towards each other on entering the house. If Ayala had accepted him at a word as they were travelling together, then there would be need of no further interference in the matter. But if not, it would be better that she should hold her peace for the present.

Ayala's first instinct was to look at the finery which had been provided for her. It was a light grey silk, almost pearl colour, as to which she had never seen anything so lovely before. She measured the waist with her eye, and knew at once that it would fit her. She threw the gauzy scarf over her shoulders and turned herself round before the large mirror which stood near the fireplace. "Dear Lady Albury!" she exclaimed; "dear Lady Albury!" It was impossible that she should have understood that Lady Albury's affection had been shown to Jonathan Stubbs much rather than to her when those presents were prepared.

She got rid of her travelling dress and her boots, and let down her hair, and seated herself before the fire, that she might think of it all in her solitude. Was she or was she not glad,—glad in sober earnest, glad now the moment of her mirth had passed by, the mirth which had made her return to Stalham so easy for her,—was she or was she not glad that this change had come upon the Colonel, this return to his old ways? She had got her friend again, but she had lost her lover. She did not want the lover. She was sure of that. She was still sure that if a lover would come to her who would be in truth acceptable,—such a lover as would enable her to give herself up to him altogether, and submit herself to him as her lord and master,—he must be something different from Jonathan Stubbs. That had been the theory of her life for many months past, a theory on which she had resolved to rely with all her might from the moment in which this man had spoken to her of his love. Would she give way and render up herself and all her dreams simply because the man was one to be liked? She had declared to herself again and again that it should not be so. There should come the Angel of Light or there should come no lover for her. On that very morning as she was packing up her boxes at Kingsbury Crescent she had arranged the words in which, should he speak to her on the subject in the railway train, she would make him understand that it could never be. Surely he would understand if she told him so simply, with a little prayer that his suit might not be repeated. His suit had not been repeated. Nothing apparently had been further from his intention. He had been droll, pleasant, friendly,—just like his old dear self. For in truth the pleasantness and the novelty of his friendship had made him dear to her. He had gone back of his own accord to the old ways, without any little prayer from her. Now was she contented? As the question would thrust itself upon her in opposition to her own will, driving out the thoughts which she would fain have welcomed, she gazed listlessly at the fire. If it were so, then for what purpose, then for what reason, had Lady Albury procured for her the pale grey pearl-coloured dress?

And why were all these grand people at Stalham so good to her,—to her, a poor little girl, whose ordinary life was devoted to the mending of linen and to the furtherance of economy in the use of pounds of butter and legs of mutton? Why was she taken out of her own sphere and petted in this new luxurious world? She had a knowledge belonging to her,—if not quite what we may call common sense,—which told her that there must be some cause. Of some intellectual capacity, some appreciation of things and words which were divine in their beauty, she was half conscious. It could not be, she felt, that without some such capacity she should have imaged to herself that Angel of Light. But not for such capacity as that had she been made welcome at Stalham. As for her prettiness, her beauty of face and form, she thought about them not at all,—almost not at all. In appearing in that pale-pearl silk, with that gauzy scarf upon her shoulders, she would take pride. Not to be shamed among other girls by the poorness of her apparel was a pride to her. Perhaps to excel some others by the prettiness of her apparel might be a pride to her. But of feminine beauty, as a great gift bestowed upon her, she thought not at all. She would look in the mirror for the effect of the scarf, but not for the effect of the neck and shoulders beneath it. Could she have looked in any mirror for the effect of the dreams she had thus dreamed,—ah! that would have been the mirror in which she would have loved yet feared to look!

Why was Lady Albury so kind to her? Perhaps Lady Albury did not know that Colonel Stubbs had changed his mind. She would know it very soon, and then, maybe, everything would be changed. As she thought of this she longed to put the pearl silk dress aside, and not to wear it as yet,—to put it aside so that it might never be worn by her if circumstances should so require. It was to be hoped that the man had changed his mind,—and to be hoped that Lady Albury would know that he had done so. Then she would soon see whether there was a change. Could she not give a reason why she should not wear the dress this night? As she sat gazing at the fire a tear ran down her cheek. Was it for the dress she would not wear, or for the lover whom she would not love?

The question as to the dress was settled for her very soon. Lady Albury's maid came into the room,—not a chit of a girl without a thought of her own except as to her own grandness in being two steps higher than the kitchen-maid,—but a well-grown, buxom, powerful woman, who had no idea of letting such a young lady as Ayala do anything in the matter of dress but what she told her. When Ayala suggested something as to the next evening in reference to the pale-pearl silk the buxom powerful woman pooh-poohed her down in a moment. What,—after Sir Harry had taken so much trouble about having it made; having actually inquired about it with his own mouth. "To-night, Miss; you must wear it to-night! My lady would be quite angry!" "My lady not know what you wear! My lady knows what all the ladies wear,—morning, noon, and night." That little plan of letting the dress lie by till she should know how she should be received after Colonel Stubbs's change of mind had been declared, fell to the ground altogether under the hands of the buxom powerful woman.

When she went into the drawing-room some of the guests were assembled. Sir Harry and Lady Albury were there, and so was Colonel Stubbs. As she walked in Sir Harry was standing well in front of the fire, in advance of the rug, so as to be almost in the middle of the room. Captain Glomax was there also, and the discussion about the foxes was going on. It had occurred to Ayala that as the dress was a present from Sir Harry she must thank him. So she walked up to him and made a little curtsey just before him. "Am I nice, Sir Harry?" she said.

"Upon my word," said Sir Harry, "that is the best spent ten-pound-note I ever laid out in my life." Then he took her by the hand and gently turned her round, so as to look at her and her dress.

"I don't know whether I am nice, but you are," she said, curtseying again. Everybody felt that she had had quite a little triumph as she subsided into a seat close by Lady Albury, who called her. As she seated herself she caught the Colonel's eye, who was looking at her. She fancied that there was a tear in it. Then he turned himself and looked away into the fire.

"You have won his heart for ever," said Lady Albury.

"Whose heart?" asked Ayala, in her confusion.

"Sir Harry's heart. As for the other, cela va sans dire. You must go on wearing it every night for a week or Sir Harry will want to know why you have left it off. If the woman had made it on you it couldn't have fitted better. Baker,—" Baker was the buxom female,—"said that she knew it was right. You did that very prettily to Sir Harry. Now go up and ask Colonel Stubbs what he thinks of it."

"Indeed, I won't," said Ayala. Lady Albury, a few minutes afterwards, when she saw Ayala walking away towards the drawing-room leaning on the Colonel's arm, acknowledged to herself that she did at last understand it. The Colonel had been able to see it all, even without the dress, and she confessed in her mind that the Colonel had eyes with which to see, and ears with which to hear, and a judgment with which to appreciate. "Don't you think that girl very lovely?" she said to Lord Rufford, on whose arm she was leaning.

"Something almost more than lovely," said Lord Rufford, with unwonted enthusiasm.

It was acknowledged now by everybody. "Is it true about Colonel Stubbs and Miss Dormer?" whispered Lady Rufford to her hostess in the drawing-room.

"Upon my word, I never inquire into those things," said Lady Albury. "I suppose he does admire her. Everybody must admire her."

"Oh yes;" said Lady Rufford. "She is certainly very pretty. Who is she, Lady Albury?" Lady Rufford had been a Miss Penge, and the Penges were supposed to be direct descendants from Boadicea.

"She is Miss Ayala Dormer. Her father was an artist, and her mother was a very handsome woman. When a girl is as beautiful as Miss Dormer, and as clever, it doesn't much signify who she is." Then the direct descendant from Boadicea withdrew, holding an opinion much at variance with that expressed by her hostess.

"Who is that young lady who sat next to you?" asked Captain Glomax of Colonel Stubbs, after the ladies had gone.

"She is a Miss Ayala Dormer."

"Did I not see her out hunting with you once or twice early in the season?"

"You saw her out hunting, no doubt, and I was there. I did not specially bring her. She was staying here, and rode one of Albury's horses."

"Take her top and bottom, and all round," said Captain Glomax, "she is the prettiest little thing I've seen for many a day. When she curtseyed to

Sir Harry in the drawing-room I almost thought that I should like to be a marrying man myself." Stubbs did not carry on the conversation, having felt displeased rather than otherwise by the admiration expressed.

"I didn't quite understand before," said Sir Harry to his wife that night, "what it was that made Jonathan so furious about that girl; but I think I see it now."

"Fine feathers make fine birds," said his wife, laughing.

"Feathers ever so fine," said Sir Harry, "don't make well-bred birds."

"To tell the truth," said Lady Albury, "I think we shall all have to own that Jonathan has been right."

This took place upstairs, but before they left the drawing-room Lady Albury whispered a few words to her young friend. "We have had a terrible trouble about you, Ayala."

"A trouble about me, Lady Albury? I should be so sorry."

"It is not exactly your fault;—but we haven't at all known what to do with that unfortunate man."

"What man?" asked Ayala, forgetful at the moment of all men except Colonel Stubbs.

"You naughty girl! Don't you know that my brother-in-law is broken-hearted about you?"

"Captain Batsby!" whispered Ayala, in her faintest voice.

"Yes; Captain Batsby. A Captain has as much right to be considered as a Colonel in such a matter as this." Here Ayala frowned, but said nothing. "Of course, I can't help it, who may break his heart, but poor Ben is always supposed to be at Stalham just at this time of the year, and now I have been obliged to tell him one fib upon another to keep him away. When he comes to know it all, what on earth will he say to me?"

"I am sure it has not been my fault," said Ayala.

"That's what young ladies always say when gentlemen break their hearts."

When Ayala was again in her room, and had got rid of the buxom female who came to assist her in taking off her new finery, she was aware of having passed the evening triumphantly. She was conscious of admiration. She knew that Sir Harry had been pleased by her appearance. She was sure that Lady Albury was satisfied with her, and she had seen something in the Colonel's glance that made her feel that he had not been indifferent. But in their conversation at the dinner table he had said nothing which any other man might not have said, if any other man could have made himself as agreeable. Those hunting days were all again described with their various incidents, with the great triumph over the brook, and Twentyman's wife and baby, and fat Lord Rufford, who was at the moment sitting there opposite to them; and the ball in London, with the lady who was thrown out of the window; and the old gentleman and the old lady of to-day who had been so peculiar in their remarks. There had been nothing else in their conversation, and it surely was not possible that a man who intended to put himself forward as a lover should have talked in such fashion as that! But then there were other things which occurred to her. Why had there been that tear in his eye? And that "cela va sans dire" which had come from Lady Albury in her railing mood;—what had that meant? Lady Albury, when she said that, could not have known that the Colonel had changed his purpose.

But, after all, what is a dress, let it be ever so pretty? The Angel of Light would not care for her dress, let her wear what she might. Were he to seek her because of her dress, he would not be the Angel of Light of whom she had dreamed. It was not by any dress that she could prevail over him. She did rejoice because of her little triumph;—but she knew that she rejoiced because she was not an Angel of Light herself. Her only chance lay in this, that the angels of yore did come down from heaven to ask for love and worship from the daughters of men.

As she went to bed, she determined that she would still be true to her dream. Not because folk admired a new frock would she be ready to give herself to a man who was only a man,—a man of the earth really; who had about him no more than a few of the real attributes of an Angel of Light.

CHAPTER VII.

GOBBLEGOOSE WOOD ON SUNDAY.

THE next two days were not quite so triumphant to Ayala as had been the evening of her arrival. There was hunting on both of those days, the gentlemen having gone on the Friday away out of Sir Harry's country to the Brake hounds. Ayala and the Colonel had arrived on the Thursday. Ayala had not expected to be asked to hunt again,—had not even thought about it. It had been arranged before on Nina's account, and Nina now was not to hunt any more. Lord George did not altogether approve of it, and Nina was quite in accord with Lord George,—though she had held up her whip and shaken it in triumph when she jumped over the Cranbury Brook. And the horse which Ayala had ridden was no longer in the stables. "My dear, I am so sorry; but I'm afraid we can't mount you," Lady Albury said. In answer to this Ayala declared that she had not thought of it for a moment. But yet the days seemed to be dull with her. Lady Rufford was,—well,—perhaps a little patronising to her, and patronage such as that was not at all to Ayala's taste. "Lady Albury seems to be quite a kind friend to you," Lady Rufford said. Nothing could be more true. The idea implied was true also,—the idea that such a one as

Ayala was much in luck's way to find such a friend as Lady Albury. It was true no doubt; but, nevertheless, it was ungracious, and had to be resented. "A very kind friend, indeed. Some people only make friends of those who are as grand as themselves."

"I am sure we should be very glad to see you at Rufford if you remain long in the country," said Lady Rufford, a little time afterwards. But even in this there was not a touch of that cordiality which might have won Ayala's heart. "I am not at all likely to stay," said Ayala. "I live with my uncle and aunt at Notting Hill, and I very rarely go away from home." Lady Rufford, however, did not quite understand it. It had been whispered to her that morning that Ayala was certainly going to marry Colonel Stubbs; and, if so, why should she not come to Rufford?

On that day, the Friday, she was taken out to dinner by Captain Glomax. "I remember quite as if it were yesterday," said the Captain. "It was the day we rode the Cranbury Brook."

Ayala looked up into his face, also remembering everything as well as it were yesterday. "Mr. Twentyman rode over it," she said, "and Colonel Stubbs rode into it."

"Oh, yes; Stubbs got a ducking; so he did." The Captain had not got a ducking, but then he had gone round by the road. "It was a good run that."

"I thought so."

"We haven't been lucky since Sir Harry has

had the hounds somehow. There doesn't seem to be the dash about 'em there used to be when I was here. I had them before Sir Harry, you know." All this was nearly in a whisper.

"Were you Master?" asked Ayala, with a tone of surprise which was not altogether pleasing to the Captain.

"Indeed I was, but the fag of it was too great, and the thanks too small, so I gave it up. They used to get four days a week out of me." During the two years that the Captain had had the hounds, there had been, no doubt, two or three weeks in which he had hunted four days.

Ayala liked hunting, but she did not care much for Captain Glomax, who, having seen her once or twice on horseback, would talk to her about nothing else. A little away on the other side of the table Nina was sitting next to Colonel Stubbs, and she could hear their voices and almost their words. Nina and Jonathan were first cousins, and, of course, could be happy together without giving her any cause for jealousy;—but she almost envied Nina. Yet she had hoped that it might not fall to her lot to be taken out again that evening by the Colonel. Hitherto she had not even spoken to him during the day. They had started to the meet very early, and the gentlemen had almost finished their breakfast before she had come down. If there had been any fault it was her fault, but yet she almost felt that there was something of a disruption between them. It was so evident to her that he was perfectly happy whilst he was talking to Nina.

After dinner it seemed to be very late before the men came into the drawing-room, and then they were still engaged upon that weary talk about hunting, till Lady Rufford, in order to put a stop to it, offered to sing. "I always do," she said, "if Rufford ventures to name a fox in the drawing-room after dinner." She did sing, and Ayala thought that the singing was more weary than the talk about hunting.

While this was going on, the Colonel hat got himself shut up in a corner of the room. Lady Albury had first taken him there, and afterwards he had been hemmed in when Lady Rufford sat down to the piano. Ayala had hardly ventured even to glance at him, but yet she knew all that he did, and heard almost every word that he spoke. The words were not many, but still when he did speak his voice was cheerful. Nina now and again had run up to him, and Lady Rufford had asked him some questions about the music. But why didn't he come out and speak to her? thought Ayala. Though all that nonsense about love was over, still he ought not to have allowed a day to pass at Stalham without speaking to her. He was the oldest friend there in that house except Nina. It was indeed no more than nine months since she had first seen him, but still it seemed to her that he was an old friend. She did feel, as she endeavoured to answer the questions that Lord Rufford was asking her, that Jonathan Stubbs was treating her unkindly.

Then came the moment in which Lady Albury

marshalled her guests out of the room towards their chambers. "Have you found yourself dull without the hunting?" the Colonel said to Ayala.

"Oh dear no; I must have a dull time if I do, seeing that I have only hunted three days in my life." There was something in the tone of her voice which, as she herself was aware, almost expressed dissatisfaction. And yet not for worlds would she have shown herself to be dissatisfied with him, could she have helped it.

"I thought that perhaps you might have regretted the little pony," he said.

"Because a thing has been very pleasant, it should not be regretted because it cannot be had always."

"To me a thing may become so pleasant, that unless I can have it always my life must be one long regret."

"The pony is not quite like that," said Ayala, smiling, as she followed the other ladies out of the room.

On the next morning the meet was nearer, and some of the ladies were taken there in an open carriage. Lady Rufford went, and Mrs. Gosling, and Nina and Ayala. "Of course there is a place for you," Lady Albury had said to her. "Had I wanted to go I would have made Sir Harry send the drag; but I've got to stop at home and see that the buttered toast is ready by the time the gentlemen all come back." The morning was almost warm, so that the sportsmen were saying evil things of violets and primroses, as is the wont of sportsmen on such occasions, and at the meet the ladies got out of the carriage and walked about among the hounds, making civil speeches to old Tony. "No, my lady," said Tony, "I don't like these sunshiny mornings at all; there ain't no kind of scent, and I goes riding about these big woods, up and down, till my shirt is as wet on my back with the sweat as though I'd been pulled through the river." Then Lady Rufford walked away and did not ask Tony any more questions.

Ayala was patting one of the hounds when the Colonel, who had given his horse to a groom, came and joined her. "If you don't regret that pony," said he, "somebody else does."

"I do regret him in one way, of course. I did like it very much; but I don't think it nice, when much has been done for me, to say that I want to have more done."

"Of course I knew what you meant."

"Perhaps you would go and tell Sir Harry, and then he would think me very ungrateful."

"Ayala," he said, "I will never say anything of you that will make anybody think evil of you. But, between ourselves, as Sir Harry is not here, I suppose I may confess that I regret the pony."

"I should like it, of course," whispered Ayala.

"And so should I,—so much! I suppose all these men here would think me an ass if they knew how little I care about the day's work,—whether we find, or whether we run, or whether we kill,—just because the pony is not here. If the pony were here I should have that feeling of expectation of joy, which is so common to girls when some much-thought-of ball or promised pleasure is just before them." Then Tony went off with his hounds, and Jonathan, mounting his horse, followed with the ruck.

Ayala knew very well what the pony meant, as spoken of by the Colonel. When he declared that he regretted the pony, it was because the pony might have carried herself. He had meant her to understand that the much-thought-of ball or promised pleasure would have been the delight of again riding with herself. And then he had again called her Ayala. She could remember well every occasion on which he had addressed her by her Christian name. It had been but seldom. Once, however, it had occurred in the full flow of their early intimacy, before that love-making had been begun. It had struck her as being almost wrong, but still as very pleasant. If it might be made right by some feeling of brotherly friendship, how pleasant would it be! And now she would like it again, if only it might be taken as a sign of friendship rather than of love. It never occurred to her to be angry as she would have been angry with any other man. How she would have looked at Captain Batsby had he dared to call her Ayala! Colonel Stubbs should call her Ayala as long as he pleased,—if it were done only in friendship.

After that they were driven about for a while, seeing what Tony did with the hounds, as tidings came to them now and again that one fox had broken this way and another had gone the other.

But Ayala, through it all, could not interest herself about the foxes. She was thinking only of Jonathan Stubbs. She knew that she was pleased because he had spoken to her, and had said kind, pleasant words to her. She knew that she had been displeased while he had sat apart from her, talking to others. But yet she could not explain to herself why she had been either pleased or displeased. She feared that there was more than friendship,—than mere friendship, in that declaration of his that he did in truth regret the pony. His voice had been, oh, so sweet as he had said it! Something told her that men do not speak in mere friendship after that fashion. Not even in the softness of friendship between a man and a woman will the man's voice become as musical as that! Young as she was, child as she was, there was an instinct in her breast which declared to her that it was so. But then, if it were so, was not everything again wrong with her? If it were so, then must that condition of things be coming back which it had been, and still was her firm resolve to avoid. And yet, as the carriage was being driven about, and as the frequent exclamations came that the fox had traversed this way or that, her pride was gratified and she was happy.

"What was Colonel Stubbs saying to you?" asked Nina, when they were at home at the house after lunch.

"He was talking about the dear pony which I used to ride."

"About nothing else?"

"No;—about nothing else." This Ayala said with a short, dry manner of utterance which she would assume when she was determined not to have a subject carried on.

"Ayala, why do you not tell me everything? I told you everything as soon as it happened."

"Nothing has happened."

"I know he asked you," said Nina.

"And I answered him."

"Is that to be everything?"

"Yes;—that is to be everything," said Ayala, with a short, dry manner of utterance. It was so plain, that even Nina could not pursue the subject.

There was nothing done on that day in the way of sport. Glomax thought that Tony had been idle, and had made a holiday of the day from the first. But Sir Harry declared that there had not been a yard of scent. The buttered toast, however, was eaten, and the regular sporting conversation was carried on. Ayala, however, was not there to hear it. Ayala was in her own room dreaming.

She was taken in to dinner by a curate in the neighbourhood,—to whom she endeavoured to make herself very pleasant, while the Colonel sat at her other side. The curate had a good deal to say as to lawn tennis. If the weather remained as it was, it was thought that they could all play lawn tennis on the Tuesday,—when there would be no hunting. The curate was a pleasant young fellow, and Ayala devoted herself to him and to their joint hopes for next Tuesday. Colonel Stubbs never once attempted to interfere with the curate's opportunity. There was Lady Rufford on the other side of him, and to Lady Rufford he said all that he did say during dinner. At one period of the repast she was more than generally lively, because she felt herself called upon to warn her husband that an attack of the gout was imminent, and would be certainly produced instantaneously if he could not deny himself the delight of a certain diet which was going the round of the table. His lordship smiled and denied himself,—thinking, as he did so, whether another wife, plus the gout, would or would not have been better for him. All this either amused Colonel Stubbs so sufficiently, or else made him so thoughtful, that he made no attempt to interfere with the curate. In the evening there was again music,—which resulted in a declaration made upstairs by Sir Harry to his wife that that wife of Rufford's was a confounded bore. "We all knew that, my dear, as soon as he married her," said Lady Albury.

"Why did he marry a bore?"

"Because he wanted a wife to look after himself, and not to amuse his friends. The wonder used to be that he had done so well."

Not a word had there been,—not a word, since that sound of "Ayala" had fallen upon her ears. No;—he was not handsome, and his name was Jonathan Stubbs;—but surely no voice so sweet had ever fallen from a man's lips! So she sat and dreamed far into the night. He, the Angel of Light, would certainly have a sweeter voice! That was an attribute without which no angel could be angelic! As to the face and the name, that would not perhaps signify. But he must have an intellect high soaring, a soul tuned to music, and a mind versed in nothing but great matters. He might be an artist, or more probably a poet;—or perhaps a musician. Yet she had read of poets, artists, and musicians, who had misused their wives, been fond of money, and had perhaps been drunkards. The Angel of Light must have the gifts, and must certainly be without the vices.

The next day was Sunday and they all went to church. In the afternoon they, as many of them as pleased, were to walk as far as Gobblegoose Wood, which was only three miles from the house. They could not hunt and therefore they must go to the very scene of the late contest and again discuss it there. Sir Harry and the Captain would walk and so would Ayala and Nina and some others. Lord Rufford did not like walking, and Lady Rufford would stay at home to console him. Ayala used her little wiles to keep herself in close company with Nina; but the Colonel's wiles were more effective;—and then, perhaps, Nina assisted the Colonel rather than Ayala. It came to pass that before they had left Gobblegoose Wood Ayala and the Colonel were together. When it was so he did not beat about the bush for a moment longer. He had fixed his opportunity for himself and he put it to use at once. "Ayala," he said, "am I to have any other answer?"

"What answer?"

"Nay, my dearest,—my own, own dearest as I

fain would have you,—who shall say what answer but you? Ayala, you know that I love you!"

"I thought you had given it up."

"Given it up. Never,—never! Does a man give up his joy,—the pride of his life,—the one only delight on which his heart has set itself! No, my darling, I have not given it up. Because you would not have it as I wished when I first spoke to you, I have not gone on troubling you. I thought I would wait till you were used again to the look of me, and to my voice. I shall never give it up, Ayala. When you came into the room that night with your new frock on——" Then he paused, and she glanced round upon him, and saw that a tear again was in his eye. "When you came in and curtseyed to Sir Harry I could hardly keep within myself because I thought you were so beautiful."

"It was the new gown which he had given me."

"No, my pet;—no! You may add a grace to a dress, but it can do but little for you. It was the little motion, the little word, the light in your eye! It twinkles at me sometimes when you glance about, so that I do not know whether it is meant for me or not. I fear that it is never meant for me."

"It is meant for nothing," said Ayala.

"And yet it goes into my very bosom. When you were talking to that clergyman at dinner I could see every sparkle that came from it. Then I wonder to myself whether you can ever be thinking of me as I am always thinking of you." She knew that she had been thinking of him every waking moment since she had been at Albury and through many of her sleeping moments also. "Ayala, one little word, one other glance from your eyes, one slightest touch from your hand upon my arm, shall tell me,—shall tell me,—shall tell me that I am the happiest, the proudest man in all the world." She walked on steadfastly, closing her very teeth against a word, with her eyes fixed before her so that no slightest glance should wander. Her two hands were in her little muff, and she kept them with her fingers clasped together, as though afraid lest one might rebel, and fly away, and touch the sleeve of his coat. "Ayala, how is it to be with me?"

"I cannot," she said sternly. And her eyes were still fixed before her, and her fingers were still bound in one with another. And yet she loved him. Yet she knew that she loved him. She could have hung upon his arm and smiled up into his face, and frowned her refusal only with mock anger as he pressed her to his bosom,—only that those dreams were so palpable to her and so dear, had been to her so vast a portion of her young life! "I cannot," she said again. "I cannot."

"Is that to be your answer for ever?" To this she made no immediate reply. "Must it be so, Ayala?"

"I cannot," she said. But the last little word was so impeded by the sobs which she could not restrain as almost to be inaudible.

"I will not make you unhappy, Ayala." Yes,

she was unhappy. She was unhappy because she knew that she could not rule herself to her own happiness; because, even at this moment, she was aware that she was wrong. If she could only release part of herself from the other, then could she fly into his arms and tell him that that spirit which had troubled her had flown. But the spirit was too strong for her, and would not fly. "Shall we go and join them?" he asked her in a voice altered, but still so sweet to her ears.

"If you think so," she replied.

"Perhaps it will be best, Ayala. Do not be angry with me now. I will not call you so again." Angry! Oh, no! She was not angry with him! But it was very bitter to her to be told that she should never hear the word again from his lips.

"The hunted fox never went up Buddlecombe Hill;—never. If he did I'll eat every fox in the Rufford and Ufford country." This was heard, spoken in most angry tones by Captain Glomax, as the Colonel and Ayala joined the rest of the party.

CHAPTER VIII.

"NO!"

AYALA, on her return from the walk to the wood, spent the remainder of the afternoon in tears. During the walk she kept close to Sir Harry, pretending to listen to the arguments about the fox, but she said nothing. Her ears were really intent on endeavouring to catch the tones of her lover's voice as he went on in front of them talking to Nina. Nothing could be more pleasant than the sound as he said a word or two now and again, encouraging Nina in her rhapsodies as to Lord George and all Lord George's family. But Ayala learned nothing from that. She had come to know the man well enough to be aware that he could tune his voice to the occasion, and could hide his feelings let them be ever so strong. She did not doubt his love now. She did not doubt but that at this moment his heart was heavy with rejected love. She quite believed in him. But nevertheless his words were pleasant and kind as he encouraged Nina.

Nor did she doubt her own love. She was alone in her room that afternoon till she told herself at last the truth. Oh, yes; she loved him. She was sure of that. But now he was gone! Why had she been so foolish? Then it seemed as though at that moment the separation took place between herself and the spirit which had haunted her. She seemed to know now,—now at this very moment,—that the man was too good for her. The knowledge had been coming to her. It had almost come when he had spoken to her in the wood. If it could only have been that he should have delayed his appeal to her yet for another day or two! She thought now that if he could have delayed it but for a few hours the cure would have been complete. If he had talked to her as he so well knew how to talk while they were in the wood together, while they were walking home,—so as to have exorcised the spirit from her by the sweetness of his words,—and then have told her that there was his love to have if she chose to have it, then she thought she would have taken it. But he had come to her while those words which she had prepared under the guidance of the spirit were yet upon her tongue. "I cannot," she had said. "I cannot." But she had not told him that she did not love him.

"I did love him," she said to herself, almost acknowledging that the spirit had been wholly exorcised. The fashion of her mind was altogether different from that which had so strongly prevailed with her. He was an honest, noble man, high in the world's repute, clever, a gentleman, a man of taste, and possessed of that gentle ever-present humour which was so inexpressibly delightful to her. She never again spoke to herself even in her thoughts of that Angel of Light,—never comforted herself again with the vision of that which was to come! There had appeared to her a man better than all other men, and when he had asked her for her hand she had simply said,—"I cannot." And yet she had loved him all the time. How foolish, how false, how wicked she had been! It was thus that she thought of it all as she sat there alone in her bedroom through the long hours of the afternoon. When they sent up for her asking her to come down, she begged that she might be allowed to remain there till dinner-time, because she was tired with her walk.

He would not come again now. Oh, no,—he was too proud, too firm, too manly for that. It was not for such a one as he to come whining after a girl,—like her cousin Tom. Would it be possible that she should even yet tell him? Could she say to him one little word, contradicting that which she had so often uttered in the wood? "Now I can," once whispered in his ear, would do it all. But as to this she was aware that there was no room for hope. To speak such a word, low as it might be spoken, simple and little as it might be, was altogether impossible. She had had her chance and had lost it,—because of those idle dreams. That the dreams had been all idle she declared to herself,—not aware that the Ayala whom her lover had loved would not have been an Ayala to be loved by him, but for the dreams. Now she must go back to her uncle and aunt and to Kingsbury Crescent, with the added sorrow that the world of dreams was closed to her for ever. When the maid came to her she consented to have the frock put on, the frock which Sir Harry had given her, boldly resolving to struggle through her sorrow till Lady Albury should have dismissed her to her home. Nobody would want her now at Stalham, and the dismissal would soon come.

While she had been alone in her room the Colonel had been closeted with Lady Albury. They had at least been thus shut up together for some half-hour during which he had told his tale. "I have to own," said he, half-laughing as he began his tale, "that I thoroughly respect Miss Dormer."

"Why is she to be called Miss Dormer?"

"Because she has shown herself worthy of my respect."

"What is it that you mean, Jonathan?"

"She knew her own mind when she told me at first that she could not accept the offer which I did myself the honour of making her, and now she sticks to her purpose. I think that a young lady who will do that should be respected."

"She has refused you again?"

"Altogether."

"As how?"

"Well, I hardly know that I am prepared to explain the 'as how' even to you. I am about as thick-skinned a man in such matters as you may find anywhere, but I do not know that even I can bring myself to tell the 'as how.' The 'as how' was very clear in one respect. It was manifest that she knew her own mind, which is a knowledge not in the possession of all young ladies. She told me that she could not marry me."

"I do not believe it."

"Not that she told me so?"

"Not that she knew her own mind. She is a little simple fool, who with some vagary in her brain is throwing away utterly her own happiness, while she is vexing you."

"As to the vexation you are right."

"Cross-grained little idiot!"

"An idiot she certainly is not; and as to being cross-grained I have never found it. A human being with the grains running more directly all in the same way I have never come across."

"Do not talk to me, Jonathan, like that," she said. "When I call her cross-grained I mean that she is running counter to her own happiness."

"I cannot tell anything about that. I should have endeavoured, I think, to make her happy. She has certainly run counter to my happiness."

"And now?"

"What;—as to this very moment! I shall leave Stalham to-morrow."

"Why should you do that? Let her go if one must go."

"That is just what I want to prevent. Why should she lose her little pleasure?"

"You don't suppose that we can make the house happy to her now! Why should we care to do so when she will have driven you away?" He sat silent for a minute or two looking at the fire, with his hands on his two knees. "You must acknowledge, Jonathan," continued she, "that I have taken kindly to this Ayala of yours."

"I do acknowledge it."

"But it cannot be that she should be the same to us simply as a young lady, staying here as it were on her own behalf, as she was when we regarded her as your possible wife. Then every little trick and grace belonging to her endeared itself to us because we regarded her as one who was about to become one of ourselves. But what are her tricks and graces to us now?"

"They are all the world to me," said the Colonel.

"But you must wipe them out of your memory,—unless, indeed, you mean to ask her again."

"Ah!—that is it."

"You will ask her again?"

"I do not say so; but I do not wish to rob myself of the chance. It may be that I shall. Of course I should to-morrow if I thought there was a hope. To-morrow there would be none,—but I should like to know, that I could find her again in hands so friendly as yours, if at the end of a month I should think myself strong enough to encounter the risk of another refusal. Would Sir Harry allow her to remain here for another month?"

"He would say, probably, nothing about it."

"My plan is this," he continued; "let her remain here, say, for three weeks or a month. Do you continue all your kindness to her,—if not for her sake then for mine. Let her feel that she is made one of yourselves, as you say."

"That will be hard," said Lady Albury.

"It would not be hard if you thought that she was going to become so at last. Try it, for my sake. Say not a word to her about me,—though not shunning my name. Be to her as though I had told you nothing of this. Then when the period is over I will come again,—if I find that I can do so. If my love is still stronger than my sense of self-respect, I shall do so." All this Lady Albury promised to do, and then the interview between them was over.

"Colonel Stubbs is going to Aldershot to-morrow," said she to Ayala in the drawing-room after dinner. "He finds now that he cannot very well remain away." There was no hesitation in her voice as she said this, and no look in her eye which taught Ayala to suppose that she had heard anything of what had occurred in the wood.

"Is he indeed?" said Ayala, trying, but in vain, to be equally undemonstrative.

"It is a great trouble to us, but we are quite unable to prevent it,—unless you indeed can control him."

"I cannot control him," said Ayala, with that fixed look of resolution with which Lady Albury had already become familiar.

That evening before they went to bed the Colonel bade them all good-bye, as he intended to start early in the morning. "I never saw such a fellow as you are for sudden changes," said Sir Harry.

"What is the good of staying here for hunting when the ground and Tony's temper are both as hard as brick-bats. If I go now I can get another week further on in March if the rain should come."

With this Sir Harry seemed to be satisfied; but Ayala felt sure that Tony's temper and the rain had had nothing to do with it.

"Good-bye, Miss Dormer," he said, with his pleasantest smile, and his pleasantest voice.

"Good-bye," she repeated. What would she not have given that her voice should be as pleasant as his, and her smile! But she failed so utterly that the little word was inaudible,—almost obliterated by the choking of a sob. How bitterly severe had that word, Miss Dormer, sounded from his mouth! Could he not have called her Ayala for the last time,——even though all the world should have heard it? She was wide awake in the morning and heard the wheels of his cart as he was driven off. As the sound died away upon her ear she felt that he was gone from her for ever. How had it been that she had said, "I cannot," so often, when all her heart was set upon "I can?"

And now it remained to her to take herself away from Stalham as fast as she might. She understood perfectly all those ideas which Lady Albury had expressed to her well-loved friend. She was nothing to anybody at Stalham, simply a young lady staying in the house;—as might be some young lady connected with them by blood, or some young lady whose father and mother had been their friends. She had been brought there to Stalham, now this second time, in order that Jonathan Stubbs might take her as his wife. Driven by some madness she had refused her destiny, and now nobody would want her at Stalham any longer. She had better begin to pack up at once,—and go. The coldness of the people, now that she had refused to do as she had been asked, would be unbearable to her. And yet she must not let it appear that Stalham was no longer dear to her merely because Colonel Stubbs had left it. She would let a day go by, and then say with all the ease she could muster that she would take her departure on the next. After that her life before her would be a blank. She had known up to this,—so at least she told herself,—that Jonathan Stubbs would afford her at any rate another chance. Now there could be no other chance.

The first blank day passed away, and it seemed to her almost as though she had no right to speak to any one. She was sure that Lady Rufford knew what had occurred, because nothing more was said as to the proposed visit. Mrs. Colonel Stubbs would have been welcome anywhere, but who was Ayala Dormer? Even though Lady Albury bade her come out in the carriage, it seemed to her to be done as a final effort of kindness. Of course they would be anxious to be rid of her. That evening the buxom woman did not come to help her dress herself. It was an accident. The buxom woman was wanted here and there till it was too late, and Ayala had left her room. Ayala, in truth, required no assistance in dressing. When the first agonizing moment of the new frock had been passed over, she would sooner have arrayed herself without assistance. But now it seemed as though the buxom woman was running away, because she, Ayala, was thought to be no longer worthy of her services.

On the next morning she began her little speech to Lady Albury. "Going away to-morrow?" said Lady Albury.

"Or perhaps the next day," suggested Ayala.

"My dear, it has been arranged that you should stay here for another three weeks."

"No."

"I say it was arranged. Everybody understood it. I am sure your aunt understood it. Because one person goes, everybody else isn't to follow so as to break up a party. Honour among thieves!"

"Thieves!"

"Well;—anything else you like to call us all. The party has been made up. And to tell the truth I don't think that young ladies have the same right of changing their minds and rushing about as men assume.. Young ladies ought to be more steady. Where am I to get another young lady at a moment's notice to play lawn tennis with Mr. Greene? Compose yourself and stay where you are like a good girl."

"What will Sir Harry say?"

"Sir Harry will probably go on talking about the Stillborough fox and quarrelling with that odious Captain Glomax. That is, if you remain here. If you go all of a sudden, he will perhaps hint——"

"Hint what, Lady Albury?"

"Never mind. He shall make no hints if you are a good girl." Nothing was said at the moment about the Colonel,—nothing further than the little allusion made above. Then there came the lawn tennis, and Ayala regained something of her spirits as she contrived with the assistance of Sir Harry to beat Nina and the curate. But on the following day Lady Albury spoke out more plainly. "It was because of Colonel Stubbs that you said that you would go away."

Ayala paused a moment, and then answered stoutly, "Yes, it was because of Colonel Stubbs."

"And why?"

Ayala paused again and the stoutness almost deserted her. "Because——"

"Well, my dear?"

"I don't think I ought to be asked," said Ayala.

"Well, you shall not be asked. I will not be cruel to you. But do you not know that if I ask anything it is with a view to your own good?"

"Oh, yes," said Ayala.

"But though I may not ask I suppose I may speak." To this Ayala made no reply, either assenting or dissenting. "You know, do you not, that I and Colonel Stubbs love each other like brother and sister,—more dearly than many brothers and sisters?"

"I suppose so."

"And that therefore he tells me everything. He told me what took place in the wood,—and because of that he has gone away."

"Of course you are angry with me;—because he has gone away."

"I am sorry that he has gone,—because of the cause of it. I always wish that he should have everything that he desires; and now I wish that he should have this thing because he desires it above all other things." Does he desire it above all other things?—thought Ayala to herself. And, if it be really so, cannot I now tell her that he shall have it? Cannot I say that I too long to get it quite as eagerly as he longs to have it? The suggestion rushed quickly to her mind; but the answer to it came as quickly. No;—she would not do so. No offer of the kind would come from her. By what she had said must she abide,—unless, indeed, he should come to her again. "But why should you go, Ayala, because he has gone? Why should you say aloud that you had come here to listen to his offer, and that you had gone away as soon as you had resolved that, for this reason or that, it was not satisfactory to you?"

"Oh, Lady Albury."

"That would be the conclusion drawn. Remain here with us, and see if you can like us well enough to be one of us."

"Dear Lady Albury, I do love you dearly."

"What he may do I cannot say. Whether he may bring himself to try once again I do not know, —nor will I ask you whether there might possibly be any other answer were he to do so."

"No!" said Ayala, driven by a sudden fit of obstinacy which she could not control.

"I ask no questions about it, but I am sure it will be better for you to remain here for a few weeks. We will make you happy if we can, and you can learn to think over what has passed without emotion." Thus it was decided that Ayala should prolong her visit into the middle of March. She could not understand her own conduct when she again found herself alone. Why had she ejaculated that sudden "No," when Lady Albury had suggested to her the possibility of changing her purpose? She knew that she would fain change it if it were possible; and yet when the idea was presented to her she replied with a sudden denial of its possibility. But still there was hope, even though the hope was faint. "Whether he may bring himself to try again I do not know." So it was that Lady Albury had spoken of him, and of what Lady Albury said to her she now believed every word. "Whether he could bring himself!" Surely such a one as he would not condescend so far as that. But if he did one word should be sufficient. By no one else would she allow it to be thought, for an instant, that she would wish to reverse her decision. It must still be No to any other person from whom such suggestion might come. But should he give her the chance she would tell him instantly the truth of everything. "Can I love you! Oh, my love, it is impossible that I should not love you!" It would be thus that the answer should be given to him, should he allow her the chance of making it.

CHAPTER IX.

"I CALL IT FOLLY."

THREE weeks passed by, and Ayala was still at Stalham. Colonel Stubbs had not as yet appeared, and very little had been said about him. Sir Harry would sometimes suggest that if he meant to see any more hunting he had better come at once, but this was not addressed to Ayala. She made up her mind that he would not come, and was sure that she was keeping him away by her presence. He could not—"bring himself to try over again," as Lady Albury had put it! Why should he—"bring himself"—to do anything on behalf of one who had treated him so badly? It had been settled that she should remain to the 25th of March, when the month should be up from the time in which Lady Albury had decided upon that as the period of her visit. Of her secret she had given no slightest hint. If he ever did come again it should not be because she had asked for his coming? As far as she knew how to carry out such a purpose, she concealed from Lady Albury anything like a feeling of regret. And she was so far successful that Lady Albury thought it expedient to bring in other assistance to help her cause,—as will be seen by a letter which Ayala received when the three weeks had passed by.

In the meantime there had been at first dismay, then wonder, and lastly, some amusement, at the condition of Captain Batsby. When Captain Batsby had first learned at Merle Park that Ayala and Jonathan Stubbs were both at Stalham, he wrote very angrily to Lady Albury. In answer to this his sister-in-law had pleaded guilty,—but still defending herself. How could she make herself responsible for the young lady,—who did not indeed seem ready to bestow her affections on any of her suitors? But still she acknowledged that a little favour was being shown to Colonel Stubbs,—wishing to train the man to the idea that, in this special matter, Colonel Stubbs must be recognised as the Stalham favourite. Then no further letters were received from the Captain, but there came tidings that he was staying at Merle Park. Ayala heard continually from her sister, and Lucy sent some revelations as to the Captain. He seemed to be very much at home at Merle Park, said Lucy; and then, at last, she expressed her own opinion that Captain Batsby and Gertrude were becoming very fond of each other. And yet the whole story of Gertrude and Mr. Houston was known, of course, to Lucy, and through Lucy to Ayala. To Ayala these sudden changes were very amusing, as she certainly did not wish to retain her own hold on the Captain, and was not specially attached to her cousin Gertrude. From Ayala the tidings went to Lady Albury, and in this way the fears which had been entertained as to the Captain's displeasure were turned to wonder and amusement. But up to this period nothing had been heard of the projected trip to Ostend.

Then came the letter to Ayala, to which allusion has been made, a letter from her old friend the Marchesa, who was now at Rome. It was ostensibly in answer to a letter from Ayala herself, but was written in great part in compliance with instructions received from Lady Albury. It was as follows;—

"Dear Ayala,—

"I was glad to get your letter about Nina. She is very happy, and Lord George is here. Indeed, to tell the truth, they arrived together,—which was not at all proper; but everything will be made proper on Tuesday, 8th April, which is the day at last fixed for the wedding. I wish you could have been here to be one of the bridesmaids. Nina says that you will have it that the Pope is to marry her. Instead of that it is going to be done by Lord George's uncle, the Dean of Dorchester, who is coming for this purpose. Then they are going up to a villa they have taken on Como, where we shall join them some time before the spring is over. After that they seem to have no plans,—except plans of connubial bliss, which is never to know any interruption.

"Now that I have come to connubial bliss, and feel so satisfied as to Nina's prospects, I have a word or two to say about the bliss of somebody else. Nina is my own child, and of course comes first. But one Jonathan Stubbs is my nephew, and is also very near to my heart. From all that I hear,

I fancy that he has set his mind also on connubial bliss. Have you not heard that it is so?

"A bird has whispered to me that you have not been kind to him. Why should it be so? Nobody knows better than I do that a young lady is entitled to the custody of her own heart, and that she should not be compelled, or even persuaded, to give her hand in opposition to her own feelings. If your feelings and your heart are altogether opposed to the poor fellow, of course there must be an end of it. But I had thought that from the time you first met him he had been a favourite of yours;—so much so that there was a moment in which I feared that you might think too much of the attentions of a man who has ever been a favourite with all who have known him. But I have found that in this I was altogether mistaken. When he came that evening to see the last of you at the theatre, taking, as I knew he did, considerable trouble to release himself from other engagements, I was pretty sure how it was going to be. He is not a man to be in love with a girl for a month and then to be in love with another the next month. When once he allowed himself to think that he was in love, the thing was done and fixed either for his great delight,—or else to his great trouble.

"I knew how it was to be, and so it has been. Am I not right in saying that on two occasions, at considerable intervals, he has come to you and made distinct offers of his hand? I fear, though I do not actually know it, that you have just as distinctly rejected those offers. I do not know it, because none but you and he can know the exact words with which you received from him the tender of all that he had to give you. I can easily believe that he, with all his intelligence, might be deceived by the feminine reserve and coyness of such a girl as you. If it be so, I do pray that no folly may be allowed to interfere with his happiness and with yours.

"I call it folly, not because I am adverse to feminine reserve, not because I am prone to quarrel even with what I call coyness; but because I know his nature so well, and feel that he would not bear rebuffs of which many another man would think nothing; that he would not bring himself to ask again, perhaps even for a seventh time, as they might do. And, if it be that by some frequent asking his happiness and yours could be insured, would it not be folly that such happiness should be marred by childish disinclination on your part to tell the truth?

"As I said before, if your heart be set against him, there must be an end of it. I can understand that a girl so young as you should fail to see the great merit of such a man. I therefore write as I do, thinking it possible that in this respect you may be willing to accept from my mouth something as to the man which shall be regarded as truth. It is on the inner man, on his nature and disposition, that the happiness of a wife must depend. A more noble nature, a more truthful spirit than his, I have never met. He is one on whom in every phase of life you may depend,—or I may depend,—as on a rock. He is one without vacillation, always steady to his purpose, requiring from himself in the way of duty and conduct infinitely more than he demands from those around him. If ever there was a man altogether manly, he is one. And yet no woman, no angel, ever held a heart more tender within his bosom. See him with children! Think of his words when he has spoken to yourself! Remember the estimation in which those friends hold him who know him best,—such as I and your friend, Lady Albury, and Sir Harry, and his cousin Nina. I could name many others, but these are those with whom you have seen him most frequently. If you can love such a man, do you not think that he would make you happy? And if you cannot, must there not be something wrong in your heart,—unless indeed it be already predisposed to some one else? Think of all this, dear Ayala, and remember that I am always

"Your affectionate friend,

"JULIA BALDONI."

Ayala's first feeling as she read the letter was a conviction that her friend had altogether wasted her labour in writing it. Of what use was it to tell her of the man's virtues,—to tell her that the man's heart was as tender as an angel's, his truth as assured as a god's, his courage that of a hero,—that he was possessed of all those attributes which should by right belong to an Angel of Light? She knew all that without requiring the evidence of a lady from Rome,—having no need of any evidence on that matter from any other human being. Of what use could any evidence be on such a subject from the most truthful lips that ever spoke! Had she not found it all out herself would any words from others have prevailed with her? But she had found it out herself. It was already her gospel. That he was tender and true, manly, heroic,—as brightly angelic as could be any Angel of Light,—was already an absolute fact to her. No!—her heart had never been predisposed to any one else. It was of him she had always dreamed even long before she had seen him. He was the man, perfect in all good things, who was to come and take her with him;—if ever man should come and take her. She wanted no Marchesa Baldoni now to tell her that the angel had in truth come and realised himself before her in all his glory.

But she had shown herself to be utterly unfit for the angel. Though she recognised him now, she had not recognised him in time;—and even when she had recognised him she had been driven by her madness to reject him. Feminine reserve and coyness! Folly! Yes, indeed; she knew all that, too, without need of telling from her elders. The kind of coyness which she had displayed had been the very infatuation of feminine imbecility. It was because nature had made her utterly unfit for such a destiny that she had been driven by coyness and feminine reserve to destroy herself! It was thus that Ayala conversed with herself.

"I know his nature so well, and feel that he would not bear rebuffs of which many another man would think nothing." Thus, she did not doubt, the Marchesa had spoken very truly. But of what value was all that now? She could not recall the rebuff. She could not now eradicate the cowardice which had made her repeat those wicked fatal words,—"I cannot." "I cannot." "I cannot." The letter had come too late, for there was nothing she could do to amend her doom. She must send some answer to her friend in Italy, but there could be nothing in her answer to her to assist her. The feminine reserve and coyness had become odious to her,—as it had been displayed by herself to him. But it still remained in full force as to any assistance from others. She could not tell another to send him back to her. She could not implore help in her trouble. If he would come himself,—himself of his own accord,—himself impelled once more by his great tenderness of heart,—himself once more from his real, real love; then there should be no more coyness. "If you will still have me,—oh yes!"

But there was the letter to be written. She so wrote it that by far the greater part of it,—the larger part at least,—had reference to Nina and her wedding. "I will think of her on the 8th of April," she said. "I shall then be at home at Kingsbury Crescent, and I shall have nothing else to think of." In that was her first allusion to her own condition with her lover. But on the last side of the sheet it was necessary that she should say more than that. Something must be said thoughtfully, carefully, and gratefully in reply to so much thought, and care, and friendship, as had been shown to her. But it must be so written that nothing of her secret should be read in it. The task was so troublesome that she was compelled to recopy the whole of her long letter, because the sentences as first written did not please her. "I am so much obliged to you," she said, "by your kindness about Colonel Stubbs. He did do me the honour of asking me to be his wife. And I felt it so. You are not to suppose that I did not understand that. It is all over now, and I cannot explain to you why I felt that it would not do. It is all over, and therefore writing about it is no good. Only I want you to be sure of two things,—that there is no one else, and that I do love you so much for all your kindness. And you may be sure of a third thing, too,—that it is all over. I do hope that he will still let me be his friend. As a friend I have always liked him so much." It was brave and bold, she thought, in answer to such words as the Marchesa's; but she did not know how to do it any better.

On Tuesday, the 25th of March, she was to return to Kingsbury Crescent. Various little words were said at Stalham indicating an intended break in the arrangement. "The Captain certainly won't come now," said Lady Albury, alluding to the arrangement as though it had been made solely with the view of saving Ayala from an encounter with her objectionable lover. "Croppy has come back," said Sir Harry one day;—Croppy being the pony which Ayala had ridden. "Miss Dormer can have him now for what little there is left of the hunting." This was said on the Saturday before she was to go. How could she ride Croppy for the rest of the hunting when she would be at Kingsbury Crescent? On neither of these occasions did she say a word, but she assumed that little look of contradiction which her friends at Stalham already knew how to read. Then, on the Sunday morning, there came a letter for Lady Albury. "What does he say?" asked Sir Harry, at breakfast. "I'll show it you before you go to church," answered his wife. Then Ayala knew that the letter was from Colonel Stubbs.

But she did not expect that the letter should be shown to her,—which, however, came to be the case. When she was in the library, waiting to start to church, Lady Albury came in and threw the letter to her across the table. "That concerns you," she said, "you had better read it." There was another lady in the room, also waiting to start on their walk across the park, and therefore it was natural that nothing else should be said at the moment. Ayala read the letter, returned it to the envelope, and then handed it back to Lady Albury,—so that there was no word spoken about it before church. The letter, which was very short, was as follows;—

"I shall be at Stalham by the afternoon train on Sunday, 30th,—in time for dinner, if you will send the dog-cart. I could not leave this most exigeant of all places this week. I suppose Albury will go on in the woodlands for a week or ten days in April, and I must put up with that. I hear that Batsby is altogether fixed by the fascinations of Merle Park. I hope that you and Albury will receive consolation in the money." Then there was a postscript. "If Croppy can be got back again, Miss Dormer might see me tumble into another river."

It was evident that Lady Albury did not expect anything to be said at present. She put the letter into her pocket, and there, for the moment, was the end of it. It may be feared that Ayala's attention was not fixed that morning so closely as it should have been on the services of the Church. There was so much in that little letter which insisted upon having all her attention! Had there been no postscript, the letter would have been very different. In that case the body of the letter itself would have intended to have no reference to her,—or rather it would have had a reference altogether opposite to that which the postscript gave it. In that case it would have been manifest to her that he had intentionally postponed his coming till she had left Stalham. Then his suggestion about the hunting would have had no interest for her. Everything would have been over. She would have been at Kingsbury Crescent, and he would have been at Stalham. But the postscript declared his intention of finding her still in the old quarters. She would not be there,—as she declared to herself. After this there would be but one other day, and then she would be gone. But even this allusion to her and to the pony made the letter something to her of intense interest. Had it not been so Lady Albury would not have shown it to her. As it was, why had Lady Albury shown it to her in that quiet, placid, friendly way,—as though it were natural that any letter from Colonel Stubbs to Stalham should be shown to her?

At lunch Sir Harry began about the pony at once. "Miss Dormer," he said, "the pony will hardly be fit to-morrow, and the distances during the rest of the week are all too great for you; you had better wait till Monday week, when Stubbs will be here to look after you."

"But I am going home on Tuesday," said Ayala.

"I've had the pony brought on purpose for you," said Sir Harry.

"You are not going at all," said Lady Albury. "All that has to be altered. I'll write to Mrs. Dosett."

"I don't think——" began Ayala.

"I shall take it very much amiss," said Sir Harry, "if you go now. Stubbs is coming on purpose."

"I don't think——" began Ayala again.

"My dear Ayala, it isn't a case for thinking," said Lady Albury. "You most positively will not leave this house till some day in April, which will have to be settled hereafter. Do not let us have a word more about it." Then, on that immediate occasion, no further word about it was spoken. Ayala was quite unable to speak as she sat attempting to eat her lunch.

CHAPTER X.

HOW LUCY'S AFFAIRS ARRANGED THEMSELVES.

We must go again to Merle Park, where the Tringle family was still living,—and from which Gertrude had not as yet been violently abducted at the period to which the reader has been brought in the relation which has been given of the affairs at Stalham. Jonathan Stubbs's little note to Lady Albury was received on Sunday, 23rd March, and Gertrude was not abducted till the 29th. On Sunday, the 30th, she was brought back,—not in great triumph. At that time the house was considerably perturbed. Sir Thomas was very angry with his daughter Augusta, having been led to believe that she had been privy to Gertrude's escapade,—so angry that very violent words had been spoken as to her expulsion from the house. Tom also was ill, absolutely ill in bed, with a doctor to see him,—and all from love, declaring that he would throw himself over the ship's side and drown himself while there was yet a chance left to him for Ayala. And in the midst of this Lady Tringle herself was by no means exempt from the paternal wrath. She was told that she must have known what was going on between her daughter and that idiot Captain,—that she encouraged the Trafficks to remain,—that she coddled up her son till he was sick from sheer lackadaisical idleness. The only one in the house who seemed to be exempt from the wrath of Sir Thomas was Lucy, — and therefore it was upon Lucy's head that fell the concentrated energy of Aunt Emmeline's revenge. When Captain Batsby was spoken of with contumely in the light of a husband,—this being always done by Sir Thomas,—Lady Tringle would make her rejoinder to this, when Sir Thomas had turned his back, by saying that a captain in Her Majesty's army, with good blood in his veins and a competent fortune, was at any rate better than a poor artist, who had, so to say, no blood, and was unable to earn his bread; and when Tom was ridiculed for his love for Ayala she would go on to explain, — always after Sir Thomas's back had been turned,—that poor Tom had been encouraged by his father, whereas Lucy had taken upon herself to engage herself in opposition to her pastors and masters. And then came the climax. It was all very well to say that Augusta was intruding,—but there were people who intruded much worse than Augusta, without half so much right. When this was said the poor sore-hearted woman felt her own cruelty, and endeavoured to withdraw the harsh words; but the wound had been given, and the venom rankled so bitterly that Lucy could no longer bear her existence among the Tringles. "I ought not to remain after that," she wrote to her lover. "Though I went into the poorhouse I ought not to remain."

"I wrote to Mr. Hamel," she said to her aunt,

"and told him that as you did not like my being here I had better,—better go away."

"But where are you to go? And I didn't say that I didn't like you being here. You oughtn't to take me up in that way."

"I do feel that I am in the way, aunt, and I think that I had better go."

"But where are you to go? I declare that everybody says everything to break my heart. Of course you are to remain here till he has got a house to keep you in." But the letter had gone and a reply had come telling Lucy that whatever might be the poor-house to which she would be destined he would be there to share it with her.

Hamel wrote this with high heart. He had already resolved, previous to this, that he would at once prepare a home for his coming bride, though he was sore distressed by the emergency of his position. His father had become more and more bitter with him as he learned that his son would in no respect be guided by him. There was a sum of money which he now declared to be due to him, and which Isadore acknowledged to have been lent to him. Of this the father demanded repayment. "If," said he, "you acknowledge anything of the obedience of a son, that money is at your disposal, —and any other that you may want. But, if you determine to be as free from my control and as deaf to my advice as might be any other young man, then you must be to me as might be any other young man." He had written to his father saying that the money should be repaid as soon as possible.

The misfortune had come to him at a trying time. It was however, before he had received Lucy's last account of her own misery at Merle Park, so that when that was received he was in part prepared.

Our Colonel, in writing to Lady Albury, had declared Aldershot to be a most exigeant place,—by which he had intended to imply that his professional cares were too heavy to allow his frequent absence; but nevertheless he would contrive occasionally to fly up to London for a little relief. Once when doing so he had found himself sitting in the sculptor's studio, and there listening to Hamel's account of Lucy's troubles at Merle Park. Hamel said nothing as to his own difficulties, but was very eager in explaining the necessity of removing Lucy from the tyranny to which she was subjected. It will perhaps be remembered that Hamel down in Scotland had declared to his friend his purpose of asking Lucy Dormer to be his wife, and also the success of his enterprise after he had gone across the lake to Glenbogie. It will be borne in mind also that should the Colonel succeed in winning Ayala to his way of thinking the two men would become the husbands of the two sisters. Each fully sympathised with the other, and in this way they had become sincere and intimate friends.

"Is she like her sister?" asked the Colonel, who was not as yet acquainted with Lucy.

"Hardly like her, although in truth there is a family likeness. Lucy is taller, with perhaps more regular features, and certainly more quiet in her manner."

"Ayala can be very quiet too," said the lover.

"Oh, yes,—because she varies in her moods. I remember her almost as a child, when she would remain perfectly still for a quarter of an hour, and then would be up and about the house everywhere, glancing about like a ray of the sun reflected from a mirror as you move it in your hand."

"She has grown steadier since that," said the Colonel.

"I cannot imagine her to be steady,—not as Lucy is steady. Lucy, if it be necessary, can sit and fill herself with her own thoughts for the hour together."

"Which of them was most like their father?"

"They were both of them like him in their thorough love for things beautiful;—but they are both of them unlike him in this, that he was self-indulgent, while they, like women in general, are always devoting themselves to others." She will not devote herself to me, thought Jonathan Stubbs to himself, but that may be because, like her father, she loves things beautiful. "My poor Lucy," continued Hamel, "would fain devote herself to those around her if they would only permit it."

"She would probably prefer devoting herself to you," said the Colonel.

"No doubt she would,—if it were expedient. If I may presume that she loves me, I may presume also that she would wish to live with me."

"Is it not expedient?" asked the other.

"It will be so, I trust, before long."

"But it seems to be so necessary just at present."

To this the sculptor at the moment made no reply. "If," continued Stubbs, "they treat her among them as you say, she ought at any rate to be relieved from her misery."

"She ought to be relieved certainly. She shall be relieved."

"But you say that it is not expedient."

"I only meant that there were difficulties;—difficulties which will have to be got over. I think that all difficulties are got over when a man looks at them steadily."

"This, I suppose, is an affair of money."

"Well, yes. All difficulties seem to me to be an affair of money. A man, of course, would wish to earn enough before he marries to make his wife comfortable. I would struggle on as I am, and not be impatient, were it not that I fear she is more uncomfortable as she is now than she would be here in the midst of my poverty."

"After all, Hamel, what is the extent of the poverty? What are the real circumstances? As you have gone so far you might as well tell me everything." Then after considerable pressure the sculptor did tell him everything. There was an income of less than three hundred a year,—which would probably become about four within the next twelvemonth. There were no funds prepared with which to buy the necessary furniture for the incoming of a wife, and there was that debt demanded by his father.

"Must that be paid?" asked the Colonel.

"I would starve rather than not pay it," said

Hamel, "if I alone were to be considered. It would certainly be paid within the next six months if I were alone, even though I should starve."

Then his friend told him that the debt should be paid at once. It amounted to but little more than a hundred pounds. And then, of course, the conversation was carried further. When a friend inquires as to the pecuniary distresses of a friend he feels himself as a matter of course bound to relieve him. He would supply also the means necessary for the incoming of the young wife. With much energy, and for a long time, Hamel refused to accept the assistance offered to him; but the Colonel insisted in the first place on what he considered to be due from himself to Ayala's sister, and then on the fact that he doubted not in the least the ultimate success which would attend the professional industry of his friend. And so before the day was over it was settled among them. The money was to be forthcoming at once, so that the debt might be paid and the preparations made, and Hamel was to write to Lucy and declare that he should be ready to receive her as soon as arrangements should be made for their immediate marriage. Then came the further outrage,—that cruel speech as to intruders, and Lucy wrote to her lover, owning that it would be well for her that she should be relieved.

The news was, of course, declared to the family at Merle Park. "I never knew anything so hard," said Aunt Emmeline. "Of course you have told him that it was all my fault." When Lucy made no answer to this, she went on with her complaint. "I know that you have told him that I have turned you out,—which is not true."

"I told him it was better I should go, as you did not like my being here."

"I suppose Lucy was in a little hurry to have the marriage come off," said Augusta,—who would surely have spared her cousin if at the moment she had remembered the haste which had been displayed by her sister.

"I thought it best," said Lucy.

"I'm sure I don't know how it is to be done," said Aunt Emmeline. "You must tell your uncle yourself. I don't know how you are to be married from here, seeing the trouble we are in."

"We shall be up in London before that," said Gertrude.

"Or from Queen's Gate either," continued Aunt Emmeline.

"I don't suppose that will much signify. I shall just go to the church."

"Like a servant-maid?" asked Gertrude.

"Yes;—like a servant-maid," said Lucy. "That is to say, a servant-maid would, I suppose, simply walk in and be married; and I shall do the same."

"I think you had better tell your uncle," said Aunt Emmeline. "But I am sure I did not mean that you were to go away like this. It will be your own doing, and I cannot help it if you will do it."

Then Lucy did tell her uncle. "And you mean to live upon three hundred a year!" exclaimed Sir

Thomas. "You don't know what you are talking about."

"I think Mr. Hamel knows."

"He is as ignorant as a babe unborn;—I mean about that kind of thing. I don't doubt he can make things in stone as well as anybody."

"In marble, Uncle Tom."

"Marble is stone, I suppose;—or in iron."

"Bronze, Uncle Tom."

"Very well. There is iron in bronze, I suppose. But he doesn't know what a wife will cost. Has he bought any furniture?"

"He is going to buy it,—just a little;—what will do?"

"Why should you want to bring him into this?" Lucy looked wistfully up into his face. He himself had been personally kind to her, and she found it to be impossible to complain to him of her aunt. "You are not happy here?"

"My aunt and cousins think that I am wrong; but I must be married to him now, Uncle Tom."

"Why did he kick up his heels when I wanted to help him?" Nevertheless, he gave his orders on the subject very much in Lucy's favour. She was to be married from Queen's Gate, and Gertrude must be her bridesmaid. Ayala no doubt would be the other. When his wife expostulated, he consented that the marriage should be very quiet, but still he would have it as he had said. Then he bestowed a cheque upon Lucy,—larger in amount than Stubbs's loan,—saying that after what had passed in Lombard Street he would not venture to send money to so independent a person as Mr. Isadore Hamel; but adding that Lucy, perhaps, would condescend to accept it. There was a smile in his eye as he said the otherwise ill-natured word, so that Lucy, without any wound to her feelings, could kiss him and accept his bounty.

"I suppose I am to have nothing to do in settling the day," said Aunt Emmeline. It was, however, settled between them that the marriage should take place on a certain day in May. Upon this Lucy was of course overjoyed, and wrote to her lover in a full flow of spirits. And she sent him the cheque, having written her name with great pride on the back of it. There was a little trouble about this as a part of it had to come back as her trousseau, but still the arrangement was pleasantly made. Then Sir Thomas again became more kind to her, in his rough manner,—even when his troubles were at the worst after the return of Gertrude. "If it will not be altogether oppressive to his pride you may tell him that I shall make you an allowance of a hundred a year as my niece,—just for your personal expenses."

"I don't know that he is so proud, Uncle Tom."

"He seemed so to me. But if you say nothing to him about it, and just buy a few gowns now and again, he will perhaps be so wrapt up in the higher affairs of his art as not to take any notice."

"I am sure he will notice what I wear," said Lucy. However she communicated her uncle's intentions to her lover, and he sent back his grateful thanks to Sir Thomas. As one effect of all this the Colonel's money was sent back to him, with an assurance that as things were now settling themselves such pecuniary assistance was not needed. But this was not done till Ayala had heard what the Angel of Light had done on her sister's behalf. But as to Ayala's feelings in that respect we must be silent here, as otherwise we should make premature allusion to the condition in which Ayala found herself before she had at last managed to escape from Stalham Park.

"Papa," said Gertrude, to her father one evening, "don't you think you could do something for me too now?" Just at this time Sir Thomas, greatly to his own annoyance, was coming down to Merle Park every evening. According to their plans as at present arranged, they were to stay in the country till after Easter, and then they were to go up to town in time to despatch poor Tom upon his long journey round the world. But poor Tom was now in bed, apparently ill, and there seemed to be great doubt whether he could be made to go on the appointed day in spite of the taking of his berth and the preparation of his outfit. Tom, if well enough, was to sail on the nineteenth of April, and there now wanted not above ten days to that time. "Don't you think you could do something for me now?" asked Gertrude. Hitherto Sir Thomas had extended no sign of pardon to his youngest daughter, and never failed to allude to her and to Captain Batsby as "those two idiots" whenever their names were mentioned before him.

"Yes, my dear; I will endeavour to do a good deal for you if you will behave yourself."

"What do you call behaving myself, papa?"

"In the first place telling me that you are very sorry for your misbehaviour with that idiot."

"Of course I am sorry if I have offended you."

"Well, that shall go for something. But how about the idiot?"

"Papa!" she exclaimed.

"Was he not an idiot? Would any one but an idiot have gone on such an errand as that?"

"Gentlemen and ladies have done it before, papa."

"I doubt it," he said. "Gentlemen have run away with young ladies before, and generally have behaved very badly when they have done so. He behaved very badly indeed, because he had come to my house, with my sanction, with the express purpose of expressing his affection for another young lady. But I think that his folly in this special running away was worse even than his conduct. How did he come to think that he could get himself married merely by crossing over the sea to Ostend? I should be utterly ashamed of him as a son-in-law,—chiefly because he has shown himself to be an idiot."

"But, papa, you will accept him, won't you?"

"No, my dear, I will not."

"Not though I love him?"

"If I were to give you a choice which you would take, him or Mr. Houston?"

"Houston is a scoundrel."

"Very likely; but then he is not an idiot. My choice would be altogether in favour of Mr. Houston.

Shall I tell you what I will do, my dear? I will consent to accept Captain Batsby as my son-in-law if he will consent to become your husband without having a shilling with you."

"Would that be kind, papa?"

"I do not think that I can show you any greater kindness than to protect you from a man who I am quite sure does not care a farthing about you. He has, you tell me, an ample income of his own."

"Oh yes, papa."

"Then he can afford to marry you without a fortune. Poor Mr. Houston could not have done so, because he had nothing of his own. I declare, as I think of it all, I am becoming very tender-hearted towards Mr. Houston. Don't you think we had better have Mr. Houston back again? I suppose he would come if you were to send for him." Then she burst into tears and went away and hid herself.

CHAPTER XI.

TOM'S LAST ATTEMPT.

WHILE Gertrude was still away on her ill-omened voyage in quest of a parson, Lady Tringle was stirred up to a great enterprise on behalf of her unhappy son. There wanted now little more than a fortnight before the starting of the ship which his father still declared should carry him out across the world, and he had progressed so far in contemplating the matter as to own to himself that it would be best for him to obey his father if there was no hope. But his mind was still swayed by a theory of love and constancy. He had heard of men who had succeeded after a dozen times of asking. If Stubbs, the hated but generous Stubbs, were in truth a successful rival, then indeed the thing would be over;—then he would go, the sooner the better; and, as he told his mother half-a-dozen times a day, it would matter nothing to him whether he were sent to Japan, or the Rocky Mountains, or the North Pole. In such case he would be quite content to go, if only for the sake of going. But how was he to be sure? He was, indeed, nearly sure in the other direction. If Ayala were in truth engaged to Colonel Stubbs it would certainly be known through Lucy. Then he had heard, through Lucy, that, though Ayala was staying at Stalham, the Colonel was not there. He had gone, and Ayala had remained week after week without him. Then, towards the end of March, he wrote a letter to his Uncle Reginald, which was very piteous in its tone;—

"Dear Uncle Reginald," the letter said,

"I don't know whether you have heard of it, but I have been very ill—and unhappy. I am now in bed, and nobody here knows that I am sending this letter to you. It is all about Ayala, and I am not such a fool as to suppose that you can do anything for me. If you could I think you would,—but of course you can't. She must choose for herself,—only I do so wish that she should choose me. Nobody would ever be more kind to her. But you can tell me really how it is. Is she engaged to marry Colonel Stubbs? I know that she refused him, because he told me so himself. If she is not engaged to him I think that I would have another shy at it. You know what the poet says,—'Faint heart never won fair lady.' Do tell me if she is or is not engaged. I know that she is with those Alburys, and that Colonel Stubbs is their friend. But they can't make her marry Colonel Stubbs any more than my friends can make her marry me. I wish they could. I mean my friends, not his.

"If she were really engaged I would go away and hide myself in the furthermost corner of the world. Siberia or Central Africa would be the same to me. They would have little trouble in getting rid of me if I knew that it was all over with me.

BUT I WILL NEVER STIR FROM THESE REALMS TILL I KNOW MY FATE!—Therefore, waiting your reply, I am your affectionate nephew,

"THOMAS TRINGLE, junior."

Mr. Dosett, when he received this letter, consulted his wife before he replied to it, and then did so very shortly;—

"MY DEAR TOM,

"As far as I know, or her aunt, your cousin Ayala is not engaged to marry any one. But I should deceive you if I did not add my belief that she is resolved not to accept the offer you have done her the honour to make her.

"Your affectionate uncle,

"REGINALD DOSETT."

The latter portion of this paragraph had no influence whatsoever on Tom. Did he not know all that before? Had he ever attempted to conceal from his relations the fact that Ayala had refused him again and again? Was not that as notorious to the world at large as a minister's promise that the income-tax should be abolished? But the income-tax was not abolished,—and, as yet, Ayala was not married to any one else. Ayala was not even engaged to any other suitor. Why should she not change her mind as well as the minister? Certainly he would not go either to the North Pole or to New York as long as there should be a hope of bliss for him in England. Then he called his mother to his bedside.

"Go to Stalham, my dear!" said his mother.

"Why not? They can't eat you. Lady Albury is no more than a Baronet's wife,—just the same as you."

"It isn't about eating me, Tom. I shouldn't know what to say to them."

"You need not tell them anything. Say that you had come to call upon your niece."

"But it would be such an odd thing to do. I never do call on Ayala,—even when I am in London."

"What does it matter being odd? You could learn the truth at any rate. If she does not care for any one else why shouldn't she have me? I could make her a baronet's wife,—that is, some day when the governor——"

"Don't, Tom;—don't talk in that way."

"I only mean in the course of nature. Sons do come after their fathers, you know. And as for money, I suppose the governor is quite as rich as those Alburys."

"I don't think that would matter."

"It does count, mother. I suppose Ayala is the same as other girls in that respect. I am sure I don't know why it is that she should have taken such an aversion to me. I suppose it is that she doesn't think me so much,—quite such a swell as some other men."

"One can't account for such things, Tom."

"No;—that is just it. And therefore she might come round without accounting for it. At any rate, you might try. You might tell her that it is ruining me;—that I shall have to go about wandering over all the world because she is so hard-hearted."

"I don't think I could, my dear," said Lady Tringle, after considering the matter for a while.

"Why not? Is it because of the trouble?"

"No, my dear; a mother does not think what trouble she may take for her child, if any good may be done. It is not the trouble. I would walk all round England to get her for you if that would do it."

"Why not, then? At any rate you might get an answer from her. She would tell you something of her intention. Mother, I shall never go away till I know more about it than I do now. The governor says that he will turn me out. Let him turn me out. That won't make me go away."

"Oh, Tom, he doesn't mean it."

"But he says it. If I knew that it was all over,—that every chance was gone, then I would go away."

"It is not the Alburys that I am afraid of," said Lady Tringle.

"What then?"

"It is your father. I cannot go if he will not let me." Nevertheless she promised before she left his bedside that she would ask Sir Thomas when he came home whether he would permit her to make the journey. All this occurred while Sir Thomas was away in quest of his daughter. And it may be imagined that immediately after his return he was hardly in a humour to yield to any such request as that which had been suggested. He was for the moment almost sick of his children, sick of Merle Park, sick of his wife, and inclined to think that the only comfort to be found in the world was to be had among his millions, in that little back parlour in Lombard Street.

It was on a Sunday that he returned, and on that day he did not see his son. On the Monday morning he went into the room, and Tom was about to press upon him the prayer which he had addressed to his mother when his lips were closed by his father's harshness. "Tom," he said, "you will be pleased to remember that you start on the nineteenth."

"But, father——"

"You start on the nineteenth," said Sir Thomas. Then he left the room, closing the door behind him with none of the tenderness generally accorded to an invalid.

"You have not asked him?" Tom said to his mother shortly afterwards.

"Not yet, my dear. His mind is so disturbed by this unfortunate affair."

"And is not my mind disturbed? You may tell him that I will not go, though he should turn me out a dozen times, unless I know more about it than I do now."

Sir Thomas came home again that evening, very sour in temper, and nothing could be said to him. He was angry with everybody, and Lady Tringle hardly dared to go near him, either then or on the following morning. On the Tuesday evening, however, he returned somewhat softened in his demeanour. The millions had perhaps gone right, though his children would go so wrong. When he spoke either to his younger daughter or of her he did so in that jeering tone which he afterwards always assumed when allusion was made to Captain Batsby, and which, disagreeable as it was, seemed to imply something of forgiveness. And he ate his dinner, and drank his glass of wine, without making any allusion to the parsimonious habits of his son-in-law, Mr. Traffick. Lady Tringle, therefore, considered that she might approach him with Tom's request.

"You go to Stalham!" he exclaimed.

"Well, my dear, I suppose I could see her?"

"And what could you learn from her?"

"I don't suppose I could learn much. She was always a pig-headed, stiff-necked creature. I am sure it wouldn't be any pleasure to me to see her."

"What good would it do?" demanded Sir Thomas.

"Well, my dear; he says that he won't go unless he can get a message from her. I am sure I don't want to go to Stalham. Nothing on earth could be so disagreeable. But perhaps I could bring back a word or two which would make him go upon his journey."

"What sort of word?"

"Why;—if I were to say that she were engaged to this Colonel Stubbs, then he would go. He says that he would start at once if he knew that his cousin were really engaged to somebody else."

"But if she be not?"

"Perhaps I could just colour it a little. It would be such a grand thing to get him away, and he in this miserable condition! If he were once on his travels, I do think he would soon begin to forget it all."

"Of course he would," said Sir Thomas.

"Then I might as well try. He has set his heart upon it, and if he thinks that I have done his bidding then he will obey you. As for turning him out, Tom, of course you do not really mean that!"

In answer to this Sir Thomas said nothing. He knew well enough that Tom couldn't be turned out. That turning out of a son is a difficult task to accomplish, and one altogether beyond the power of Sir Thomas. The chief cause of his sorrow lay in the fact that he, as the head of Travers and Treason, was debarred from the assistance and companionship of his son. All Travers and Treason was nothing to him, because his son would run so far away from the right path. There was nothing he would not do to bring him back. If Ayala could have been bought by any reasonable, or even unreasonable, amount of thousands, he would have bought her willingly for his boy's delight. It was a thing wonderful to him that Tom should have been upset so absolutely by his love. He did appreciate the feeling so far that he was willing to condone all those follies already committed if Tom would only put himself in the way of recovery. That massacreing of the policeman, those ill-spent nights at the Mountaineers and at Bolivia's, that foolish challenge, and the almost more foolish blow under the portico at the Haymarket, should all be forgiven if Tom would only consent to go through some slight purgation which would again fit him for Travers and Treason. And the purgation should be made as pleasant as possible. He should travel about the world with his pocket full of money and with every arrangement for luxurious comfort. Only he must go. There was no other way in which he could be so purged as to be again fit for Travers and Treason. He did not at all believe that Ayala could now be purchased. Whether pig-headed or not, Ayala was certainly self-willed. No good such as Tom expected would come from this projected visit to Stalham. But if he would allow it to be made in obedience to Tom's request,—then perhaps some tidings might be brought back which, whether strictly true or not, might induce Tom to allow himself to be put on board the ship. Arguing thus with himself, Sir Thomas at last gave his consent.

It was a most disagreable task which the mother thus undertook. She could not go from Merle Park to Stalham and back in one day. It was necessary that she should sleep two nights in London. It was arranged, therefore, that she should go up to London on the Thursday; then make her journey down to Stalham and back on the Friday, and get home on the Saturday. There would then still remain nearly a fortnight before Tom would have to leave Merle Park. After much consideration it was decided that a note should be written to Ayala apprising her of her aunt's coming. "I hope Lady Albury will not be surprised at my visit," said the note, "but I am so anxious to see you, just for half-an-hour, upon a matter of great importance, that I shall run my chance." She would prefer to have seen the girl without any notice; but then, had no notice been given, the girl would perhaps have been out of the way. As it was a telegram was received back in reply. "I shall be at home. Lady Albury will be very glad to see you at lunch. She says there shall be a room all ready if you will sleep."

"I certainly shall not stay there," Lady Tringle said to Mrs. Traffick, "but it is as well to know that they will be civil to me."

"They are stuck-up sort of people I believe," said Augusta; "just like that Marchesa Baldoni, who is one of them. But, as to their being civil, that is a matter of course. They would hardly be uncivil to any one connected with Lord Boardotrade!"

Then came the Thursday on which the journey was to be commenced. As the moment came near Lady Tringle was very much afraid of the task before her. She was afraid even of her niece Ayala, who had assumed increased proportions in her eyes since she had persistently refused not only Tom but also Colonel Stubbs and Captain Batsby, and then in spite of her own connexion with Lord Boardotrade,—of whom since her daughter's marriage she had learned to think less than she had done before,—she did feel that the Alburys were fashionable people, and that Ayala as their guest had achieved something for herself. Stalham was, no doubt, superior in general estimation to Merle Park, and with her there had been always a certain awe of Ayala which she had not felt in reference to Lucy. Ayala's demand that Augusta should go upstairs and fetch the scrap-book had had its effect, —as had also her success in going up St. Peter's and to the Marchesa's dance; and then there would be Lady Albury herself,—and all the Alburys! Only that Tom was very anxious, she would even now have abandoned the undertaking.

"Mother," said Tom, on the last morning, "you will do the best you can for me."

"Oh yes, my dear."

"I do think that, if you would make her understand the real truth, she might have me yet. She wouldn't like that a fellow should die."

"I am afraid that she is hard-hearted, Tom."

"I do not believe it, mother. I have seen her when she wouldn't kill even a fly. If she could only be made to see all the good she could do."

"I am afraid she won't care for that unless she can bring herself really to love you."

"Why shouldn't she love me?"

"Ah, my boy; how am I to tell you? Perhaps if you hadn't loved her so well it might have been different. If you had scorned her——"

"Scorn her! I couldn't scorn her. I have heard of that kind of thing before, but how is one to help oneself? You can't scorn a friend just because you choose to say so to yourself. When I see her she is something so precious to me that I could not be rough to her to save my life. When she first came it wasn't so. I could laugh at her then. But now——! They talk about goddesses, but I am sure she is a goddess to me."

"If you had made no more than a woman of her it might have been better, Tom." All that was too late now. The doctrine which Lady Tringle was enunciating to her son, and which he repudiated, is one that has been often preached and never practised. A man when he is conscious of the presence of a mere woman, to whom he feels that no worship is due, may for his own purpose be able to tell a lie to her, and make her believe that he acknowledges a divinity in her presence. But, when he feels the goddess, he cannot carry himself before her as though she were a mere woman, and, as such, inferior to himself in her attributes. Poor Tom had felt the touch of something divine, and had fallen immediately prostrate before the shrine with his face to the ground. His chance with Ayala could in no circumstances have been great; but she was certainly not one to have yielded to a prostrate worshipper.

"Mother!" said Tom, recalling Lady Tringle as she was leaving the room.

"What is it, my dear? I must really go now or I shall be too late for the train."

"Mother, tell her, tell her,—tell her that I love her." His mother ran back, kissed his brow, and then left the room.

Lady Tringle spent that evening in Queen's Gate, where Sir Thomas remained with her. The hours passed heavily, as they had not much present to their mind with which to console each other. Sir Thomas had no belief whatever in the journey except in so far as it might help to induce his son to proceed upon his travels;—but his wife had been so far softened by poor Tom's sorrows as to hope a little, in spite of her judgment, that Ayala might yet relent. Her heart was soft towards her son, so that she felt that the girl would deserve all manner of punishment unless she would at last yield to Tom's wishes. She was all but sure that it could not be so, and yet, in spite of her convictions, she hoped.

On the next morning the train took her safely to the Stalham Road Station, and as she approached the end of her journey her heart became heavier within her. She felt that she could not but fail to give any excuse to the Alburys for such a journey,—unless, indeed, Ayala should do as she would have her. At the station she found the Albury carriage, with the Albury coachman, and the Albury footman, and the Albury liveries, waiting for her. It was a closed carriage, and for a moment she thought that Ayala might be there. In that case she could have performed her commission in the carriage, and then have returned to London without going to the house at all. But Ayala was not there. Lady Tringle was driven up to the house, and then taken through the hall into a small sitting-room, where for a moment she was alone. Then the door opened, and Ayala, radiant with beauty, in all the prettiness of her best morning costume, was in a moment in her arms. She seemed in her brightness to be different from that Ayala who had been known before at Glenbogie and in Rome. "Dear aunt," said Ayala, "I am so delighted to see you at Stalham!"

CHAPTER XII.

IN THE CASTLE THERE LIVED A KNIGHT.

Ayala was compelled to consent to remain at Stalham. The "I don't think" which she repeated so often was, of course, of no avail to her. Sir Harry would be angry, and Lady Albury would be disgusted, were she to go,—and so she remained. There was to be a week before Colonel Stubbs would come, and she was to remain not only for the week but also for some short time afterwards,—so that there might be yet a few days left of hunting under the Colonel. It could not, surely, have been doubtful to her after she had read that letter,—with the postscript,—that if she remained her happiness would be insured! He would not have come again and insisted on her being there to receive him if nothing were to come of it. And yet she had fought for permission to return to Kingsbury Crescent after her little fashion, and had at last yielded, as she told Lady Albury,—because Sir Harry seemed to wish it. "Of course he wishes it," said Lady Albury. "He has got the pony on purpose, and nobody likes being disappointed when he has done a thing so much as Sir Harry." Ayala, delighted as she was, did not make her secret known. She was fluttered, and apparently uneasy,—so that her friend did not know what to make of it, or which way to take it. Ayala's secret was to herself a secret still to be maintained with holy reticence. It might still be possible that Jonathan Stubbs should never say another word to her of his love. If he did,—why then all the world might know. Then there would be no secret. Then she could sit and discuss her love, and his love, all night long with Lady Albury, if Lady Albury would listen to her. In the meantime the secret must be a secret. To confess her love, and then to have her love disappointed,—that would be death to her!

And thus it went on through the whole week, Lady Albury not quite knowing what to make of it. Once she did say a word, thinking that she would thus extract the truth, not as yet understanding how potent Ayala could be to keep her secret. "That man has, at any rate, been very true to you," she said. Ayala frowned, and shook her head, and would not say a word upon the subject. "If she did not mean to take him now, surely she would have gone," Lady Albury said to her husband.

"She is a pretty little girl enough," said Sir Harry, "but I doubt whether she is worth all the trouble."

"Of course she is not. What pretty little girl ever was? But as long as he thinks her worth it the trouble has to be taken."

"Of course she'll accept him?"

"I am not at all so sure of it. She has been

made to believe that you wanted her to stay, and therefore she has stayed. She is quite master enough of herself to ride out hunting with him again and then to refuse him." And so Lady Albury doubted up to the Sunday, and all through the Sunday,—up to the very moment when the last preparations were to be made for the man's arrival.

The train reached the Stalham Road Station at 7 P.M., and the distance was five miles. On Sundays they usually dined at Stalham at 7·30. The hour fixed was to be 8 on this occasion,—and even with this there would be some bustling. The house was now nearly empty, there being no visitors there except Mr. and Mrs. Gosling and Ayala. Lady Albury gave many thoughts to the manner of the man's reception, and determined at last that Jonathan should have an opportunity of saying a word to Ayala immediately on his arrival if he so pleased. "Mind you are down at half-past seven," she said to Ayala, coming to her in her bedroom.

"I thought we should not dine till eight."

"There is no knowing. Sir Harry is so fussy. I shall be down, and I should like you to be with me." Then Ayala promised. "And mind you have his frock on."

"You'll make me wear it out before any one else sees it," she said, laughing. But again she promised. She got a glimmer of light from it all, nearly understanding what Lady Albury intended. But against such intentions as these she had no reason to fight. Why should she not be ready to see him? Why should she not have on her prettiest dress when he came? If he meant to say the word,—then her prettiest dress would all be too poor, and her readiest ears not quick enough to meet so great a joy. If he were not to say the other word,—then should she shun him by staying behind, or be afraid of the encounter? Should she be less gaily attired because it would be unnecessary to please his eye?

Oh, no! "I'll be there at half-past seven," she said. "But I know the train will be late, and Sir Harry won't get his dinner till nine."

"Then, my dear, great as the Colonel is, he may come in and get what is left for him in the middle. Sir Harry will not wait a minute after eight."

The buxom woman came and dressed her. The buxom woman probably knew what was going to happen;—was perhaps more keenly alive to the truth than Lady Albury herself. "We have taken great care of it, haven't we, Miss?" she said, as she fastened the dress behind. "It's just as new still."

"New!" said Ayala. "It has got to be new with me for the next two years."

"I don't know much about that, Miss. Somebody will have to pay for a good many more new dresses before two years are over, I take it." To this Ayala made no answer, but she was quite sure that the buxom woman intended to imply that Colonel Stubbs would have to pay for the new dresses.

Punctually at half-past seven she was in the drawing-room, and there she remained alone for a few minutes. She endeavoured to sit down and be quiet, but she found it impossible to compose herself. Almost immediately he would be there, and then,—as she was quite sure,—her fate would be known to her instantly. She knew that the first moment of his presence in the room with her would tell her everything. If that were told to her which she desired to hear, everything should be re-told to him as quickly. But, if it were otherwise, then she thought that when the moment came she would still have strength enough to hide her sorrow. If he had come simply for the hunting,—simply that they two might ride a-hunting together so that he might show to her that all traces of his disappointment were gone,—then she would know how to teach him to think that her heart towards him was as it had ever been. The thing to be done would be so sad as to call from her tears almost of blood in her solitude; but it should be so done that no one should know that any sorrow such as this had touched her bosom. Not even to Lucy should this secret be told.

There was a clock on the mantelpiece to which her eye was continually turned. It now wanted twenty minutes to eight, and she was aware that if the train was punctual he might now be at the hall-door. At this moment Lady Albury entered the room. "Your knight has come at last," she said; "I hear his wheels on the gravel."

"He is no knight of mine," said Ayala, with that peculiar frown of hers.

"Whose ever knight he is, there he is. Knight or not, I must go and welcome him." Then Lady Albury hurried out of the room and Ayala was again alone. The door had been left partly open, so that she could hear the sound of voices and steps across the inner hall or billiard-room. There were the servants waiting upon him, and Sir Harry bidding him to go up and dress at once so as not to keep the whole house waiting, and Lady Albury declaring that there was yet ample time as the dinner certainly would not be on the table for half-an-hour. She heard it all, and heard him to whom all her thoughts were now given laughing as he declared that he had never been so cold in his life, and that he certainly would not dress himself till he had warmed his fingers. She was far away from the door, not having stirred from the spot on which she was standing when Lady Albury left her; but she fancied that she heard the murmur of some slight whisper, and she told herself that Lady Albury was telling him where to seek her. Then she heard the sound of the man's step across the billiard-room, she heard his hand upon the door, and there he was in her presence!

When she thought of it all afterwards, as she did so many scores of times, she never could tell how it had occurred. When she accused him in her playfulness, telling him that he had taken for granted that of which he had had no sign, she never knew whether there had been aught of truth in her accusation. But she did know that he had hardly closed the door behind him when she was in his arms, and felt the burning love of his kisses upon her cheeks. There had been no more asking whether he was to have any other answer. Of that she was quite sure. Had there been such further question she would have answered him, and some remembrance of her own words would have remained with her. She was quite sure that she had answered no question. Some memory of mingled granting and denying, of repulses and assents all quickly huddled upon one another, of attemps to escape while she was so happy to remain, and then of a deluge of love terms which fell upon her ears,—"his own one, his wife, his darling, his Ayala, at last his own sweet Ayala,"—this was what remained to her of that little interview. She had not spoken a word. She thought she was sure of that. Her breath had left her,—so that she could not speak. And yet it had been taken for granted,—though on former occasions he had pleaded with slow piteous words! How had it been that he had come to know the truth so suddenly? Then she became aware that Lady Albury was speaking to Mrs. Gosling in the billiard-room outside, detaining her other guest till the scene within should be over. At that moment she did speak a word which she remembered afterwards. "Go;—go; you must go now." Then there had been one other soft repulse, one other sweet assent, and the man had gone. There was just a moment for her, in which to tell herself that the Angel of Light had come for her, and had taken her to himself.

Mrs. Gosling, who was a pretty little woman, crept softly into the room, hiding her suspicion if she had any. Lady Albury put out her hand to Ayala behind the other woman's back, not raising it high, but just so that her young friend might touch it if she pleased. Ayala did touch it, sliding her little fingers into the offered grasp. "I thought it would be so," whispered Lady Albury. "I thought it would be so."

"What the deuce are you all up to," said Sir Harry, bursting into the room. "It's eight now, and that man has only just gone up to his room."

"He hasn't been in the house above five minutes yet," said Lady Albury, "and I think he has been very quick." Ayala thought so too.

During dinner and afterwards they were very full of hunting for the next day. It was wonderful to Ayala that there should be thought for such a trifle when there was such a thing as love in the world. While there was so much to fill her heart, how could there be thoughts of anything else? But Jonathan,—he was Jonathan to her now, her Jonathan, her Angel of Light,—was very keen upon the subject. There was but one week left. He thought that Croppy might manage three days as there was to be but one week. Croppy would have leisure and rest enough afterwards. "It's a little sharp," said Sir Harry.

"Oh, pray don't," said Ayala.

But Lady Albury and Jonathan together silenced Sir Harry, and Mrs. Gosling proved the absurdity of the objection by telling the story of a pony who had carried a lady three days running. "I should not have liked to be either the pony, or the owner, or the lady," said Sir Harry. But he was silenced. What did it matter though the heavens fell, so that Ayala was pleased? What is too much to be done for a girl who proves herself to be an angel by accepting the right man at the right time?

She had but one moment alone with her lover that night. "I always loved you," she whispered to him as she fled away. The Colonel did not quite understand the assertion, but he was contented with it as he sat smoking his cigar with Sir Harry and Mr. Gosling.

But, though she could have but one word that night with her lover, there were many words between her and Lady Albury before they went to bed. "And so, like wise people, you have settled it all between you at last," said Lady Albury.

"I don't know whether he is wise."

"We will take that for granted. At any rate he has been very true."

"Oh, yes."

"And you,—you knew all about it."

"No;—I knew nothing. I did not think he would ever ask again. I only hoped."

"But why on earth did you give him so much trouble?"

"I can't tell you," said Ayala, shaking her head.

"Do you mean that there is still a secret?"

"No, not that. I would tell you anything that I could tell, because you have been so very, very good to me. But I cannot tell. I cannot explain even to myself. Oh, Lady Albury, why have you been so good to me?"

"Shall I say because I have loved you?"

"Yes;—if it be true."

"But it is not true."

"Oh, Lady Albury!"

"I do love you dearly. I shall always love you now. I do hope I shall love you now, because you will be his wife. But I have not been kind to you as you call it because I loved you."

"Then why?"

"Because I loved him. Cannot you understand that? Because I was anxious that he should have all that he wanted. Was it not necessary that there should be some house in which he might meet you? Could there have been much of a pleasant time for wooing between you in your aunt's drawing-room in Kingsbury Crescent?"

"Oh, no," said Ayala.

"Could he have taken you out hunting unless you had been here? How could he and you have known each other at all unless I had been kind to you? Now you will understand."

"Yes," said Ayala, "I understand now. Did he ask you?"

"Well,—he consulted me. We talked you all over, and made up our minds, between us, that if we petted you down here that would be the best way to win you. Were we not right?"

"It was a very nice way. I do so like to be petted."

"Sir Harry was in the secret, and he did his petting by buying the frock. That was a success too, I think."

"Did he care about that, Lady Albury?"

"What he?"

"Jonathan," said Ayala, almost stumbling over

the word, as she pronounced it aloud for the first time.

"I think he liked it. But whether he would have persevered without it you must ask yourself. If he tells you that he would never have said another word to you only for this frock, then I think you ought to thank Sir Harry, and give him a kiss."

"I am sure he will not tell me that," said Ayala, with mock indignation.

"And now, my dear, as I have told you all my secret, and have explained to you how we laid our heads together, and plotted against you, I think you ought to tell me your secret. Why was it that you refused him so pertinaciously on that Sunday when you were out walking, and yet you knew your mind about it so clearly as soon as he arrived to-day?"

"I can't explain it," said Ayala.

"You must know that you liked him."

"I always liked him."

"You must have more than liked on that Sunday."

"I adored him."

"Then I don't understand you."

"Lady Albury, I think I fell in love with him the first moment I saw him. The Marchesa took me to a party in London, and there he was."

"Did he say anything to you then?"

"No. He was very funny,—as he often is, Don't you know his way? I remember every word he said to me. He came up without any introduction and ordered me to dance with him."

"And you did?"

"Oh yes. Whatever he told me I should have done. Then he scolded me because I did not stand up quick enough. And he invented some story about a woman who was engaged to him and would not marry him because he had red hair and his name was Jonathan. I knew it was all a joke, and yet I hated the woman."

"That must have been love at first sight."

"I think it was. From that day to this I have always been thinking about him."

"And yet you refused him twice over?"

"Yes."

"At ever so long an interval?" Ayala bobbed her head at her companion. "And why?"

"Ah;—that I can't tell. I shall try to tell him some day, but I know that I never shall. It was because ——. But, Lady Albury, I cannot tell it. Did you ever picture anything to yourself in a waking dream?"

"Build castles in the air?" suggested Lady Albury.

"That's just it."

"Very often. But they never come true."

"Never have come true,—exactly. I had a castle in the air, and in the castle lived a knight." She was still ashamed to say that the inhabitant of the castle was an Angel of Light. "I wanted to find out whether he was the knight who lived there. He was."

"And you were not quite sure till to-day?"

"I have been sure a long time. But when we

walked out on that Sunday I was such an idiot that I did not know how to tell him. Oh, Lady Albury, I was such a fool! What should I have done if he hadn't come back?"

"Sent for him."

"Never;—never! I should have been miserable always! But now I am so happy."

"He is the real knight?"

"Oh, yes; indeed. He is the real,—real knight, that has always been living in my castle."

Ayala's promotion was now so firmly fixed that the buxom female came to assist her off with her clothes when Lady Albury had left her. From this time forth it was supposed that such assistance would be necessary. "I take it, Miss," said the buxom female, "there will be a many new dresses before the end of this time two years." From which Ayala was quite sure that everybody in the house knew all about it.

* * * * *

But it was now, now when she was quite alone, that the great sense of her happiness came to her. In the fulness of her dreams there had never been more than the conviction that such a being, and none other, could be worthy of her love. There had never been faith in the hope that such a one would come to her,—never even though she would tell herself that angels had come down from heaven and had sought in marriage the hands of the daughters of men. Her dreams had been to her a barrier against love rather than an encouragement. But now he that she had in truth dreamed of had come for her. Then she brought out the Marchesa's letter and read that description of her lover. Yes; he was all that; true, brave, tender,—a very hero. But then he was more than all that,—for he was in truth the very "Angel of Light."

CHAPTER XIII.

GOBBLEGOOSE WOOD AGAIN.

THE Monday was devoted to hunting. I am not at all sure that riding about the country with a pack of hounds is an amusement specially compatible with that assured love entertainment which was now within the reach of Ayala and her Angel. For the rudiments of love-making, for little endearing attentions, for a few sweet words to be whispered with shortened breath as one horse gallops beside another, perhaps for a lengthened half-hour together, amidst the mazes of a large wood when opportunities are no doubt given for private conversation, hunting may be very well. But for two persons who are engaged, with the mutual consent of all their friends, a comfortable sofa is perhaps preferable. Ayala had heard as yet but very little of her lover's intentions;—was acquainted only with that one single intention which he had declared in asking her to be his wife. There were a thousand things to be told,—the how, the where, and the when. She knew hitherto the why, and that was all. Nothing could be told her while she was galloping about a big wood on Croppy's back. "I am delighted to see you again in these parts, Miss," said Larry Twentyman, suddenly.

"Oh, Mr. Twentyman; how is the baby?"

"The baby is quite well, Miss. His mamma has been out ever so many times."

"I ought to have asked for her first. Does baby come out too?"

"Not quite. But when the hounds are near mamma comes for an hour or so. We have had a wonderful season,—quite wonderful. You have heard, perhaps, of our great run from Dillsborough Wood. We found him there, close to my place, you know, and run him down in the Brake country after an hour and forty minutes. There were only five or six of them. You'd have been one, Miss, to a moral, if you'd have been here on the pony. I say we never changed our fox."

Ayala was well disposed towards Larry Twentyman, and was quite aware that, according to the records and established usages of that hunt, he was a man with whom she might talk safely. But she did not care about the foxes so much as she had done before. There was nothing now for which she cared much, except Jonathan Stubbs. He was always riding near her throughout the day, so that he might be with her should there arise anything special to be done; but he was not always close to her,—as she would have had him. He had gained his purpose, and he was satisfied. She had entered in upon the fruition of positive bliss, but enjoyed it in perfection only when she heard the sound of his voice, or could look into his eyes as she spoke to him. She did not care much about the great run from Dillsborough, or even for the compliment with which Mr. Twentyman finished his narrative. They were riding about the big woods all day, not without killing a fox, but with none of the excitement of a real run. "After that Croppy will be quite fit to come again on Wednesday," suggested the Colonel on their way home. To which Sir Harry assented.

"What do you folks mean to do to-day?" asked Lady Albury at breakfast on the following morning. Ayala had her own little plan in her head, but did not dare to propose it publicly. "Will you choose to be driven, or will you choose to walk?" said Lady Albury, addressing herself to Ayala. Ayala, in her present position, was considered to be entitled to special consideration. Ayala thought she would prefer to walk. At last there came a moment in which she could make her request to the person chiefly concerned. "Walk with me to the wood with that absurd name," suggested Ayala.

"Gobblegoose Wood," suggested the Colonel. Then that was arranged according to Ayala's wishes.

A walk in a wood is perhaps almost as good as a comfortable seat in a drawing-room, and is, perhaps, less liable to intrusion. They started and walked the way which Ayala remembered so well when she had trudged along, pretending to listen to Sir Harry and Captain Glomax as they carried on their discussion about the hunted fox, but giving all her ears to the Colonel, and wondering whether he would say anything to her before the day was over.

Then her mind had been in a perturbed state which she herself had failed to understand. She was sure that she would say "No" to him, should he speak, and yet she desired that it should be "Yes." What a fool she had been, she told herself as she walked along now, and how little she had deserved all the good that had come to her!

The conversation was chiefly with him as they went. He told her much now of the how, and the when, and the where. He hoped there might be no long delay. He would live, he said, for the next year or two at Aldershot, and would be able to get a house fit for her on condition that they should be married at once. He did not explain why the house could not be taken even though their marriage were delayed two or three months,—but as to this she asked no questions. Of course they must be married in London if Mrs. Dosett wished it; but if not it might be arranged that the wedding should take place at Stalham. Upon all this and many other things he had much to propose, and all that he said Ayala accepted as gospel. As the Angel of Light had appeared,—as the knight who was lord of the castle had come forth,—of course he must be obeyed in everything. He could hardly have made a suggestion to which she would not have acceded. When they had entered the wood Ayala in her own quiet way led him to the very spot in which on that former day he had asked her his question. "Do you remember this path?" she asked.

"I remember that you and I were walking here together," he said.

"Ay, but this very turn? Do you remember this branch?"

"Well, no; not the branch."

"You put your hand on it when you said that 'never—never,' to me."

"Did I say 'never,—never'?"

"Yes, you did;—when I was so untrue to you."

"Were you untrue?" he asked.

"Jonathan, you remember nothing about it. It has all passed away from you just as though you were talking to Captain Glomax about the fox."

"Has it, dear?"

"I remember every word of it. I remember how you stood and how you looked, even to the hat you wore and the little switch you held in your hand,—when you asked for one little word, one glance, one slightest touch. There, now;—you shall have all my weight to bear." Then she leant upon him with both her hands, turned round her arm, glanced up into his face, and opened her lips as though speaking that little word. "Do you remember that I said I thought you had given it all up?"

"I remember that, certainly."

"And was not that untrue? Oh, Jonathan, that was such a story. Had I thought so I should have been miserable."

"Then why did you swear to me so often that you could not love me?"

"I never said so," replied Ayala; "never."

"Did you not?" he asked.

"I never said so. I never told you such a story as that. I did love you then, almost as well as

I do now. Oh, I had loved you for so long a time!"

"Then why did you refuse me?"

"Ah; that is what I would explain to you now,—here on this very spot,—if I could. Does it not seem odd that a girl should have all that she wants offered to her, and yet not be able to take it?"

"Was it all that you wanted?"

"Indeed it was. When I was in church that morning I told myself that I never, never, could be happy unless you came to me again."

"But when I did come you would not have me."

"I knew how to love you," she said, "but I did not know how to tell you that I loved you. I can tell you now; cannot I?" and then she looked up at him and smiled. "Yes, I think I shall never be tired of telling you now. It is sweet to hear you say that you love me, but it is sweeter still to be always telling you. And yet I could not tell you then. Suppose you had taken me at my word?"

"I told you that I should never give you up."

"It was only that that kept me from being altogether wretched. I think that I was ashamed to tell you the truth when I had once refused to do as you would have me. I had given you so much trouble all for nothing. I think that if you had asked me on that first day at the ball in London I should have said yes, if I had told the truth."

"That would have been very sudden. I had never seen you before that."

"Nevertheless it was so. I don't mind owning it to you now, though I never, never, would own it to any one else. When you came to us at the theatre I was sure that no one else could ever have been so good. I certainly did love you then."

"Hardly that, Ayala."

"I did," she said. "Now I have told you everything, and if you choose to think I have been bad, —why you must think so, and I must put up with it."

"Bad, my darling?"

"I suppose it was bad to fall in love with a man like that; and very bad to give him the trouble of coming so often. But now I have made a clean breast of it, and if you want to scold me you must scold me now. You may do it now, but you must never scold me afterwards,—because of that." It may be left to the reader to imagine the nature of the scolding which she received.

Then on their way home she thanked him for all the good that he had done to all those belonging to her. "I have heard it all from Lucy;—how generous you have been to Isadore."

"That has all come to nothing," he said.

"How come to nothing? I know that you sent him the money."

"I did offer to lend him something, and, indeed, I sent him a cheque; but two days afterwards he returned it. That tremendous uncle of yours——"

"Uncle Tom?"

"Yes, your Uncle Tom; the man of millions! He came forward and cut me out altogether. I don't know what went on down there in Sussex, but when he heard that they intended to be married shortly he put his hand into his pocket, as a magnificent uncle, overflowing with millions, ought to do."

"I did not hear that."

"Hamel sent my money back at once."

"And poor Tom! You were so good to poor Tom."

"I like Tom."

"But he did behave badly."

"Well; yes. One gentleman shouldn't strike another, even though he be ever so much in love. It's an uncomfortable proceeding, and never has good results. But then, poor fellow, he has been so much in earnest."

"Why couldn't he take a No when he got it?"

"Why didn't I take a No when I got it?"

"That was very different. He ought to have taken it. If you had taken it you would have been very wrong, and have broken a poor girl's heart. I am sure you knew that all through."

"Did I?"

"And then you were too good-natured. That was it. I don't think you really love me;—not as I love you. Oh, Jonathan, if you were to change your mind now! Suppose you were to tell me that it was a mistake! Suppose I were to awake and find myself in bed at Kingsbury Crescent?"

"I hope there may be no such waking as that!"

"I should go mad,—stark mad. Shake me till I find out whether it is real waking, downright, earnest. But, Jonathan, why did you call me Miss Dormer when you went away? That was the worst of all. I remember when you called me Ayala first. It went through and through me like an electric shock. But you never saw it;—did you?"

On that afternoon when she returned home she wrote to her sister Lucy, giving a sister's account to her sister of all her happiness. "I am sure Isadore is second best, but Jonathan is best. I don't want you to say so; but if you contradict me I shall stick to it. You remember my telling you that the old woman in the railway said that I was perverse. She was a clever old woman, and knew all about it, for I was perverse. However, it has come all right now, and Jonathan is best of all. Oh, my man,—my man! Is it not sweet to have a man of one's own to love?" If this letter had been written on the day before,—as would have been the case had not Ayala been taken out hunting,—it would have reached Merle Park on the Wednesday, the news would have been made known to Aunt Emmeline, and so conveyed to poor Tom, and that disagreeable journey from Merle Park to Stalham would have been saved. But there was no time for writing on the Monday. The letter was sent away in the Stalham post-bag on the Tuesday evening, and did not reach Merle Park till the Thursday, after Lady Tringle had left the house. Had it been known on that morning that Ayala was engaged to Colonel Stubbs that would have sufficed to send Tom away upon his travels without any more direct messenger from Stalham.

On the Wednesday there was more hunting, and on this day Ayala, having liberated her mind to her lover in Gobblegoose Wood, was able to devote herself more satisfactorily to the amusement in hand. Her engagement was now an old affair. It had already become matter for joking to Sir Harry, and had been discussed even with Mrs. Gosling. It was, of course, "a joy for ever,"—but still she was beginning to descend from the clouds and to walk the earth,—no more than a simple queen. When, therefore, the hounds went away and Larry told her that he knew the best way out of the wood, she collected her energies and rode "like a little brick," as Sir Harry said when they got back to Stalham. On that afternoon she received the note from her aunt and replied to it by telegram.

On the Thursday she stayed at home and wrote various letters. The first was to the Marchesa, and then one to Nina,—in both of which much had to be said about "Jonathan." To Nina also she could repeat her idea of the delight of having a man to love. Then there was a letter to Aunt Margaret,—which certainly was due, and another to Aunt Emmeline,—which was not however received until after Lady Tringle's visit to Stalham. There was much conversation between her and Lady Albury as to the possible purpose of the visit which was to be made on the morrow. Lady Albury was of opinion that Lady Tringle had heard of the engagement, and was coming with the intention of setting it on one side on Tom's behalf. "But she can't do that, you know," said Ayala, with some manifest alarm. "She is nothing to me now, Lady

Albury. She got rid of me, you know. I was changed away for Lucy."

"If there had been no changing away, she could do nothing," said Lady Albury.

About a quarter of an hour before the time for lunch on the following day Lady Tringle was shown into the small sitting-room which has been mentioned in a previous chapter, and Ayala, radiant with happiness and beauty, appeared before her. There was a look about her of being at home at Stalham, as though she were almost a daughter of the house, that struck her aunt with surprise. There was nothing left of that submissiveness which, though Ayala herself had not been submissive, belonged, as of right, to girls so dependent as she and her sister Lucy. "I am so delighted to see you at Stalham," said Ayala, as she embraced her aunt.

"I am come to you," said Lady Tringle, "on a matter of very particular business." Then she paused, and assumed a look of peculiar solemnity.

"Have you got my letter?" demanded Ayala.

"I got your telegram, and I thought it very civil of Lady Albury. But I cannot stay. Your poor cousin Tom is in such a condition that I cannot leave him longer than I can help."

"But you have not got my letter?"

"I have had no letter from you, Ayala."

"I have sent you such news,—oh, such news, Aunt Emmeline?"

"What news, my dear?" Lady Tringle as she asked the question seemed to become more solemn than ever.

"Oh, Aunt Emmeline——; I am——"

"You are what, Ayala?"

"I am engaged to be married to Colonel Jonathan Stubbs."

"Engaged!"

"Yes, Aunt Emmeline;—engaged. I wrote to you on Tuesday to tell you all about it. I hope you and Uncle Tom will approve. There cannot possibly be any reason against it,—except only that I have nothing to give him in return; that is in the way of money. Colonel Stubbs, Aunt Emmeline, is not what Uncle Tom will call a rich man, but everybody here says that he has got quite enough to be comfortable. If he had nothing in the world it could not make any difference to me. I don't understand how anybody is to love any one or not to love him just because he is rich or poor."

"But you are absolutely engaged!" exclaimed Lady Tringle.

"Oh dear yes. Perhaps you would like to ask Lady Albury about it. He did want it before, you know."

"But now you are engaged to him?" In answer to this Ayala thought it sufficient simply to nod her head. "It is all over then?"

"All over!" exclaimed Ayala. "It is just going to begin."

"All over for poor Tom," said Lady Tringle.

"Oh yes. It was always over for him, Aunt Emmeline. I told him ever so many times that it never could be so. Don't you know, Aunt Emmeline, that I did?"

"But you said that to this man just the same."

"Aunt Emmeline," said Ayala, putting on all the serious dignity which she knew how to assume, "I am engaged to Colonel Stubbs, and nothing on earth that anybody can say can change it. If you want to hear all about it, Lady Albury will tell you. She knows that you are my aunt, and therefore she will be quite willing to talk to you. Only nothing that anybody can say can change it."

"Poor Tom!" ejaculated the rejected lover's mother.

"I am very sorry if my cousin is displeased."

"He is ill,—terribly ill. He will have to go away and travel all about the world, and I don't know that ever he will come back again. I am sure this Stubbs will never love you as he has done."

"Oh, aunt, what is the use of that?"

"And then Tom will have twice as much. But, however——" Ayala stood silent, not seeing that any good could be done by addition to her former assurances. "I will go and tell him, my dear, that's all. Will you not send him some message, Ayala?"

"Oh, yes; any message that I can that shall go along with my sincere attachment to Colonel Stubbs. You must tell him that I am engaged to Colonel Stubbs. You will tell him, Aunt Emmeline?"

"Oh, yes; if it must be so."

"It must," said Ayala. "Then you may give him my love, and tell him that I am very unhappy that I should have been a trouble to him, and that

I hope he will soon be well, and come back from his travels." By this time Aunt Emmeline was dissolved in tears. "I could not help it, Aunt Emmeline, could I?" Her aunt had once terribly outraged her feelings by telling her that she had encouraged Tom. Ayala remembered at this moment the cruel words and the wound which they had inflicted on her; but, nevertheless, she behaved tenderly, and endeavoured to be respectful and submissive. "I could not help it,—could I, Aunt Emmeline?"

"I suppose not, my dear."

After that Lady Tringle declared that she would return to London at once. No;—she would rather not go in to lunch. She would rather go back at once to the station if they would take her. She had been weeping, and did not wish to show her tears. Therefore, at Ayala's request, the carriage came round again,—to the great disgust, no doubt, of the coachman,—and Lady Tringle was taken back to the station without having seen any of the Albury family.

CHAPTER XIV.

CAPTAIN BATSBY IN LOMBARD STREET.

It was not till Colonel Stubbs had been three or four days at Stalham, basking in the sunshine of Ayala's love, that any of the Stalham family heard of the great event which had occurred in the life of Ayala's third lover. During that walk to and from Gobblegoose Wood something had been said between the lovers as to Captain Batsby,—something, no doubt, chiefly in joke. The idea of the poor Captain having fallen suddenly into so melancholy a condition was droll enough. "But he never spoke to me," said Ayala. "He doesn't speak very much to any one," said the Colonel, "but he thinks a great deal about things. He has had ever so many affairs with ever so many ladies, who generally, I fancy, want to marry him because of his money. How he has escaped so long nobody knows." A man when he has just engaged himself to be married is as prone as ever to talk of other men "escaping," feeling that, though other young ladies were no better than evils to be avoided, his young lady is to be regarded as almost a solitary instance of a blessing. Then, two days afterwards, arrived the news of the trip to Ostend. Sir Harry received a letter from a friend in which an account was given of his half-brother's adventure. "What do you think has happened?" said Sir Harry, jumping up from his chair at the breakfast table.

"What has happened?" asked his wife.

"Benjamin has run off to Ostend with a young lady."

"Benjamin,—with a young lady!" exclaimed Lady Albury. Ayala and Stubbs were equally astonished, each of them knowing that the Captain had been excluded from Stalham because of the ardour of his unfortunate love for Ayala. "Ayala, that is your doing!"

"No!" said Ayala. "But I am very glad if he's happy."

"Who is the young lady?" asked Stubbs.

"It is that which makes it so very peculiar," said Sir Harry, looking at Ayala. He had learned something of the Tringle family, and was aware of Ayala's connection with them.

"Who is it, Harry?" demanded her ladyship.

"Sir Thomas Tringle's younger daughter."

"Gertrude!" exclaimed Ayala, who also knew of the engagement with Mr. Houston.

"But the worst of it is," continued Sir Harry, "that he is not at all happy. The young lady has come back, while nobody knows what has become of Benjamin."

"Benjamin never will get a wife," said Lady Albury. Thus all the details of the little event became known at Stalham,—except the immediate condition and whereabouts of the lover.

Of the Captain's condition and whereabouts something must be told. When the great disruption came, and he had been abused and ridiculed by Sir Thomas at Ostend, he felt that he could neither remain there where the very waiters knew what had happened, nor could he return to Dover in the same vessel with Sir Thomas and his daughter. He therefore took the first train and went to Brussels.

But Brussels did not offer him many allurements in his present frame of mind. He found nobody there whom he particularly knew, and nothing particular to do. Solitude in a continental town with no amusements beyond those offered by the table d'hôte and the theatre is oppressing. His time he endeavoured to occupy with thinking of the last promise he had made to Gertrude. Should he break it or should he keep it? Sir Thomas Tringle was, no doubt, a very rich man,—and then there was the fact which would become known to all the world, that he had run off with a young lady. Should he ultimately succeed in marrying the young lady the enterprise would bear less of an appearance of failure than it would do otherwise. But then, should the money not be forthcoming, the consolation coming from the possession of Gertrude herself would hardly suffice to make him a happy man. Sir Thomas, when he came to consider the matter, would certainly feel that his daughter had compromised herself by her journey, and that it would be good for her to be married to the man who had taken her. It might be that Sir Thomas would yield, and consent to make, at any rate, some compromise. A rumour had reached his ears that

Traffick had received £200,000 with the elder daughter. He would consent to take half that sum. After a week spent amidst the charms of Brussels he returned to London, without any public declaration of his doing so,—"sneaked back," as a friend of his said of him at the club;—and then went to work to carry out his purpose as best he might. All that was known of it at Stalham was that he had returned to his lodgings in London.

On Friday, the 11th of April, when Ayala was a promised bride of nearly two weeks' standing, and all the uncles and aunts were aware that her lot in life had been fixed for her, Sir Thomas was alone in the back-room in Lombard Street, with his mind sorely diverted from the only joy of his life. The whole family were now in town, and Septimus Traffick with his wife was actually occupying a room in Queen's Gate. How it had come to pass Sir Thomas hardly knew. Some word had been extracted from him signifying a compliance with a request that Augusta might come to the house for a night or two until a fitting residence should be prepared for her. Something had been said of Lord Boardotrade's house being vacated for her and her husband early in April. An occurrence to which married ladies are liable was about to take place with Augusta, and Sir Thomas certainly understood that the occurrence was to be expected under the roof of the coming infant's noble grandfather. Something as to ancestral halls had been thrown out in the chance way of conversation. Then he certainly had assented to some minimum of London hospitality for his daughter,—as certainly not including the presence of his son-in-law; and now both of them were domiciled in the big front spare bed-room at Queen's Gate! This perplexed him sorely. And then Tom had been brought up from the country still as an invalid, his mother moaning and groaning over him as though he were sick almost past hope of recovery. And yet the nineteenth of the month, now only eight days distant, was still fixed for his departure. Tom, on the return of his mother from Stalham, had to a certain extent accepted as irrevocable the fact of which she bore the tidings. Ayala was engaged to Stubbs, and would, doubtless, with very little delay, become Mrs. Jonathan Stubbs. "I knew it," he said; "I knew it. Nothing could have prevented it unless I had shot him through the heart. He told me that she had refused him; but no man could have looked like that after being refused by Ayala." Then he never expressed a hope again. It was all over for him as regarded Ayala. But still he refused to be well, or even, for a day or two, to leave his bed. He had allowed his mother to understand that if the fact of her engagement were indubitably brought home to him he would gird up his loins for his journey and proceed at once wherever it might be thought good to send him. His father had sternly reminded him of his promise; but, when so reminded, Tom had turned himself in his bed and uttered groans instead of replies. Now he had been brought up to London and was no longer actually in bed; but even yet he had not signified his intention of girding up his loins and proceeding upon his journey. Nevertheless the preparations were going on, and, under Sir Thomas's directions, the portmanteaus were already being packed. Gertrude also was a source of discomfort to her father. She considered herself to have been deprived of her two lovers, one after the other, in a spirit of cruel parsimony. And with this heavy weight upon her breast she refused to take any part in the family conversations. Everything had been done for Augusta, and everything was to be done for Tom. For her nothing had been done, and nothing had been promised;—and she was therefore very sulky. With these troubles all around him, Sir Thomas was sitting oppressed and disheartened in Lombard Street on Friday, the 11th of April.

Then there entered to him one of the junior clerks with a card announcing the name of Captain Batsby. He looked at it for some seconds before he gave any notification of his intention, and then desired the young man to tell the gentleman that he would not see him. The message had been delivered, and Captain Batsby with a frown of anger on his brow was about to shake the dust off from his feet on the uncourteous threshold when there came another message saying that Captain Batsby could go in and see Sir Thomas if he wished it. Upon this he turned round and was shown into the little sitting-room. "Well, Captain Batsby," said Sir Thomas; "what can I do for you now? I am glad to see that you have come back safely from foreign parts."

"I have called," said the Captain, "to say something about your daughter."

"What more can you have to say about her?"

At this the Captain was considerably puzzled. Of course Sir Thomas must know what he had to say. "The way in which we were separated at Ostend was very distressing to my feelings."

"I dare say."

"And also I should think to Miss Tringle's."

"Not improbably. I have always observed that when people are interrupted in the performance of some egregious stupidity their feelings are hurt. As I said before, what can I do for you now?"

"I am very anxious to complete the alliance which I have done myself the honour to propose to you."

"I did not know that you had proposed anything. You came down to my house under a false pretence; and then you persuaded my daughter,—or else she persuaded you,—to go off together to Ostend. Is that what you call an alliance?"

"That, as far as it went was,—was an elopement."

"Am I to understand that you now want to arrange another elopement, and that you have come to ask my consent?"

"Oh dear no."

"Then what do you mean by completing an alliance?"

"I want to make," said the Captain, "an offer for the young lady's hand in a proper form. I consider myself to be in a position which justifies me in doing so. I am possessed of the young lady's affections, and have means of my own equal to those which I presume you will be disposed to give her."

"Very much better means I hope, Captain Batsby. Otherwise I do not see what you and your wife would have to live upon. I will tell you exactly what my feelings are in this matter. My daughter has gone off with you, forgetting all the duty that she owed to me and to her mother, and throwing aside all ideas of propriety. After that I will not say that you shall not marry her if both of you think fit. I do not doubt your means, and I have no reason for supposing that you would be cruel to her. You are two fools, but after all fools must live in the world. What I do say is, that I will not give a sixpence towards supporting you in your folly. Now, Captain Batsby, you can complete the alliance or not as you please."

Captain Batsby had been called a fool also at Ostend, and there, amidst the distressing circumstances of his position, had been constrained to bear the opprobrious name, little customary as it is for one gentleman to allow himself to be called a fool by another; but now he had collected his thoughts, had reminded himself of his position in the world, and had told himself that it did not become him to be too humble before this City man of business. It might have been all very well at Ostend; but he was not going to be called a fool in London without resenting it. "Sir Thomas," said he, "fool and folly are terms which I cannot allow you to use to me."

"If you do not present yourself to me here, Captain Batsby, or at my own house,—or, perhaps I may say, at Ostend,—I will use no such terms to you."

"I suppose you will acknowledge that I am entitled to ask for your daughter's hand."

"I suppose you will acknowledge that when a man runs away with my daughter I am entitled to express my opinion of his conduct."

"That is all over now, Sir Thomas. What I did I did for love. There is no good in crying over spilt milk. The question is as to the future happiness of the young lady."

"That is the only wise word I have heard you say, Captain Batsby. There is no good in crying after spilt milk. Our journey to Ostend is done and gone. It was not very agreeable, but we have lived through it. I quite think that you show a good judgment in not intending to go there again in quest of a clergyman. If you want to be married there are plenty of them in London. I will not oppose your marriage, but I will not give you a shilling. No man ever had a better opportunity of showing the disinterestedness of his affection. Now, good morning."

"But, Sir Thomas——"

"Captain Batsby, my time is precious. I have told you all that there is to tell." Then he stood up, and the Captain with a stern demeanour and angry brow left the room and took himself in silence away from Lombard Street.

"Do you want to marry Captain Batsby?" Sir

Thomas said to his daughter that evening, having invited her to come apart with him after dinner.

"Yes, I do."

"You think that you prefer him on the whole to Mr. Houston?"

"Mr. Houston is a scoundrel. I wish that you would not talk about him, papa."

"I like him so much the best of the two," said Sir Thomas. "But of course it is for you to judge. I could have brought myself to give something to Houston. Luckily, however, Captain Batsby has got an income of his own."

"He has, papa."

"And you are sure that you would like to take him as your husband?"

"Yes, papa."

"Very well. He has been with me to-day."

"Is he in London?"

"I tell you that he has been with me to-day in Lombard Street."

"What did he say? Did he say anything about me?"

"Yes, my dear. He came to ask me for your hand."

"Well, papa."

"I told him that I should make no objection,—that I should leave it altogether to you. I only interfered with one small detail as to my own wishes. I assured him that I should never give him or you a single shilling. I don't suppose it will matter much to him, as he has, you know, means of his own." It was thus that Sir Thomas punished his daughter for her misconduct.

Captain Batsby and the Trafficks were acquainted with each other. The Member of Parliament had, of course, heard of the journey to Ostend from his wife, and had been instigated by her to express an opinion that the young people ought to be married. "It is such a very serious thing," said Augusta to her husband, "to be four hours on the sea together! And then you know——!" Mr. Traffick acknowledged that it was serious, and was reminded by his wife that he, in the capacity of brother, was bound to interfere on his sister's behalf. "Papa, you know, understands nothing about these kind of things. You, with your family interest, and your seat in Parliament, ought to be able to arrange it." Mr. Traffick probably knew how far his family interest and his seat in Parliament would avail. They had, at any rate, got him a wife with a large fortune. They were promising for him, still further, certain domiciliary advantages. He doubted whether he could do much for Batsby; but still he promised to try. If he could arrange these matters it might be that he would curry fresh favour with Sir Thomas by doing so. He therefore made it his business to encounter Captain Batsby on the Sunday afternoon at a club to which they both belonged. "So you have come back from your little trip?" said the Member of Parliament.

The Captain was not unwilling to discuss the question of their family relations with Mr. Traffick. If anybody would have influence with Sir Thomas it might probably be Mr. Traffick. "Yes; I have come back."

"Without your bride."

"Without my bride,—as yet. That is a kind of undertaking in which a man is apt to run many dangers before he can carry it through."

"I dare say. I never did anything of the kind myself. Of course you know that I am the young lady's brother-in-law."

"Oh yes."

"And therefore you won't mind me speaking. Don't you think you ought to do something further?"

"Something further! By George, I should think so," said the Captain, exultingly. "I mean to do a great many things further. You don't suppose I am going to give it up?"

"You oughtn't, you know. When a man has taken a girl off with him in that way, he should go on with it. It's a deuced serious thing, you know."

"It was his fault in coming after us."

"That was a matter of course. If he hadn't done it, I must. I have made the family my own, and, of course, must look after its honour." The noble scion of the house of Traffick, as he said this, showed by his countenance that he perfectly understood the duty which circumstances had imposed upon him.

"He made himself very rough, you know," said the Captain.

"I dare say he would."

"And said things,—well,—things which he ought not to have said."

"In such a case as that a father may say pretty nearly what comes uppermost."

"That was just it. He did say what came uppermost,—and very rough it was."

"What does it matter?"

"Not much if he'd do as he ought to do now. As you are her brother-in-law, I'll tell you just how it stands. I have been to him and made a regular proposal."

"Since you have been back?"

"Yes; the day before yesterday. And what do you think he says?"

"What does he say?"

"He gives his consent; only——"

"Only what?"

"He won't give her a shilling! Such an idea, you know! As though she were to be punished after marriage for running away with the man she did marry."

"Take your chance, Batsby," said the Member of Parliament.

"What chance?"

"Take your chance of the money. I'd have done it; only, of course, it was different with me. He was glad to catch me, and therefore the money was settled."

"I've got a tidy income of my own, you know," said the Captain, thinking that he was entitled to be made more welcome as a son-in-law than the younger son of a peer who had no income.

"Take your chance," continued Traffick. "What on earth can a man like Tringle do with his money except give it to his children? He is rough, as you say, but he is not hard-hearted, nor yet stubborn. I can do pretty nearly what I like with him."

"Can you, though?"

"Yes; by smoothing him down the right way. You run your chance, and we'll get it all put right for you." The Captain hesitated, rubbing his head carefully to encourage the thoughts which were springing up within his bosom. The Honourable Mr. Traffick might perhaps succeed in getting the affair put right, as he called it, in the interest rather of the elder than of the second daughter. "I don't see how you can hesitate now, as you have been off with the girl," said Mr. Traffick.

"I don't know about that. I should like to see the money settled."

"There would have been nothing settled if you had married her at Ostend."

"But I didn't," said the Captain. "I tell you what you might do. You might talk him over and make him a little more reasonable. I should be ready to-morrow if he'd come forward."

"What's the sum you want?"

"The same as yours, I suppose."

"That's out of the question," said Mr. Traffick, shaking his head. "Suppose we say sixty thousand pounds." Then after some chaffering on the subject it was decided between them that Mr. Traffick should use his powerful influence with his father-in-law to give his daughter on her marriage,—say a hundred thousand pounds if it were possible, or sixty thousand pounds at the least.

CHAPTER XV.

MR. TRAFFICK IN LOMBARD STREET.

Mr. Traffick entertained some grand ideas as to the house of Travers and Treason. Why should not he become a member, and ultimately the leading member, of that firm? Sir Thomas was not a young man, though he was strong and hearty. Tom had hitherto succeeded only in making an ass of himself. As far as transacting the affairs of the firm, Tom,—so thought Mr. Traffick,—was altogether out of the question. He might perish in those extensive travels which he was about to take. Mr. Traffick did not desire any such catastrophe;—but the young man might perish. There was a great opening. Mr. Traffick, with his thorough knowledge of business, could not but see that there was a great opening. Besides Tom, there were but two daughters, one of whom was his own wife. Augusta, his wife, was, he thought, certainly the favourite at the present moment. Sir Thomas could, indeed, say rough things even to her; but then Sir Thomas was of his nature rough. Now, at this time, the rough things said to Gertrude were very much the rougher. In all these circumstances the wisdom of interfering in Gertrude's little affairs was very clear to Mr. Traffick. Gertrude would, of course, get herself married sooner or later, and almost any other husband would obtain a larger portion than that which would satisfy Batsby. Sir Thomas was now constantly saying good things about Mr. Houston. Mr. Houston would be much more objectionable than Captain Batsby,—much more likely to interfere. He would require more money at once, and might possibly come forward himself in the guise of a partner. Mr. Traffick saw his way clearly. It was incumbent upon him to see that Gertrude should become Mrs. Batsby with as little delay as possible.

But one thing he did not see. One thing he had failed to see since his first introduction to the Tringle family. He had not seen the peculiar nature of his father-in-law's foibles. He did not understand either the weakness or the strength of Sir Thomas,—either the softness or the hardness. Mr. Traffick himself was blessed with a very hard skin. In the carrying out of a purpose there was nothing which his skin was not sufficiently serviceable to endure. But Sir Thomas, rough as he was, had but a thin skin;—a thin skin and a soft heart. Had Houston and Gertrude persevered he would certainly have given way. For Tom, in his misfortune, he would have made any sacrifice. Though he had given the broadest hints which he had been able to devise he had never as yet brought himself absolutely to turn Traffick out of his house. When Ayala was sent away he still kept her name in his will, and added also that of Lucy as soon as Lucy had been entrusted to him. Had things gone a little more smoothly between him and Hamel when they met,—had he not unluckily advised that all the sculptor's grand designs should be sold by auction for what they would fetch,—he would have put Hamel and Lucy upon their legs. He was a soft-hearted man;—but there never was one less willing to endure interference in his own affairs.

At the present moment he was very sore as to the presence of Traffick in Queen's Gate. The Easter parliamentary holidays were just at hand, and there was no sign of any going. Augusta had whispered to her mother that the poky little house in Mayfair would be very uncomfortable for the coming event,—and Lady Tringle, though she had not dared to say even as much as that in plain terms to her husband, had endeavoured to introduce the subject by little hints,—which Sir Thomas had clearly understood. He was hardly the man to turn a daughter and an expected grandchild into the streets; but he was, in his present mood, a father-in-law who would not unwillingly have learned that his son-in-law was without a shelter except that afforded by the House of Commons. Why on earth should he have given up one hundred and twenty thousand pounds,—£6,000 a-year as it was under his fostering care,—to a man who could not even keep a house over his wife's head? This was the humour of Sir Thomas when Mr. Traffick undertook to prevail with him to give an adequate fortune to his youngest daughter on her marriage with Captain Batsby.

The conversation between Traffick and Batsby took place on a Sunday. On the following day the

Captain went down to the House and saw the Member. "No; I have not spoken to him yet."

"I was with him on Friday, you know," said Batsby. "I can't well go and call on the ladies in Queen's Gate till I hear that he has changed his mind."

"I should. I don't see what difference it would make."

Then Captain Batsby was again very thoughtful. "It would make a difference, you know. If I were to say a word to Gertrude now,—as to being married or anything of that kind,—it would seem that I meant to go on whether I got anything or not."

"And you should seem to want to go on," said Traffick, with all that authority which the very surroundings of the House of Commons always give to the words and gait of a Member.

"But then I might find myself dropped in a hole at last."

"My dear Batsby, you made that hole for yourself when you ran off with the young lady."

"We settled all that before."

"Not quite. What we did settle was that we'd do our best to fill the hole up. Of course you ought to go and see them. You went off with the young lady,—and since that have been accepted as her suitor by her father. You are bound to go and see her."

"Do you think so?"

"Certainly! Certainly! It never does to talk to Tringle about business at his own house. I'll make an hour to see him in the City to-morrow. I'm so pressed by business that I can hardly get away from the House after twelve;—but, I'll do it. But, while I'm in Lombard Street, do you go to Queen's Gate." The Captain after further consideration said that he would go to Queen's Gate.

At three o'clock on the next day he did go to Queen's Gate. He had many misgivings, feeling that by such a step he would be committing himself to matrimony with or without the money. No doubt he could so offer himself, even to Lady Tringle, as a son-in-law, that it should be supposed that the offer would depend upon the father-in-law's goodwill. But then the father-in-law had told him that he would be welcome to the young lady,—without a farthing. Should he go on with his matrimonial purpose, towards which this visit would be an important step, he did not see the moment in which he could stop the proceedings by a demand for money. Nevertheless he went, not being strong enough to oppose Mr. Traffick.

Yes;—the ladies were at home, and he found himself at once in Lady Tringle's presence. There was at the time no one with her, and the Captain acknowledged to himself that a trying moment had come to him. "Dear me! Captain Batsby!" said her ladyship, who had not seen him since he and Gertrude had gone off together.

"Yes, Lady Tringle. As I have come back from abroad I thought that I might as well come and call. I did see Sir Thomas in the City."

"Was not that a very foolish thing you did?"

"Perhaps it was, Lady Tringle. Perhaps it would have been better to ask permission to address your daughter in the regular course of things. There was, perhaps,—perhaps a little romance in going off in that way."

"It gave Sir Thomas a deal of trouble."

"Well, yes; he was so quick upon us you know. May I be allowed to see Gertrude now?"

"Upon my word I hardly know," said Lady Tringle, hesitating.

"I did see Sir Thomas in the City."

"But did he say you were to come and call?"

"He gave his consent to the marriage."

"But I am afraid there was to be no money," whispered Lady Tringle. "If money is no matter I suppose you may see her." But before the Captain had resolved how he might best answer this difficult suggestion the door opened, and the young lady herself entered the room, together with her sister.

"Benjamin," said Gertrude, "is this really you?" And then she flew into his arms.

"My dear," said Augusta, "do control your emotions."

"Yes, indeed, Gertrude," said the mother. "As the things are at present you should control yourself. Nobody as yet knows what may come of it."

"Oh, Benjamin!" again exclaimed Gertrude, tearing herself from his arms, throwing herself on the sofa, and covering her face with both her hands. "Oh, Benjamin,—so you have come at last."

"I am afraid he has come too soon," said

Augusta, who however had received her lesson from her husband, and had communicated some portion of her husband's tidings to her sister.

"Why too soon?" exclaimed Gertrude. "It can never be too soon. Oh, mamma, tell him that you make him welcome to your bosom as your second son-in-law."

"Upon my word, my dear, I do not know, without consulting your father."

"But papa has consented," said Gertrude.

"But only if——"

"Oh, mamma," said Mrs. Traffick, "do not talk about matters of business on such an occasion as this. All that must be managed between the gentlemen. If he is here as Gertrude's acknowledged lover, and if papa has told him that he shall be accepted as such, I don't think that we ought to say a word about money. I do hate money. It does make things so disagreeable."

"Nobody can be more noble in everything of that kind than Benjamin," said Gertrude. "It is only because he loves me with all his heart that he is here. Why else was it that he took me off to Ostend?"

Captain Batsby as he listened to all this felt that he ought to say something. And yet how dangerous might a word be! It was apparent to him, even in his perturbation, that the ladies were in fact asking him to renew his offer, and to declare that he renewed it altogether independently of any money consideration. He could not bring himself quite to agree with that noble sentiment in expressing which Mrs. Traffick had declared her hatred of money. In becoming the son-in-law of a millionaire he would receive the honest congratulations of all his friends,—on condition that he received some comfortable fraction out of the millions, but he knew well that he would subject himself to their ridicule were he to take the girl and lose the plunder. If he were to answer them now as they would have him answer he would commit himself to the girl without any bargain as to the plunder. And yet what else was there for him to do? He must be a brave man who can stand up before a girl and declare that he will love her for ever,—on condition that she shall have so many thousand pounds; but he must be more than brave, he will be heroic, who can do so in the presence not only of the girl but of the girl's mother and married sister as well. Captain Batsby was no such hero. "Of course," he said at last.

"Of course what?" asked Augusta.

"It was because I loved her."

"I knew that he loved me," sobbed Gertrude.

"And you are here, because you intend to make her your wife in presence of all men?" asked Augusta.

"Oh certainly."

"Then I suppose that it will be all right," said Lady Tringle.

"It will be all right," said Augusta. "And now, mamma, I think that we may leave them alone together." But to this Lady Tringle would not give her assent. She had not had confided to her the depth of Mr. Traffick's wisdom, and declared herself opposed to any absolute overt love-making until Sir Thomas should have given his positive consent.

"It is all the same thing, Benjamin, is it not?" said Augusta, assuming already the familiarity of a sister-in-law.

"Oh quite," said the Captain.

But Gertrude looked as though she did not think it to be exactly the same. Such deficiency as that, however, she had to endure; and she received from her sister after the Captain's departure full congratulations as to her lover's return. "To tell you the truth," said Augusta, "I didn't think that you would ever see him again. After what papa said to him in the City he might have got off and nobody could have said a word to him. Now he's fixed."

Captain Batsby effected his escape as quickly as he could, and went home a melancholy man. He, too, was aware that he was fixed; and, as he thought of this, a dreadful idea fell upon him that the Honourable Mr. Traffick had perhaps played him false.

In the meantime Mr. Traffick was true to his word and went into the City. In the early days of his married life his journeys to Lombard Street were frequent. The management and investing of his wife's money had been to him a matter of much interest, and he had felt a gratification in discussing any money matter with the man who handled millions. In this way he had become intimate with the ways of the house, though latterly his presence there had not been encouraged. "I suppose I can go in to Sir Thomas," he said, laying his hand upon a leaf in the counter, which he had been accustomed to raise for the purpose of his own entrance. But here he was stopped. His name should be taken in, and Sir Thomas duly apprised. In the meantime he was relegated to a dingy little waiting-room, which was odious to him, and there he was kept waiting for half-an-hour. This made him angry, and he called to one of the clerks. "Will you tell Sir Thomas that I must be down at the House almost immediately, and that I am particularly anxious to see him on business of importance?" For another ten minutes he was still kept, and then he was shown into his father-in-law's presence. "I am very sorry, Traffick," said Sir Thomas, "but I really can't turn two Directors of the Bank of England out of my room, even for you."

"I only thought I would just let you know that I am in a hurry."

"So am I, for the matter of that. Have you gone to your father's house to-day, so that you would not be able to see me in Queen's Gate?"

This was intended to be very severe, but Mr. Traffick bore it. It was one of those rough things which Sir Thomas was in the habit of saying, but which really meant nothing. "No. My father is still at his house as yet, though they are thinking of going every day. It is about another matter, and I did not want to trouble you with it at home."

"Let us hear what it is."

"Captain Batsby has been with me."

"Oh, he has, has he?"

"I've known him ever so long. He's a foolish fellow."

"So he seems."

"But a gentleman."

"Perhaps I am not so good a judge of that. His folly I did perceive."

"Oh yes; he's a gentleman. You may take my word for that. And he has means."

"That's an advantage."

"While that fellow Houston is hardly more than a beggar. And Batsby is quite in earnest about Gertrude."

"If the two of them wish it he can have her to-morrow. She has made herself a conspicuous ass by running away with him, and perhaps it's the best thing she can do."

"That's just it. Augusta sees it quite in the same light."

"Augusta was never tempted. You wouldn't have run away."

"It wasn't necessary, Sir Thomas, was it? There he is,—ready to marry her to-morrow. But, of course, he is a little anxious about the money."

"I dare say he is."

"I've been talking to him,—and the upshot is, that I have promised to speak to you. He isn't at all a bad fellow."

"He'd keep a house over his wife's head, you think?" Sir Thomas had been particularly irate that morning, and before the arrival of his son-in-law had sworn to himself that Traffick should go. Augusta might remain, if she pleased, for the occurrence; but the Honourable Septimus should no longer eat and drink as an inhabitant of his house.

"He'd do his duty by her as a man should do," said Traffick, determined to ignore the disagreeable subject.

"Very well. There she is."

"But of course he would like to hear something about money."

"Would he?"

"That's only natural."

"You found it so,—did you not? What's the good of giving a girl money when her husband won't spend it. Perhaps this Captain Batsby would expect to live at Queen's Gate or Merle Park."

It was impossible to go on enduring this without notice. Mr. Traffick, however, only frowned and shook his head. It was clear at last that Sir Thomas intended to be more than rough, and it was almost imperative upon Mr. Traffick to be rough in return. "I am endeavouring to do my duty by the family," he said.

"Oh indeed."

"Gertrude has eloped with this man, and the thing is talked about everywhere. Augusta feels it very much."

"She does, does she?"

"And I have thought it right to ask his intentions."

"He didn't knock you down, or anything of that sort?"

"Knock me down?"

"For interfering. But he hasn't pluck for that. Houston would have done it immediately. And I should have said he was right. But if you have got anything to say, you had better say it. When you have done, then I shall have something to say."

"I've told him that he couldn't expect as much as you would have given her but for this running away."

"You told him that?"

"Yes; I told him that. Then some sum had to be mentioned. He suggested a hundred thousand pounds."

"How very modest. Why should he have put up with less than you, seeing that he has got something of his own?"

"He hasn't my position, Sir. You know that well enough. Now to make a long and short of it, I suggested sixty."

"Out of your own pocket?"

"Not exactly."

"But out of mine?"

"You're her father, and I suppose you intend to provide for her."

"And you have come here to dictate to me the provision which I am to make for my own child! That is an amount of impudence which I did not expect even from you. But suppose that I agree to the terms. Will he, do you think, consent to have a clause put into the settlement?"

"What clause?"

"Something that shall bind him to keep a house

for his own wife's use, so that he should not take my money and then come and live upon me afterwards."

"Sir Thomas," said the Member of Parliament, "that is a mode of expression so uncourteous that I cannot bear it even from you."

"Is there any mode of expression that you cannot bear?"

"If you want me to leave your house, say it at once."

"Why I have been saying it for the last six months! I have been saying it almost daily since you were married."

"If so you should have spoken more clearly, for I have not understood you."

"Heavens and earth," ejaculated Sir Thomas.

"Am I to understand that you wish your child to leave your roof during this inclement weather in her present delicate condition?"

"Are you in a delicate condition?" asked Sir Thomas. To this Mr. Traffick could condescend to make no reply. "Because, if not, you, at any rate, had better go,—unless you find the weather too inclement."

"Of course I shall go," said Mr. Traffick. "No consideration on earth shall induce me to eat another meal under your roof until you shall have thought good to have expressed regret for what you have said."

"Then it is very long before I shall have to give you another meal."

"And now what shall I say to Captain Batsby?"

"Tell him from me," said Sir Thomas, "that he cannot possibly set about his work more injudiciously than by making you his ambassador." Then Mr. Traffick took his departure.

It may be as well to state here that Mr. Traffick kept his threat religiously,—at any rate, to the end of the Session. He did not eat another meal during that period under his father-in-law's roof. But he slept there for the next two or three days until he had suited himself with lodgings in the neighbourhood of the House. In doing this, however, he contrived to get in and out without encountering Sir Thomas. His wife in her delicate condition,—and because of the inclemency of the weather,—awaited the occurrence at Queen's Gate.

CHAPTER XVI.

TREGOTHNAN.

THE writer, in giving a correct chronicle of the doings of the Tringle family at this time, has to acknowledge that Gertrude, during the prolonged absence of Captain Batsby at Brussels,—an absence that was cruelly prolonged for more than a week,—did make another little effort in another direction. Her father, in his rough way, had expressed an opinion that she had changed very much for the worse in transferring her affections from Mr. Houston to Captain Batsby, and had almost gone so far as to declare that had she been persistent with her

Houston the money difficulty might have been overcome. This was imprudent,—unless, indeed, he was desirous of bringing back Mr. Houston into the bosom of the Tringles. It instigated Gertrude to another attempt,—which, however, she did not make till Captain Batsby had been away from her for at least four days without writing a letter. Then it occurred to her that if she had a preference it certainly was for Frank Houston. No doubt the general desirability of marriage was her chief actuating motive. Will the world of British young ladies be much scandalised if I say that such is often an actuating motive? They would be justly scandalised if I pretended that many of its members were capable of the speedy transitions which Miss Tringle was strong enough to endure; but transitions do take place, and I claim, on behalf of my young lady, that she should be regarded as more strong-minded and more determined than the general crowd of young ladies. She had thought herself to be off with the old love before she was on with the new. Then the "new" had gone away to Brussels,—or heaven only knows where,—and there seemed to be an opportunity of renewing matters with the "old." Having perceived the desirability of matrimony, she simply carried out her purpose with a determined will. It was with a determined will, but perhaps with deficient judgment, that she had written as follows:

"Papa has altered his mind altogether. He speaks of you in the highest terms, and says that had you persevered he would have yielded about the money. Do try him again. When hearts have been united it is terrible that they should be dragged asunder." Mr. Traffick had been quite right in telling his father-in-law that "the thing had been talked about everywhere." The thing talked about had been Gertrude's elopement. The daughter of a baronet and a millionaire cannot go off with the half-brother of another baronet and escape that penalty. The journey to Ostend was in everybody's mouth, and had surprised Frank Houston the more because of the recent termination of his own little affair with the lady. That he should already have re-accommodated himself with Imogene was intelligible to him, and seemed to admit of valid excuse before any jury of matrons. It was an old affair, and the love,—real, true love,—was already existing. He, at any rate, was going back to the better course,—as the jury of matrons would have admitted. But Gertrude's new affair had had to be arranged from the beginning, and shocked him by its celerity. "Already!" he had said to himself,—"gone off with another man already?" He felt himself to have been wounded in a tender part, and was conscious of a feeling that he should like to injure the successful lover,—blackball him at a club, or do him some other mortal mischief. When, therefore, he received from the young lady the little billet above given, he was much surprised. Could it be a hoax? It was certainly the young lady's handwriting. Was he to be enticed once again into Lombard Street, in order that the clerks might set upon him in a body and maltreat him? Was he to be decoyed into Queen's Gate, and made a sacrifice of by the united force of the housemaids? Not understanding the celerity of the young lady, he could hardly believe the billet.

When he received the note of which we have here spoken two months had elapsed since he had seen Imogene and had declared to her his intention of facing the difficulties of matrimony in conjunction with herself as soon as she would be ready to undergo the ceremony with him. The reader will remember that her brother, Mudbury Docimer, had written to him with great severity, abusing both him and Imogene for the folly of their intention. And Houston, as he thought of their intention, thought to himself that perhaps they were foolish. The poverty, and the cradles, and the cabbages, were in themselves evils. But still he encouraged himself to think that there might be an evil worse even than folly. After that scene with Imogene, in which she had offered to sacrifice herself altogether, and to be bound to him, even though they should never be married, on condition that he should take to himself no other wife, he had quite resolved that it behoved him not to be exceeded by her in generosity. He had stoutly repudiated her offer, which he had called a damnable compact. And then there had been a delightful scene between them, in which it had been agreed that they should face the cradles and the cabbages with bold faces. Since that he had never allowed himself to fluctuate in his purpose. Had Sir Thomas come to him with Gertrude in one hand and the much-desired £120,000 in the other, he would have repudiated the lot of them. He declared to himself with stern resolution that he had altogether washed his hands from dirt of that kind. Cabbages and cradles for ever was the unpronounced cry of triumph with which he buoyed up his courage. He set himself to work earnestly, if not altogether steadfastly, to alter the whole tenor of his life. The champagne and the woodcocks,—or whatever might be the special delicacies of the season,—he did avoid. For some few days he absolutely dined upon a cut of mutton at an eating-house, and as he came forth from the unsavoury doors of the establishment regarded himself as a hero. Cabbages and cradles for ever! he would say to himself, as he went away to drink a cup of tea with an old maiden aunt, who was no less surprised than gratified by his new virtue. Therefore, when it had at last absolutely come home to him that the last little note had in truth been written by Gertrude with no object of revenge, but with the intention of once more alluring him into the wealth of Lombard Street, he simply put it into his breastcoat-pocket, and left it there unanswered.

Mudbury Docimer did not satisfy himself with writing the very uncourteous letter which the reader has seen, but proceeded to do his utmost to prevent the threatened marriage. "She is old enough to look after herself," he had said, as though all her future actions must be governed by her own will. But within ten days of the writing of that letter he had found it expedient to go down into the country, and to take his sister with him. As the head of the

Docimer family he possessed a small country-house almost in the extremity of Cornwall; and thither he went. It was a fraternal effort made altogether on his sister's behalf, and was so far successful that Imogene was obliged to accompany him. It was all very well for her to feel that as she was of age she could do as she pleased. But a young lady is constrained by the exigencies of society to live with somebody. She cannot take a lodging by herself, as her brother may do. Therefore, when Mudbury Docimer went down to Cornwall, Imogene was obliged to accompany him.

"Is this intended for banishment?" she said to him, when they had been about a week in the country.

"What do you call banishment? You used to like the country in the spring." It was now the middle of April.

"So I do, and in summer also. But I like nothing under constraint."

"I am sorry that circumstances should make it imperative upon me to remain here just at present."

"Why cannot you tell the truth, Mudbury?"

"Have I told you any falsehood?"

"Why do you not say outright that I have been brought down here to be out of Frank Houston's way?"

"Because Frank Houston is a name which I do not wish to mention to you again,—at any rate for some time."

"What would you do if he were to show himself here?" she asked.

"Tell him at once that he was not welcome. In other words, I would not have him here. It is very improbable I should think that he would come without a direct invitation from me. That invitation he will never have until I feel satisfied that you and he have changed your mind again, and that you mean to stick to it."

"I do not think we shall do that."

"Then he shall not come down here; nor, as far as I am able to arrange it, shall you go up to London."

"Then I am a prisoner?"

"You may put it as you please," said her brother. "I have no power of detaining you. Whatever influence I have I think it right to use. I am altogether opposed to this marriage, believing it to be an absurd infatuation. I think that he is of the same opinion."

"No!" said she, indignantly.

"That I believe to be his feeling," he continued, taking no notice of her assertion. "He is as perfectly aware as I am that you two are not adapted to live happily together on an income of a few hundreds a year. Some time ago it was agreed between you that it was so. You both were quite of one mind, and I was given to understand that the engagement was at an end. It was so much at an end that he made an arrangement for marrying another woman. But your feelings are stronger than his, and you allowed them to get the better of you. Then you enticed him back from the purpose on which you had both decided."

"Enticed!" said she. "I did nothing of the kind!"

"Would he have changed his mind if you had not enticed him?"

"I did nothing of the kind. I offered to remain just as we are."

"That is all very well. Of course he could not accept such an offer. Thinking as I do, it is my duty to keep you apart as long as I can. If you contrive to marry him in opposition to my efforts, the misery of both of you must be on your head. I tell you fairly that I do not believe he wishes anything of the kind."

"I am quite sure he does," said Imogene.

"Very well. Do you leave him alone; stay down here, and see what will come of it. I quite agree that such a banishment, as you call it, is not a happy prospect for you;—but it is happier than that of a marriage with Frank Houston. Give that up, and then you can go back to London and begin the world again."

Begin the world again! She knew what that meant. She was to throw herself into the market, and look for such other husband as Providence might send her. She had tried that before, and had convinced herself that Providence could never send her any that could be acceptable. The one man had taken possession of her, and there never could be a second. She had not known her own strength,—or her own weakness as the case might be,—when she had agreed to surrender the man she loved because there had been an alteration in their prospects of an income. She had struggled with herself, had attempted to amuse herself with the world, had told herself that somebody would come who would banish that image from her thoughts and heart. She had bade herself to submit to the separation for his welfare. Then she had endeavoured to quiet herself by declaring to herself that the man was no hero,—was unworthy of so much thinking. But it had all been of no avail. Gertrude Tringle had been a festering sore to her. Frank, whether a hero or only a commonplace man, was,—as she owned to herself,—hero enough for her. Then came the opening for a renewal of the engagement. Frank had been candid with her, and had told her everything. The Tringle money would not be forthcoming on his behalf. Then,—not resolving to entice him back again,—she had done so. The word was odious to her, and was rejected with disdain when used against her by her brother;—but, when alone, she acknowledged to herself that it was true. She had enticed her lover back again,—to his great detriment. Yes; she certainly had enticed him back. She certainly was about to sacrifice him because of her love. "If I could only die, and there be an end of it!" she exclaimed to herself.

Though Tregothnan Hall, as the Docimers' house was called, was not open to Frank Houston, there was the post running always. He had written to her half-a-dozen times since she had been in Cornwall, and had always spoken of their engagement as an affair at last irrevocably fixed. She, too, had written little notes, tender and loving, but still tinged by that tone of despondency which had become common to her. "As for naming a day," she said once, "suppose we fix the first of January, ten years hence. Mudbury's opposition will be worn out by old age, and you will have become thoroughly sick of the pleasures of London." But joined to this there would be a few jokes, and then some little word of warmest, most enduring, most trusting love. "Don't believe me if I say that I am not happy in knowing that I am altogether your own." Then there would come a simple "I" as a signature, and after that some further badinage respecting her "Cerberus," as she called her brother.

But after that word, that odious word, "enticed," there went another letter up to London of altogether another nature.

"I have changed my mind again," she said, "and have become aware that, though I should die in doing it,—though we should both die if it were possible,—there should be an end of everything between you and me. Yes, Frank; there! I send you back my troth, and demand my own in return. After all why should not one die;—hang oneself if it be necessary? To be self-denying is all that is necessary,—at any rate to a woman. Hanging or lying down and dying, or lingering on and saying one's prayers and knitting stockings, is altogether immaterial. I have sometimes thought Mudbury to be brutal to me, but I have never known him to be untrue,—or even, as I believe, mistaken. He sees clearly and knows what will happen. He tells me that I have enticed you back. I am not true as he is. So I threw him back the word in his teeth,—though its truth at the moment was going like a dagger through my heart. I know myself to have been selfish, unfeeling, unfeminine, when I induced you to surrender yourself to a mode of life which will make you miserable. I have sometimes been proud of myself because I have loved you so truly; but now I hate myself and despise myself because I have been incapable of the first effort which love should make. Love should at any rate be unselfish.

"He tells me that you will be miserable and that the misery will be on my head,—and I believe him. There shall be an end of it. I want no promise from you. There may, perhaps, be a time in which Imogene Docimer as a sturdy old maid shall be respected and serene of mind. As a wife who had enticed her husband to his misery she would be respected neither by him nor by herself,—and as for serenity it would be quite out of the question. I have been unfortunate. That is all;—but not half so unfortunate as others that I see around me.

"*Pray, pray*, PRAY, take this as final, and thus save me from renewed trouble and renewed agony.

"Now I am yours truly,

—"never again will I be affectionate to any one with true feminine love,

"IMOGENE DOCIMER."

Houston when he received the above letter of course had no alternative but to declare that it could not possibly be regarded as having any avail. And indeed he had heart enough in his bosom to be warmed to something like true heat by such words as these. The cabbages and cradles ran up in his estimation. The small house at Pau, which in some of his more despondent moments had assumed an unqualified appearance of domestic discomfort, was now ornamented and accoutred till it seemed to be a little paradise. The very cabbages blossomed into roses, and the little babies in the cradles produced a throb of paternal triumph in his heart. If she were woman enough to propose to herself such an agony of devotion, could he not be man enough to demand from her a devotion of a different kind? As to Mudbury Docimer's truth, he believed in it not at all, but was quite convinced of the man's brutality. Yes; she should hang herself —but it should be round his neck. The serenity should be displayed by her not as an aunt but as a wife and mother. As for enticing, did he not now,—just in this moment of his manly triumph,—acknowledge to himself that she had enticed him to his happiness, to his glory, to his welfare? In this frame of mind he wrote his answer as follows;—

"MY DEAREST,

"You have no power of changing your mind again. There must be some limit to vacillations, and that has been reached. Something must be fixed at last. Something has been fixed at last, and I most certainly shall not consent to any further unfixing. What right has Mudbury to pretend to know my feelings? or, for the matter of that, what right have you to accept his description of them? I tell you now that I place my entire happiness in the hope of making you my wife. I call upon you to ignore all the selfish declarations as to my own ideas which I have made in times past. The only right which you could now possibly have to separate yourself from me would come from your having ceased to love me. You do not pretend to say that such is the case; and therefore, with considerable indignation, but still very civilly, I desire that Mudbury with his hard-hearted counsels may go to the ——

"Enticed! Of course you have enticed me. I suppose that women do as a rule entice men, either to their advantage or disadvantage. I will leave it to you to say whether you believe that such enticement, if it be allowed its full scope, will lead to one or the other as far as I am concerned. I never was so happy as when I felt that you had enticed me back to the hopes of former days.

"Now I am yours, as always, and most affectionately,

"FRANK HOUSTON.

"I shall expect the same word back from you by return of post scored under as eagerly as those futile 'prays.'"

Imogene when she received this was greatly disturbed,—not knowing how to carry herself in her great resolve,—or whether indeed that resolve must not be again abandoned. She had determined, should her lover's answer be as she had certainly intended it to be when she wrote her letter, to go at once to her brother and to declare to him that the danger was at an end, and that he might return to London without any fear of a relapse on her part. But she could not do so with such a reply as that she now held in her pocket. If that reply could, in very truth, be true, then there must be another revulsion, another change of purpose, another yielding to absolute joy. If it could be the case that Frank Houston no longer feared the dangers that he had feared before, if he had in truth reconciled himself to a state of things which he had once described as simple poverty, if he really placed his happiness on the continuation of his love, then,—then, why should she make the sacrifice? Why should she place such implicit confidence in her brother's infallibility against error, seeing that by doing so she would certainly shipwreck her own happiness,—and his too, if his words were to be trusted?

He called upon her to write to him again by return of post. She was to write to him and unsay those prayers, and comfort him with a repetition of that dear word which she had declared that she would never use again with all its true meaning. That was his express order to her. Should she obey it, or should she not obey it? Should she vacillate again, or should she leave his last letter unanswered with stern obduracy? She acknowledged to herself that it was a dear letter, deserving the best treatment at her hands, giving her lover credit, probably, for more true honesty than he deserved. What was the best treatment? Her brother had plainly shown his conviction that the best treatment would be to leave him without meddling with him any further. Her sister-in-law, though milder in her language, was, she feared, of the same opinion. Would it not be better for him not to be meddled with? Ought not that to be her judgment, looking at the matter all round?

She did not at any rate obey him at all points, for she left his letter in her pocket for three or four days, while she considered the matter backwards and forwards.

CHAPTER XVII.

AUNT ROSINA.

DURING this period of heroism it had been necessary to Houston to have some confidential friend to whom from time to time he could speak of his purpose. He could not go on eating slices of boiled mutton at eating-houses, and drinking dribblets of bad wine out of little decanters no bigger than the bottles in a cruet stand, without having some one to encourage him in his efforts. It was a hard apprenticeship, and, coming as it did rather late in life for such a beginning, and after much luxurious indulgence, required some sympathy and consolation. There were Tom Shuttlecock and Lord John Battledore at the club. Lord John was the man as to whose expulsion because of his contumacious language so much had been said, but who lived through that and various other dangers. These had been his special friends, and to them he had confided everything in regard to the Tringle marriage. Shuttlecock had ridiculed the very idea of love, and had told him that everything else was to be thrown to the dogs in pursuit of a good income. Battledore had reminded him that there was "a deuced deal of cut-and-come-again in a hundred and twenty thousand pounds." They had been friends, not always altogether after his own heart, but friends who had served his purpose when he was making his raid upon Lombard Street. But they were not men to whom he could descant on the wholesomeness of cabbages as an article of daily food, or who would sympathise with the struggling joys of an embryo father. To their thinking, women were occasionally very convenient as being the depositaries of some of the accruing wealth of the world. Frank had been quite worthy of their friendship as having "spotted" and nearly "run down" for himself a well-laden city heiress. But now Tom Shuttlecock and Lord John Battledore were distateful to him,—as would he be to them. But he found the confidential friend in his maiden aunt.

Miss Houston was an old lady,—older than her time, as are some people,—who lived alone in a small house in Green Street. She was particular in calling it Green Street, Hyde Park. She was very anxious to have it known that she never occupied it during the months of August, September, and October,—though it was often the case with her that she did not in truth expatriate herself for more than six weeks. She was careful to have a fashionable seat in a fashionable church. She dearly loved to see her name in the papers when she was happy enough to be invited to a house whose entertainments were chronicled. There were a thousand little tricks,—I will not be harsh enough to call them unworthy,—by which she served Mammon. But she did not limit her service to the evil spirit. When in her place in church she sincerely said her prayers. When in London, or out of it, she gave a modicum of her slender income to the poor. And, though she liked to see her name in the papers as one of the fashionable world, she was a great deal too proud of the blood of the Houstons to toady any one or to ask for any favour. She was a neat, clean, nice-looking old lady, who understood that if economies were to be made in eating and drinking they should be effected at her own table and not at that of the servants who waited upon her. This was the confidential friend whom Frank trusted in his new career.

It must be explained that Aunt Rosina, as Miss Houston was called, had been well acquainted with her nephew's earlier engagement, and had approved of Imogene as his future wife. Then had come the unexpected collapse in the uncle's affairs, by which Aunt Rosina as well as others in the family had suffered,—and Frank, much to his aunt's displeasure, had allowed himself to be separated from the lady of his love on account of his comparative poverty. She had heard of Gertrude Tringle and all her money, but from a high standing of birth and social belongings had despised all the Tringles and all their money. To her, as a maiden lady, truth in love was everything. To her, as a well-born lady, good blood was everything. Therefore, though there had been no quarrel between her and Frank, there had been a cessation of sympathetic interest, and he had been thrown into the hands of the Battledores and Shuttlecocks. Now again the old sympathies were revived, and Frank found it convenient to drink tea with his aunt when other engagements allowed it.

"I call that an infernal interference," he said to his aunt, showing her Imogene's letters.

"My dear Frank, you need not curse and swear," said the old lady.

"Infernal is not cursing nor yet swearing." Then Miss Houston, having liberated her mind by her remonstrance, proceeded to read the letter. "I call that abominable," said Frank, alluding of course to the allusions made in the letter to Mudbury Docimer.

"It is a beautiful letter;—just what I should have expected from Imogene. My dear, I will tell you what I propose. Remain as you are both of you for five years."

"Five years. That's sheer nonsense."

"Five years, my dear, will run by like a dream. Five years to look back upon is as nothing."

"But these five years are five years to be looked forward to. It is out of the question."

"But you say that you could not live as a married man."

"Live! I suppose we could live." Then he thought of the cabbages and the cottage at Pau. "There would be seven hundred a-year I suppose."

"Couldn't you do something, Frank?"

"What, to earn money? No; I don't think I could. If I attempted to break stones I shouldn't break enough to pay for the hammers."

"Couldn't you write a book?"

"That would be worse than the stones. I sometimes thought I could paint a picture,—but, if I did, nobody would buy it. As to making money that is hopeless. I could save some, by leaving off gloves and allowing myself only three clean shirts a-week."

"That would be dreadful, Frank."

"It would be dreadful, but it is quite clear that I must do something. An effort has to be made." This he said with a voice the tone of which was almost heroic. Then they discussed the matter at great length, in doing which Aunt Rosina thoroughly encouraged him in his heroism. That idea of remaining unmarried for another short period of five years was allowed to go by the board, and when they parted on that night it was understood that steps were to be taken to bring about a marriage as speedily as possible.

"Perhaps I can do a little to help," said Aunt Rosina, in a faint whisper as Frank left the room.

Frank Houston, when he showed Imogene's letter to his aunt, had already answered it. Then he waited a day or two, not very patiently, for a further rejoinder from Imogene,—in which she of course was to unsay all that she had said before. But when, after four or five days, no rejoinder had come, and his fervour had been increased by his expectation, then he told his aunt that he should immediately take some serious step. The more ardent he was the better his aunt loved him. Could he have gone down and carried off his bride, and married her at once, in total disregard of the usual wedding-cake and St.-George's-Hanover-Square ceremonies to which the Houston family had always been accustomed, she could have found it in her heart to forgive him. "Do not be rash, Frank," she said. He merely shook his head, and as he again left her declared that he was not going to be driven this way or that by such a fellow as Mudbury Docimer.

"As I live, there's Frank coming through the gate." This was said by Imogene to her sister-in-law, as they were walking up and down the road which led from the lodge to the Tregothnan house. The two ladies were at that moment discussing Imogene's affairs. No rejoinder had as yet been made to Frank's last letter, which, to Imogene's feeling, was the most charming epistle which had ever come from the hands of a true lover. There had been passion and sincerity in every word of it; —even when he had been a little too strong in his language as he denounced the hard-hearted counsels of her brother. But yet she had not responded to all this sincerity, nor had she as yet withdrawn the resolution which she had herself declared. Mrs. Docimer was of opinion that that resolution should not be withdrawn, and had striven to explain that the circumstances were now the same as when, after full consideration, they had determined that the engagement should come to an end. At this very moment she was speaking words of wisdom to this effect, and as she did so Frank appeared, walking up from the gate.

"What will Mudbury say?" was Mrs. Docimer's first ejaculation. But Imogene, before she had considered how this danger might be encountered, rushed forward and gave herself up,—I fear we must confess,—into the arms of her lover. After that it was felt at once that she had withdrawn all her last resolution and had vacillated again. There was no ground left even for an argument now that she had submitted herself to be embraced. Frank's words of affection need not here be repeated, but they were of a nature to leave no doubt on the minds of either of the ladies.

Mudbury had declared that he would not receive Houston in his house as his sister's lover, and had expressed his opinion that even Houston would not have the face to show his face there. But Houston had come, and something must be done with him. It was soon ascertained that he had walked over from Penzance, which was but two miles off, and had left his portmanteau behind him. "I wouldn't bring anything," said he. "Mudbury would find it easier to maltreat my things than myself. It would look so foolish to tell the man with a fly to carry them back at once. Is he in the house?"

"He is about the place," said Mrs. Docimer, almost trembling.

"Is he very fierce against me?"

"He thinks it had better be all over."

"I am of a different way of thinking, you see. I cannot acknowledge that he has any right to dictate to Imogene."

"Nor can I," said Imogene.

"Of course he can turn me out."

"If he does I shall go with you," said Imogene.

"We have made up our minds to it," said Frank, "and he had better let us do as we please. He can make himself disagreeable, of course; but he has got no power to prevent us." Now they had reached the house, and Frank was of course allowed to enter. Had he not entered neither would Imogene, who was so much taken by this further instance of her lover's ardour that she was determined now to be led by him in everything. His explanation of that word "enticed" had been so thoroughly satisfactory to her that she was no longer in the least angry with herself because she had enticed him. She had quite come to see that it is the duty of a young woman to entice a young man.

Frank and Imogene were soon left alone, not from any kindness of feeling on the part of Mrs. Docimer, but because the wife felt it necessary to find her husband. "Oh, Mudbury, who do you think has come? He is here!"

"Houston!"

"Yes; Frank Houston!"

"In the house?"

"He is in the house. But he hasn't brought anything. He doesn't mean to stay."

"What does that matter? He shall not be asked even to dine here."

"If he is turned out she will go with him! If she says so she will do it. You cannot prevent her. That's what would come of it if she were to insist on going up to London with him."

"He is a scoundrel!"

"No; Mudbury;—not a scoundrel. You cannot call him a scoundrel. There is something firm about him; isn't there?"

"To come to my house when I told him not?"

"But he does really love her."

"Bother!"

"At any rate there they are in the breakfast-parlour, and something must be done. I couldn't tell him not to come in. And she wouldn't have come without him. There will be enough for them to live upon. Don't you think you'd better?" Docimer, as he returned to the house, declared that he "did not think he'd better." But he had to confess to himself that, whether it were better or whether it were worse, he could do very little to prevent it.

The greeting of the two men was anything but pleasant. "What I have got to say I would rather say outside," said Docimer.

"Certainly," said Frank. "I suppose I'm to be allowed to return?"

"If he does not,"—said Imogene, who at her brother's request had left the room, but still stood at the open door,—"if he does not I shall go to him in Penzance. You will hardly attempt to keep me a prisoner."

"Who says that he is not to return? I think that you are two idiots, but I am quite aware that I cannot prevent you from being married if you are both determined." Then he led the way out through the hall, and Frank followed him. "I cannot understand that any man should be so fickle," he said, when they were both out on the walk together.

"Constant, I should suppose you mean."

"I said fickle, and I meant it. It was at your own suggestion that you and Imogene were to be separated."

"No doubt; it was at my suggestion, and with her consent. But you see that we have changed our minds."

"And will change them again."

"We are steady enough in our purpose, now, at any rate. You hear what she says. If I came down here to persuade her to alter her purpose,—to talk her into doing something of which you disapproved, and as to which she agreed with you,—then you might do something by quarrelling with me. But what's the use of it, when she and I are of one mind? You know that you cannot talk her over."

"Where do you mean to live?"

"I'll tell you all about that if you'll allow me to

send into Penzance for my things. I cannot discuss matters with you if you proclaim yourself to be my enemy. You say we are both idiots."

"I do."

"Very well. Then you had better put up with idiots. You can't cure their idiocy. Nor have you any authority to prevent them from exhibiting it." The argument was efficacious though the idiocy was acknowledged. The portmanteau was sent for, and before the evening was over Frank had again been received at Tregothnan as Imogene's accepted lover.

Then Frank had his story to tell and his new proposition to make. Aunt Rosina had offered to join her means with his. The house in Green Street, no doubt, was small, but room it was thought could be made, at any rate till the necessity had come for various cribs and various cradles. "I cannot imagine that you will endure to live with Aunt Rosina," said the brother.

"Why on earth should I object to Aunt Rosina?" said Imogene. "She and I have always been friends." In her present mood she would hardly have objected to live with any old woman, however objectionable. "And we shall be able to have a small cottage somewhere," said Frank. "She will keep the house in London, and we shall keep the cottage."

"And what on earth will you do with yourself?"

"I have thought of that too," said Frank. "I shall take to painting pictures in earnest;—portraits probably. I don't see why I shouldn't do as well as anybody else."

"That head of yours of old Mrs. Jones," said Imogene, "was a great deal better than dozens of things one sees every year in the Academy."

"Bother!" exclaimed Docimer.

"I don't see why he should not succeed, if he really will work hard," said Mrs. Docimer.

"Bother!"

"Why should it be bother?" said Frank, put upon his mettle. "Ever so many fellows have begun and have got on, older than I am. And, even if I don't earn anything, I've got an employment."

"And is the painting-room to be in Green Street also?" asked Docimer.

"Just at present I shall begin by copying things at the National Gallery," explained Houston, who was not as yet prepared with his answer to that difficulty as to a studio in the little house in Green Street.

When the matter had been carried as far as this it was manifest enough that anything like opposition to Imogene's marriage was to be withdrawn. Houston remained at Tregothnan for a couple of days and then returned to London. A week afterwards the Docimers followed him, and early in the following June the two lovers, after all their troubles and many vacillations, were made one at St. George's church, to the great delight of Aunt Rosina. It cannot be said that the affair gave equal satisfaction to all the bridegroom's friends, as may be learnt from the following narration of two conversations which took place in London very shortly after the wedding.

"Fancy after all that fellow Houston going and marrying such a girl as Imogene Docimer, without a single blessed shilling to keep themselves alive." This was said in the smoking-room of Houston's club by Lord John Battledore to Tom Shuttlecock; but it was said quite aloud, so that Houston's various acquaintances might be enabled to offer their remarks on so interesting a subject; and to express their pity for the poor object of their commiseration.

"It's the most infernal piece of folly I ever heard in my life," said Shuttlecock. "There was that Tringle girl with two hundred thousand pounds to be had just for the taking;—Traffick's wife's sister you know."

"There was something wrong about that," said another. "Benjamin Batsby, that stupid fellow who used to be in the twentieth, ran off with her just when everything had been settled between Houston and old Tringle."

"Not a bit of it," said Battledore. "Tringle had quarrelled with Houston before that. Batsby did go with her, but the governor wouldn't come down with the money. Then the girl was brought back and there was no marriage." Upon that the condition of poor Gertrude in reference to her lovers and her fortune was discussed by those present with great warmth; but they all agreed that Houston had proved himself to be a bigger fool than any of them had expected.

"By George, he's going to set up for painting portraits," said Lord John, with great disgust.

In Queen's Gate the matter was discussed by the ladies there very much in the same spirit. At this time Gertrude was engaged to Captain Batsby, if not with the full approbation at any rate with the consent both of her father and mother, and therefore she could speak of Frank Houston and his bride, if with disdain, still without wounded feelings. "Here it is in the papers, Francis Houston and Imogene Docimer," said Mrs. Traffick.

"So she has really caught him at last!" said Gertrude.

"There was not much to catch," rejoined Mrs. Traffick. "I doubt whether they have got £500 a year between them."

"It does seem so very sudden," said Lady Tringle.

"Sudden!" said Gertrude. "They have been about it for the last five years. Of course he has tried to wriggle out of it all through. I am glad that she has succeeded at last, if only because he deserves it."

"I wonder where they'll find a place to live in," said Augusta. This took place in the bedroom which Mrs. Traffick still occupied in Queen's Gate, when she had been just a month a mother.

Thus, with the kind assistance of Aunt Rosina, Frank Houston and Imogene Docimer were married at last, and the chronicler hereby expresses a hope that it may not be long before Frank may see a picture of his own hanging on the walls of the Academy, and that he may live to be afraid of the coming of no baby.

CHAPTER XVIII.

TOM TRINGLE GOES UPON HIS TRAVELS.

WE must again go back and pick up our threads to April, having rushed forward to be present at the wedding of Frank Houston and Imogene Docimer, which did not take place till near Midsummer. This we must do at once in regard to Tom Tringle, who, if the matter be looked at aright, should be regarded as the hero of this little history. Ayala indeed, who is no doubt the real heroine among so many young ladies who have been more or less heroic, did not find in him the angel of whom she had dreamed, and whose personal appearance on earth was necessary to her happiness. But he had been able very clearly to pick out an angel for himself, and, though he had failed in his attempts to take the angel home with him, had been constant in his endeavours as long as there remained to him a chance of success. He had shown himself to be foolish, vulgar, and ignorant. He had given way to Bolivian champagne and Faddle intimacies. He had been silly enough to think that he could bribe his Ayala with diamonds for herself, and charm her with cheaper jewelry on his own person. He had thought to soar high by challenging his rival to a duel, and had then been tempted by pot courage to strike him in the streets.

A very vulgar and foolish young man! But a young man capable of a persistent passion! Young men not foolish and not vulgar are, perhaps, common enough. But the young men of constant heart and capable of such persistency as Tom's are not to be found every day walking about the streets of the metropolis. Jonathan Stubbs was constant, too; but it may be doubted whether the Colonel ever really despaired. The merit is to despair and yet to be constant. When a man has reason to be assured that a young lady is very fond of him, he may always hope that love will follow,—unless indeed the love which he seeks has been already given away elsewhere. Moreover, Stubbs had many substantial supports at his back; the relationship of the Marchesa, the friendship of Lady Albury, the comforts of Stalham—and not least, if last, the capabilities and prowess of Croppy. Then, too, he was neither vulgar nor foolish nor ignorant. Tom Tringle had everything against him,—everything that would weigh with Ayala; and yet he fought his battle out to the last gasp. Therefore, I desire my hearers to regard Tom Tringle as the hero of the transactions with which they have been concerned, and to throw their old shoes after him as he starts away upon his grand tour.

"Tom, my boy, you have to go, you know, in four days," said his father to him. At this time Tom had as yet given no positive consent as to his departure. He had sunk into a low state of moaning and groaning, in which he refused even to accede to the doctrine of the expediency of a manly bearing. "What's the good of telling a lie about it?" he would say to his mother. "What's the good of manliness when a fellow would rather be drowned?" He had left his bed indeed, and had once or twice sauntered out of the house. He had been instigated by his sister to go down to his club, under the idea that by such an effort he would shake off the despondency which overwhelmed him. But he had failed in the attempts, and had walked by the doors of the Mountaineers, finding himself unable to face the hall-porter. But still the preparations for his departure were going on. It was presumed that he was to leave London for Liverpool on the Friday, and his father had now visited him in his own room on the Tuesday evening with the intention of extorting from him his final consent. Sir Thomas had on that morning expressed himself very freely to his son-in-law Mr. Traffick, and on returning home had been glad to find that his words had been of avail, at any rate as regarded the dinner-hour. He was tender-hearted towards his son, and disposed to tempt him rather than threaten him into obedience.

"I haven't ever said I would go," replied Tom.

"But you must, you know. Everything has been packed up, and I want to make arrangements with you about money. I have got a cabin for you to yourself, and Captain Merry says that you will have a very pleasant passage. The equinoxes are over."

"I don't care about the equinoxes," said Tom. "I should like bad weather if I am to go."

"Perhaps you may have a touch of that, too."

"If the ship could be dashed against a rock I should prefer it!" exclaimed Tom.

"That's nonsense. The Cunard ships never are dashed against rocks. By the time you've been three days at sea you'll be as hungry as a hunter. Now, Tom, how about money?"

"I don't care about money," said Tom.

"Don't you? Then you're very unlike anybody else that I meet. I think I had better give you power to draw at New York, San Francisco, Yokohama, Pekin, and Calcutta."

"Am I to go to Pekin?" asked Tom, with renewed melancholy.

"Well, yes;—I think so. You had better see what the various houses are doing in China. And then from Calcutta you can go up the country. By that time I dare say we shall have possession of Cabul. With such a government as we have now, thank God! the Russians will have been turned pretty nearly out of Asia by this time next year." *

"Am I to be away more than a year?"

"If I were you," said the father, glad to catch the glimmer of assent which was hereby implied,—"if I were you I would do it thoroughly whilst I was about it. Had I seen so much when I was young I should have been a better man of business."

"It's all the same to me," said Tom. "Say ten years, if you like it! Say twenty! I shan't ever want to come back again. Where am I to go after Cabul?"

* It has to be stated that this story was written in 1878.

"I didn't exactly fix it that you should go to Cabul. Of course you will write home and give me your own opinion as you travel on. You will stay two or three months probably in the States."

"Am I to go to Niagara?" he asked.

"Of course you will, if you wish it. The Falls of Niagara, I am told, are very wonderful."

"If a man is to drown himself," said Tom, "it's the sort of place to do it effectually."

"Oh, Tom!" exclaimed his father. "Do you speak to me in that way when I am doing everything in my power to help you in your trouble?"

"You cannot help me," said Tom.

"Circumstances will. Time will do it. Employment will do it. A sense of your dignity as a man will do it, when you find yourself amongst others who know nothing of what you have suffered. You revel in your grief now because those around you know that you have failed. All that will be changed when you are with strangers. You should not talk to your father of drowning yourself!"

"That was wrong. I know it was wrong," said Tom, humbly. "I won't do it if I can help it,—but perhaps I had better not go there. And how long ought I to stay at Yokohama? Perhaps you had better put it all down on a bit of paper." Then Sir Thomas endeavoured to explain to him that all that he said now was in the way of advice. That it would be in truth left to himself to go almost where he liked, and to stay at each place almost as long as he liked;—that he would be his own master, and that within some broad and undefined limits he would have as much money as he pleased to spend. Surely no preparations for a young man's tour were ever made with more alluring circumstances! But Tom could not be tempted into any expression of satisfaction.

This, however, Sir Thomas did gain,—that before he left his son's room it was definitely settled,—that Tom should take his departure on the Friday, going down to Liverpool by an afternoon train on that day. "I tell you what," said Sir Thomas; "I'll go down with you, see you on board the ship, and introduce you to Captain Merry. I shall be glad of an opportunity of paying a visit to Liverpool." And so the question of Tom's departure was settled.

On the Wednesday and Thursday he seemed to take some interest in his bags and portmanteaus, and began himself to look after those assuagements of the toils of travel which are generally dear to young men. He interested himself in a fur coat, in a well-arranged despatch box, and in a very neat leathern case which was intended to hold two brandy flasks. He consented to be told of the number of his shirts, and absolutely expressed an opinion that he should want another pair of dress-boots. When this occurred every female bosom in the house, from Lady Tringle's down to the kitchenmaid's, rejoiced at the signs of recovery which evinced themselves. But neither Lady Tringle nor the kitchenmaid, nor did any of the intermediate female bosoms, know how he employed himself when he left the house on that Thursday afternoon. He walked across the

Park, and, calling at Kingsbury Crescent, left a note addressed to his aunt. It was as follows:—"I start to-morrow afternoon,—I hardly know whither. It may be for years or it may be for ever. I should wish to say a word to Ayala before I go. Will she see me if I come at twelve o'clock exactly to-morrow morning? I will call for an answer in half-an-hour. T. T., junior. Of course I am aware that Ayala is to become the bride of Colonel Jonathan Stubbs." In half-an-hour he returned, and got his answer. "Ayala will be glad to have an opportunity of saying good-bye to you to-morrow morning."

From this it will be seen that Ayala had at that time returned from Stalham to Kingsbury Crescent. She had come back joyful in heart, thoroughly triumphant as to her angel, with everything in the world sweet and happy before her,—desirous if possible to work her fingers off in mending the family linen, if only she could do something for somebody in return for all the joy that the world was giving her. When she was told that Tom wished to see her for the last time,—for the last time at any rate before her marriage,—she assented at once. "I think you should see him as he asks it," said her aunt.

"Poor Tom! Of course I will see him." And so the note was written which Tom received when he called the second time at the door.

At half-past eleven he skulked out of the house in Queen's Gate, anxious to avoid his mother and sisters, who were on their side anxious to devote every remaining minute of the time to his comfort and welfare. I am afraid it must be acknowledged that he went with all his jewelry. It could do no good. At last he was aware of that. But still he thought that she would like him better with his jewelry than without it. Stubbs wore no gems, not even a ring, and Ayala when she saw her cousin enter the room could only assure herself that the male angels certainly were never be-jewelled. She was alone in the drawing-room, Mrs. Dosett having arranged that at the expiration of ten minutes, which were to be allowed to Tom for his private adieux, she would come down to say good-bye to her nephew. "Ayala!" said Tom.

"So you are going away,—for a very long journey, Tom."

"Yes, Ayala; for a very long journey; to Pekin and Cabul, if I live through, to get to those sort of places."

"I hope you will live through, Tom."

"Thank you, Ayala. Thank you. I daresay I shall. They tell me I shall get over it. I don't feel like getting over it now."

"You'll find some beautiful young lady at Pekin, perhaps."

"Beauty will never have any effect upon me again, Ayala. Beauty indeed! Think what I have suffered from beauty! From the first moment in which you came down to Glenbogie I have been a victim to it. It has destroyed me,—destroyed me!"

"I am sure you will come back quite well," said Ayala, hardly knowing how to answer the last appeal.

"Perhaps I may. If I can only get my heart to turn to stone, then I shall. I don't know why I should have been made to care so much about it. Other people don't."

"And now we must say, Good-bye, I suppose."

"Oh, yes;—good-bye! I did want to say one or two words if you ain't in a hurry. Of course you'll be his bride now."

"I hope so," said Ayala.

"I take that for granted. Of course I hate him."

"Oh, Tom; you shan't say that."

"It's human nature! I can tell a lie if you want it. I'd do anything for you. But you may tell him this: I'm very sorry I struck him."

"He knows that, Tom. He has said so to me."

"He behaved well to me,—very well,—as he always does to everybody."

"Now, Tom, that is good of you. I do like you so much for saying that."

"But I hate him!"

"No!"

"The evil spirits always hate the good ones. I am conscious of an evil spirit within my bosom. It is because my spirit is evil that you would not love me. He is good, and you love him."

"Yes; I do," said Ayala.

"And now we will change the conversation. Ayala, I have got a little present which you must take from me."

"Oh, no!" said Ayala, thinking of the diamond necklace.

"It's only a little thing,—and I hope you will."

Then he brought out from his pocket a small brooch which he had selected from his own stock of jewelry for the occasion. "We are cousins, you know."

"Yes, we are cousins," said Ayala, accepting the brooch, but still accepting it unwillingly.

"He must be very disdainful if he would object to such a little thing as this," said Tom, referring to the Colonel.

"He is not at all disdainful. He will not object in the least. I am sure of that, Tom. I will take it then, and I will wear it sometimes as a memento that we have parted like friends,—as cousins should do."

"Yes, as friends," said Tom, who thought that even that word was softer to his ear than cousins. Then he took her by the hand and looked into her face wistfully, thinking what might be the effect if for the last and for the first time he should snatch a kiss. Had he done so I think she would have let it pass without rebuke under the guise of cousinship. It would have been very disagreeable;—but then he was going away for so long a time, for so many miles! But at the moment Mrs. Dosett came in, and Ayala was saved. "Good-bye," he said; "good-bye," and without waiting to take the hand which his aunt offered him he hurried out of the room, out of the house, and back across the Gardens to Queen's Gate.

At Queen's Gate there was an early dinner, at three o'clock, at which Sir Thomas did not appear, as he had arranged to come out of the city and meet his son at the railway station. There were, therefore, sitting at the board for the last time the mother and the two sisters with the intending traveller. "Oh, Tom," said Lady Tringle, as soon as the servant had left them together, "I do so hope you will recover."

"Of course he will recover," said Augusta.

"Why shouldn't he recover?" asked Gertrude. "It's all in a person's mind. If he'd only make up his mind not to think about her the thing would be done, and there would be nothing the matter with him."

"There are twenty others, ever so much better than Ayala, would have him to-morrow," said his mother.

"And be glad to catch him," said Gertrude. "He's not like one of those who haven't got anything to make a wife comfortable with."

"As for Ayala," said Augusta, "she didn't deserve such good luck. I am told that that Colonel Stubbs can't afford to keep any kind of carriage for her. But then, to be sure, she has never been used to a carriage."

"Oh, Tom, do look up," said his mother, "and say that you will try to be happy."

"He'll be all right in New York," said Gertrude. "There's no place in the world, they say, where the girls put themselves forward so much, and make things so pleasant for the young men."

"He will soon find some one there," said Augusta, "with a deal more to say for herself than Ayala, and a great deal better-looking."

"I hope he will find some one who will really love him," said his mother.

Tom sat silent while he listened to all this encouragement, turning his face from one speaker to the other. It was continued, with many other similar promises of coming happiness, and assurances that he had been a gainer in losing all that he lost, when he suddenly turned sharply upon them, and strongly expressed his feelings to his sisters. "I don't believe that either of you know anything about it," he said.

"Don't know anything about what?" said Augusta, who as a lady who had been married over twelve months, and was soon about to become a mother, felt that she certainly did know all about it.

"Why don't we know as well as you?" asked Gertrude, who had also had her experiences.

"I don't believe you do know anything about it;—that's all," said Tom. "And now there's the cab. Good-bye, mother! Good-bye, Augusta. I hope you'll be all right." This alluded to the baby. "Good-bye, Gertrude. I hope you'll get all right too some day." This alluded to Gertrude's two lovers. Then he left them, and as he got into his cab declared to himself that neither of them had ever, or would ever, know anything of that special trouble which had so nearly overwhelmed himself.

"Upon my word, Tom," said his father, walking about the vessel with him, "I wish I were going to New York myself with you;—it all looks so comfortable."

"Yes," said Tom, "it's very nice."

"You'll enjoy yourself amazingly. There is that Mrs. Thompson has two as pretty daughters with her as ever a man wished to see." Tom shook his head. "And you're fond of smoking. Did you see the smoking-room? They've got everything on board these ships now. Upon my word I envy you the voyage."

"It's as good as anything else, I dare say," said Tom. "Perhaps it's better than London."

Then his father, who had been speaking aloud to him, whispered a word in his ear. "Shake yourself, Tom;—shake yourself, and get over it."

"I am trying," said Tom.

"Love is a very good thing, Tom, when a man can enjoy it, and make himself warm with it, and protect himself by it from selfishness and hardness of heart. But when it knocks a man's courage out of him, and makes him unfit for work, and leaves him to bemoan himself, there's nothing good in it. It's as bad as drink. Don't you know that I am doing the best I can for you, to make a man of you?"

"I suppose so."

"Then shake yourself, as I call it. It is to be done, if you set about it in earnest. Now, God bless you, my boy." Then Sir Thomas got into his boat, and left his son to go upon his travels and get himself cured by a change of scene.

I have no doubt that Tom was cured, if not before he reached New York, at any rate before he left that interesting city;—so that when he reached Niagara, which he did do in company with Mrs. Thompson and her charming daughters, he entertained no idea of throwing himself down the Falls. We cannot follow him on that prolonged tour to Japan and China, and thence to Calcutta and Bombay. I fancy that he did not go on to Cabul, as before that time the Ministry in England was unfortunately changed, and the Russians had not as yet been expelled from Asia;—but I have little doubt that he obtained a great deal of very useful mercantile information, and that he will live to have a comfortable wife and a large family, and become in the course of years the senior partner in the great house of Travers and Treason. Let us, who have soft hearts, now throw our old shoes after him.

CHAPTER XIX.

HOW VERY MUCH HE LOVED HER.

We have seen how Mr. Traffick was finally turned out of his father-in-law's house;—or, rather, not quite finally when we last saw him, as he continued to sleep at Queen's Gate for two or three nights after that, until he had found shelter for his head. This he did without encountering Sir Thomas, Sir Thomas pretending the while to believe that he was gone; and then in very truth his last pair of boots was removed. But his wife remained, awaiting the great occurrence with all the paternal comforts around her, Mr. Traffick having been quite right in surmising that the father would not expose his daughter in her delicate condition to the inclemencies of the weather.

But this no more than natural attention on the

part of the father and grandfather to the needs of his own daughter and grandchild did not in the least mitigate in the bosom of the Member of Parliament the wrath which he felt at his own expulsion. It was not, as he said to himself, the fact that he was expelled, but the coarseness of the language used. "The truth is," he said to a friend in the House, "that, though it was arranged I should remain there till after my wife's confinement, I could not bear his language." It will probably be acknowledged that the language was of a nature not to be borne.

When, therefore, Captain Batsby went down to the House on the day of Tom's departure to see his counsellor he found Mr. Traffick full rather of anger than of counsel. "Oh, yes," said the Member, walking with the Captain up and down some of the lobbies, "I spoke to him, and told him my mind very freely. When I say I'll do a thing, I always do it. And as for Tringle, nobody knows him better than I. It does not do to be afraid of him. There is a little bit of the cur about him."

"What did he say?"

"He didn't like it. The truth is——. You know I don't mind speaking to you openly."

"Oh, no," said Batsby.

"He thinks he ought to do as well with the second girl as he has done with the first." Captain Batsby at this opened his eyes, but he said nothing. Having a good income of his own, he thought much of it. Not being the younger son of a lord, and not being a Member of Parliament, he thought less of the advantages of those high privileges. It did not suit him, however, to argue the question at the present moment. "He is proud of his connection with our family, and looks perhaps even more than he ought to do to a seat in the House."

"I could get in myself if I cared for it," said Batsby.

"Very likely. It is more difficult than ever to find a seat just now. A family connection of course does help one. I had to trust to that a good deal before I was known myself."

"But what did Sir Thomas say?"

"He made himself uncommonly disagreeable;—I can tell you that. He couldn't very well abuse me, but he wasn't very particular in what he said about you. Of course he was cut up about the elopement. We all felt it. Augusta was very much hurt. In her precarious state it was so likely to do a mischief."

"It can't be undone now."

"No;—it can't be undone. But it makes one feel that you can't make a demand for money as though you set about it in the other way. When I made up my mind to marry I stated what I thought I had a right to demand, and I got it. He knew very well that I shouldn't take a shilling less. It does make a difference when he knows very well that you've got to marry the girl whether with or without money."

"I haven't got to marry the girl at all."

"Haven't you? I rather think you have, old fellow. It is generally considered that when a gentleman has gone off with a girl he means to marry her."

"Not if the father comes after her and brings her back."

"And when he has gone afterwards to the family house and proposed himself again in the mother's presence." In all this Mr. Traffick received an unfair advantage from the communications which were made to him by his wife. "Of course you must marry her. Sir Thomas knows that, and, knowing it, why should he be flush with his money? I never allowed myself to say a single word they could use against me till the ready-money-down had been all settled."

"What was it he did say?" Batsby was thoroughly sick of hearing his counsellor tell so many things as to his own prudence and his own success, and asked the question in an angry tone.

"He said that he would not consider the question of money at all till the marriage had been solemnised. Of course he stands on his right. Why shouldn't he? But, rough as he is, he isn't stingy. Give him his due. He isn't stingy. The money's there all right; and the girl is his own child. You'll have to wait his time;—that's all."

"And have nothing to begin with?"

"That'll be about it, I think. But what does it matter, Batsby? You are always talking about your income."

"No, I ain't; not half so much as you do of your seat in Parliament,—which everybody says you are likely to lose at the next election." Then, of course, there was a quarrel. Mr. Traffick took his offended dignity back to the House,—almost doubting whether it might not be his duty to bring Captain Batsby to the bar for contempt of privilege; and the Captain took himself off in thorough disgust.

Nevertheless there was the fact that he had engaged himself to the young lady a second time. He had run away with her with the object of marrying her, and had then, according to his own theory in such matters,—been relieved from his responsibility by the appearance of the father and the re-abduction of the young lady. As the young lady had been taken away from him it was to be supposed that the intended marriage was negatived by a proper authority. When starting for Brussels he was a free man; and had he been wise he would have remained there, or at some equally safe distance from the lady's charms. Then, from a distance, he might have made his demand for money, and the elopement would have operated in his favour rather than otherwise. But he had come back, and had foolishly allowed himself to be persuaded to show himself at Queen's Gate. He had obeyed Traffick's advice, and now Traffick had simply thrown him over and quarrelled with him. He had too promised, in the presence both of the mother and the married sister, that he would marry the young lady without any regard to money. He felt it all and was very angry with himself, consoling himself as best he might with the reflection that Sir Thomas's money was certainly safe, and that Sir Thomas himself was a liberal man. In his present condition it would be well for him, he thought, to remain inactive and see what circumstances would do for him.

But circumstances very quickly became active. On his return to his lodgings, after leaving Mr. Traffick, he found a note from Queen's Gate. "Dearest Ben,—Mamma wants you to come and lunch to-morrow. Papa has taken poor Tom down to Liverpool, and won't be back till dinner-time.—G." He did not do as he was bid, alleging some engagement of business. But the persecution was continued in such a manner as to show him that all opposition on his part would be hopeless unless he were to proceed on some tour as prolonged as that of his future brother-in-law. "Come and walk at three o'clock in Kensington Gardens to-morrow." This was written on the Saturday after his note had been received. What use would there be in continuing a vain fight? He was in their hands, and the more gracefully he yielded the more probable it would be that the father would evince his generosity at an early date. He therefore met his lady-love on the steps of the Albert Memorial, whither she had managed to take herself all alone from the door of the family mansion.

"Ben," she said, as she greeted him, "why did you not come for me to the house?"

"I thought you would like it best."

"Why should I like it best? Of course mamma knows all about it. Augusta would have come with me just to see me here, only that she cannot walk out just at present." Then he said something to her about the Monument, expressed his admiration of the Prince's back, abused the east wind, remarked that the buds were coming on some of the trees, and suggested that the broad road along by the Round Pond would be drier than the little paths. It was not interesting, as Gertrude felt; but she had not expected him to be interesting. The interest she knew must be contributed by herself. "Ben," she said, "I was so happy to hear what you said to mamma the other day."

"What did I say?"

"Why, of course, that, as papa has given his consent, our engagement is to go on just as if——"

"Just as if what?"

"As if we had found the clergyman at Ostend."

"If we had done that we should have been married now," suggested Batsby.

"Exactly. And it's almost as good as being married;—isn't it?"

"I suppose it comes to the same thing."

"Hadn't you better go to papa again and have it all finished?"

"He makes himself so very unpleasant."

"That's only because he wants to punish us for running away. I suppose it was wrong. I shall never be sorry, because it made me know how very, very much you loved me. Didn't it make you feel how very, very dearly I loved you,—to trust myself all alone with you in that way?"

"Oh, yes; of course."

"And papa can't bite you, you know. You go to him, and tell him that you hope to be received in the house as my,—my future husband, you know."

"Shall I say nothing else?"

"You mean about the day?"

"I was meaning about money."

"I don't think I would. He is very generous, but he does not like to be asked. When Augusta was to be married he arranged all that himself after they were engaged."

"But Traffick demanded a certain sum?" This question Captain Batsby asked with considerable surprise, remembering what Mr. Traffick had said to him in reference to Augusta's fortune.

"Not at all. Septimus knew nothing about it till after the engagement. He was only too glad to get papa's consent. You mustn't believe all that Septimus says, you know. You may be sure of this, —that you can trust papa's generosity." Then, before he landed her at the door in Queen's Gate, he had promised that he would make another journey to Lombard Street, with the express purpose of obtaining Sir Thomas's sanction to the marriage,— either with or without money.

"How are you again?" said Sir Thomas, when the Captain was for the third time shown into the little back parlour. "Have you had another trip to the continent since I saw you?" Sir Thomas was in a good humour. Tom had gone upon his travels; Mr. Traffick had absolutely taken himself out of the house; and the millions were accommodating themselves comfortably.

"No, Sir Thomas; I haven't been abroad since

then. I don't keep on going abroad constantly in that way."

"And what can I do for you now?"

"Of course it's about your daughter. I want to have your permission to consider ourselves engaged."

"I explained to you before that if you and Gertrude choose to marry each other I shall not stand in your way."

"Thank you, Sir."

"I don't know that it is much to thank me for. Only that she made a fool of herself by running away with you I should have preferred to wait till some more sensible candidate had proposed himself for her hand. I don't suppose you'll ever set the Thames on fire."

"I did very well in the army."

"It's a pity you did not remain there, and then, perhaps, you would not have gone to Ostend with my daughter. As it is, there she is. I think she might have done better with herself; but that is her fault. She has made her bed and she must lie upon it."

"If we are to be married I hope you won't go on abusing me always, Sir Thomas."

"That's as you behave. You didn't suppose that I should allow such a piece of tomfoolery as that to be passed over without saying anything about it! If you marry her and behave well to her I will——" Then he paused.

"What will you do, Sir Thomas?"

"I'll say as little as possible about the Ostend journey."

"And as to money, Sir Thomas?"

"I think I have promised quite enough for you. You are not in a position, Captain Batsby, to ask me as to money;—nor is she. You shall marry her without a shilling,—or you shall not marry her at all. Which is it to be? I must have an end put to all this. I won't have you hanging about my house unless I know the reason why. Are you two engaged to each other?"

"I suppose we are," said Batsby, lugubriously.

"Suppose is not enough."

"We are," said Batsby, courageously.

"Very well. Then, from this moment, Ostend shall be as though there weren't such a seaport anywhere in Europe. I will never allude to the place again,—unless, perhaps, you should come and stay with me too long when I am particularly anxious to get rid of you. Now you had better go and settle about the time and all that with Lady Tringle, and tell her that you mean to come and dine to-morrow or next day, or whenever it suits. Come and dine as often as you please, only do not bring your wife to live with me pertinaciously when you're not asked." All this Captain Batsby did not understand, but, as he left Lombard Street, he made up his mind that of all the men he had ever met, Sir Thomas Tringle, his future father-in-law, was the most singular. "He's a better fellow than Traffick," said Sir Thomas to himself when he was alone, "and as he has trusted me so far I'll not throw him over."

The Captain now had no hesitation in taking

himself to Queen's Gate. As he was to be married he might as well make the best of such delights as were to be found in the happy state of mutual affection. "My dear, dearest Benjamin, I am so happy," said Lady Tringle, dissolved in tears as she embraced her son-in-law that was to be. "You will always be so dear to me!" In this she was quite true. Traffick was not dear to her. She had at first thought much of Mr. Traffick's position and noble blood, but, of late, she too had become very tired of Mr. Traffick. Augusta took almost too much upon herself, and Mr. Traffick's prolonged presence had been an eyesore. Captain Batsby was softer, and would be much more pleasant as a son-in-law. Even the journey to Ostend had had a good effect in producing a certain humility.

"My dear Benjamin," said Augusta, "we shall always be so happy to entertain you as a brother. Mr. Traffick has a great regard for you, and said from the first that if you behaved as you ought to do after that little journey he would arrange that everything should go straight between you and papa. I was quite sure that you would come forward at once as a man."

But Gertrude's delight was, of course, the strongest, and Gertrude's welcoming the warmest, as was proper. "When I think of it," she said to him, "I don't know how I should ever have looked anybody in the face again,—after our going away with our things mixed up in that way."

"I am glad rather now that we didn't find the clergyman."

"Oh, certainly," said Gertrude. "I don't suppose anybody would have given me anything. Now there'll be a regular wedding, and, of course, there will be the presents."

"And, though nothing is to be settled, I suppose he will do something."

"And it would have been very dreadful, not having a regular trousseau," said Gertrude. "Mamma will, of course, do now just as she did about Augusta. He allowed her £300! Only think;—if we had been married at Ostend you would have had to buy things for me before the first month was out. I hadn't more than half-a-dozen pair of stockings with me."

"He can't but say now that we have done as he would have us," added the Captain. "I do suppose that he will not be so unnatural as not to give something when Augusta had £200,000."

"Indeed, she had not. But you'll see that sooner or later papa will do for me quite as well as for Augusta." In this way they were happy together, consoling each other for any little trouble which seemed for a while to cloud their joys, and basking in the full sunshine of their permitted engagement.

The day was soon fixed, but fixed not entirely in reference to the wants of Gertrude and her wedding. Lucy had also to be married from the same house, and the day for her marriage had already been arranged. Sir Thomas had ordered that everything should be done for Lucy as though she were a daughter of the house, and her wedding had been arranged for the last week in May. When he heard that Ayala and Colonel Stubbs were also engaged he was anxious that the two sisters should be "buckled," as he called it, on the same occasion, —and he magnanimously offered to take upon himself the entire expense of the double arrangement, intimating that the people in Kingsbury Crescent had hardly room enough for a wedding. But Ayala, acting probably under Stalham influences, would not consent to this. Lady Albury, who was now in London, was determined that Ayala's marriage should take place from her own house; and, as Aunt Margaret and Uncle Reginald had consented, that matter was considered as settled. But Sir Thomas, having fixed his mind upon a double wedding, resolved that Gertrude and Lucy should be the joint brides. Gertrude, who still suffered perhaps a little in public estimation from the Ostend journey, was glad enough to wipe out that stain as quickly as possible, and did not therefore object to the arrangement. But to the Captain there was something in it by which his more delicate feelings were revolted. It was a matter of course that Ayala should be present at her sister's wedding, and would naturally appear there in the guise of a bridesmaid. She would also, now, act as a bridesmaid to Gertrude,—her future position as Mrs. Colonel Stubbs giving her, as was supposed, sufficient dignity for that honourable employment. But Captain Batsby, not so very long ago, had appeared among the suitors for Ayala's hand; and therefore, as he said to Gertrude, he felt a little shamefaced about it. "What does that signify?" said Gertrude. "If you say nothing to her about it, I'll be bound she'll say nothing to you." And so it was on the day of the wedding. Ayala did not say a word to Captain Batsby, nor did Captain Batsby say very much to Ayala.

On the day before his marriage Captain Batsby paid a fourth visit to Lombard Street in obedience to directions from Sir Thomas. "There, my boy," said he, "though you and Gertrude did take a little journey on the sly to a place which we will not mention, you shan't take her altogether empty-handed." Then he explained certain arrangements which he had made for endowing Gertrude with an allowance, which under the circumstance the bridegroom could not but feel to be liberal. It must be added, that, considering the shortness of time allowed for getting them together, the amount of wedding presents bestowed was considered by Gertrude to be satisfactory. As Lucy's were exhibited at the same time the show was not altogether mean. "No doubt I had twice as much as the two put together," said Mrs. Traffick to Ayala up in her bedroom, "but then of course Lord Boardotrade's rank would make people give."

CHAPTER XX.

AYALA AGAIN IN LONDON.

AFTER that last walk in Gobblegoose Wood, after Lady Tringle's unnecessary journey to Stalham on the Friday, and the last day's hunting with Sir Harry's hounds,—which took place on the Saturday, Ayala again became anxious to go home. Her anxiety was in its nature very different from that which had prompted her to leave Stalham on an appointed day lest she should seem to be waiting for the coming of Colonel Stubbs. "No; I don't wan't to run away from him any more," she said to Lady Albury. "I want to be with him always, and I hope he won't run away from me. But I've got to be somewhere where I can think about it all for a little time."

"Can't you think about it here?"

"No;—one can never think about a thing where it has all taken place. I must be up in my own little room in Kingsbury Crescent, and must have Aunt Margaret's work around me,—so that I may realise what is going to come. Not but what I mean to do a great deal of work always."

"Mend his stockings?"

"Yes,—if he wears stockings. I know he doesn't. He always wears socks. He told me so. Whatever he has, I'll mend,—or make if he wants me.

'I can bake and I can brew,
And I can make an Irish stew;—
Wash a shirt, and iron it too.'"

Then, as she sang her little song, she clapped her hands together.

"Where did you get all your poetry?"

"He taught me that. We are not going to be fine people,—except sometimes when we may be invited to Stalham. But I must go on Thursday, Lady Albury. I came for a week, and I have been here ever since the middle of February. It seems years since the old woman told me I was perverse, and he said that she was right."

"Think how much you have done since that time."

"Yes, indeed. I very nearly destroyed myself; —didn't I?"

"Not very nearly."

"I thought I had. It was only when you showed me his letter on that Sunday morning that I began to have any hopes. I wonder what Mr. Greene preached about that morning. I didn't hear a word. I kept on repeating what he said in the postscript."

"Was there a postscript?"

"Of course there was. Don't you remember?"

"No, indeed; not I."

"The letter would have been nothing without the postscript. He said that Croppy was to come back for me. I knew he wouldn't say that unless he meant to be good to me. And yet I wasn't quite sure of it. I know it now; don't I? But I must go, Lady Albury. I ought to let Aunt Margaret know all about it." Then it was settled that she should go on the Thursday,—and on the Thursday she went. As it was now considered quite wrong that she should travel by the railway alone,—in dread, probably, lest the old lady should tell her again how perverse she had been,—Colonel Stubbs accompanied her. It had then been decided that the wedding must take place at Stalham, and many messages were sent to Mr. and Mrs. Dosett assuring them that they would be made very welcome on the occasion. "My own darling Lucy will be away at that time with her own young man," said Ayala, in answer to further invitations from Lady Albury.

"And so you've taken Colonel Stubbs at last," said her Aunt Margaret.

"He has taken me, aunt. I didn't take him."

"But you refused him ever so often."

"Well;—yes. I don't think I quite refused him."

"I thought you did."

"It was a dreadful muddle, Aunt Margaret;—but it has come right at last, and we had better not talk about that part of it."

"I was so sure you didn't like him."

"Not like him? I always liked him better than anybody else in the world that I ever saw."

"Dear me!"

"Of course I shouldn't say so if it hadn't come right at last. I may say whatever I please about it now, and I declare that I always loved him. A girl can be such a fool! I was, I know. I hope you are glad, aunt."

"Of course I am. I am glad of anything that makes you happy. It seemed such a pity that, when so many gentlemen were falling in love with you all round, you couldn't like anybody."

"But I did like somebody, Aunt Margaret. And I did like the best,—didn't I?" In answer to this Mrs. Dosett made no reply, having always had an aunt's partiality for poor Tom, in spite of all his chains.

Her uncle's congratulations were warmer even than her aunt's.

"My dear girl," he said, "I am rejoiced indeed that you should have before you such a prospect of happiness. I always felt how sad for you was your residence here, with two such homely persons as your aunt and myself."

"I have always been happy with you," said Ayala,—perhaps straining the truth a little in her anxiety to be courteous. "And I know," she added, "how much Lucy and I have always owed you since poor papa's death."

"Nevertheless, it has been dull for a young girl like you. Now you will have your own duties, and if you endeavour to do them properly the world will never be dull to you." And then there were some few words about the wedding. "We have no feeling, my dear," said her uncle, "except to do the best we can for you. We should have been glad to see you married from here if that had suited. But, as this lover of yours has grand friends of his own, I dare say their place may be the better." Ayala could hardly explain to her uncle that she had acceded to Lady Albury's proposal because, by doing so, she would spare him the necessary expense of the wedding.

But Ayala's great delight was in meeting her sister. The two girls had not seen each other since the engagement of either of them had been ratified by their friends. The winter and spring, as passed by Lucy at Merle Park, had been very unhappy for her. Things at Merle Park had not been pleasant to any of the residents there, and Lucy had certainly had her share of the unpleasantness. Her letters to Ayala had not been triumphant when Aunt Emmeline had more than once expressed her wish to be rid of her, and when the news reached her that Uncle Tom and Hamel had failed to be gracious to each other. Nor had Ayala written in a spirit of joy before she had been able to recognise the Angel of Light in Jonathan Stubbs. But now they were to meet after all their miseries, and each could be triumphant.

It was hard for them to know exactly how to begin. To Lucy, Isadore Hamel was, at the present moment, the one hero walking the face of this sublunary globe; and to Ayala, as we all know, Jonathan Stubbs was an Angel of Light, and, therefore, more even than a hero. As each spoke, the "He's" intended took a different personification; so that to any one less interested than the young ladies themselves there might be some confusion as to which "He" might at that moment be under discussion. "It was bad," said Lucy, "when Uncle

Tom told him to sell those magnificent conceptions of his brain by auction!"

"I did feel for him certainly," said Ayala.

"And then when he was constrained to say that he would take me at once without any preparation because Aunt Emmeline wanted me to go, I don't suppose any man ever behaved more beautifully than he did."

"Yes indeed," said Ayala. And then she felt herself constrained to change the subject by the introduction of an exaggerated superlative in her sister's narrative. Hamel, no doubt, had acted beautifully, but she was not disposed to agree that nothing could be more beautiful. "Oh, Lucy," she said, "I was so miserable when he went away after that walk in the wood. I thought he never would come back again when I had behaved so badly. But he did. Was not that grand in him?"

"I suppose he was very fond of you."

"I hope he was. I hope he is. But what should I have done if he had not come back? No other man would have come back after that. You never behaved unkindly to Isadore?"

"I think he would have come back a thousand times," said Lucy; "only I cannot imagine that I should ever have given him the necessity of coming back even a second. But then I had known him so much longer."

"It wasn't that I hadn't known him long enough," said Ayala. "I seemed to know all about him almost all at once. I knew how good he was, and how grand he was, long before I had left the

Marchesa up in London. But I think it astounded me that such a one as he should care for me." And so it went on through an entire morning, each of the sisters feeling that she was bound to listen with rapt attention to the praises of the other's "him" if she wished to have an opportunity of singing those of her own.

But Lucy's marriage was to come first by more than two months, and therefore in that matter she was allowed precedence. And at her marriage Ayala would be present, whereas with Ayala's Lucy would have no personal concern. Though she did think that Uncle Tom had been worse than any Vandal in that matter of selling her lover's magnificent works, still she was ready to tell of his generosity. In a manner of his own he had sent the money which Hamel had so greatly needed, and had now come forward to provide, with a generous hand, for the immediate necessities, and more than the necessities, of the wedding. It was not only that she was to share the honours of the two wedding-cakes with Gertrude, and that she was to be taken as a bride from the gorgeous mansion in Queen's Gate, but that he had provided for her bridal needs almost as fully as for those of his own daughter. "Never mind what she'll be able to do afterwards," he said to his wife, who ventured on some slight remonstrance with him as to the unnecessary luxuries he was preparing for the wife of a poor man. "She won't be the worse for having a dozen new petticoats in her trunk, and, if she don't want to blow her nose with as many handkerchiefs this year as Gertrude does, she'll be able to keep them for next year." Then Aunt Emmeline obeyed without further hesitation the orders which were given her.

Nor was his generosity confined to the niece who for the last twelve months had been his property. Lucy was still living in Queen's Gate, though at this time she spent much of each day in Kingsbury Crescent, and on one occasion she brought with her a little note from Uncle Tom. "Dear Ayala," said the little note,

"As you are going to be married too, you, I suppose, will want some new finery. I therefore send a cheque. Write your name on the back of it, and give it to your uncle. He will let you have the money as you want it.

"Yours affectionately,

"T. Tringle."

"I hope your Colonel Stubbs will come and see me some day."

"You must go and see him," she said to her Colonel Stubbs, when he called one day in Kingsbury Crescent. "Only for him I shouldn't have any clothes to speak of at all, and I should have to be married in my old brown morning frock."

"It would be just as good as any other for my purpose," said the Colonel.

"But it wouldn't for mine, Sir. Fine feathers make fine birds, and I mean to be as fine as Lady Albury's big peacock. So if you please you'll go to Queen's Gate, and Lombard Street too, and show yourself. Oh, Jonathan, I shall be so proud that everybody who knows me should see what sort of a man has chosen to love me."

Then there was a joint visit paid by the two sisters to Mr. Hamel's studio,—an expedition which was made somewhat on the sly. Aunt Margaret in Kingsbury Crescent knew all about it, but Aunt Emmeline was kept in the dark. Even now, though the marriage was sanctioned and was so nearly at hand, Aunt Emmeline would not have approved of such a visit. She still regarded the sculptor as improper,—at any rate not sufficiently proper to be treated with full familiarity,—partly on account of his father's manifest improprieties, and partly because of his own relative poverty and unauthorised position in the world. But Aunt Margaret was more tolerant, and thought that the sister-in-law was entitled to visit the workshop in which her sister's future bread was to be earned. And then, starting from Kingsbury Crescent, they could go in a cab; whereas any such proceeding emanating from Queen's Gate would have required the carriage. There was a wickedness in this starting off in a Hansom cab to call on an unmarried young man, doing it in a manner successfully concealed from Aunt Emmeline, on which Ayala expatiated with delight when she next saw Colonel Stubbs.

"You don't come and call on me," said the Colonel.

"What!—all the way down to Aldershot? I should like, but I don't quite dare to do that."

The visit was very successful. Though it was

expected, Hamel was found in his artist's costume, with a blouse or loose linen tunic fitted close round his throat, and fastened with a belt round his waist. Lucy thought that in this apparel he was certainly as handsome as could ever have been any Apollo,—and, so thinking, had contrived her little plans in such a way that he should certainly be seen at his best. To her thinking Colonel Stubbs was not a handsome man. Hamel's hair was nearly black, and she preferred dark hair. Hamel's features were regular, whereas the Colonel's hair was red, and he was known for a large mouth and broad nose, which were not obliterated though they were enlightened by the brightness of his eyes. "Yes," said Ayala to herself, as she looked at Hamel; "he is very good looking, but nobody would take him for an Angel of Light."

"Ayala has come to see you at your work," said Lucy, as they entered the studio.

"I am delighted to see her. Do you remember where we last met, Miss Dormer?"

"Miss Dormer, indeed," said Ayala. "I am not going to call you Mr. Hamel. Yes; it was high up among the seats of the Coliseum. There has a great deal happened to us all since then."

"And I remember you at the bijou."

"I should think so. I knew then so well what was going to happen," said Ayala.

"What did you know?"

"That you and Lucy were to fall in love with each other."

"I had done my part of it already," said he.

"Hardly that, Isadore," said Lucy, "or you would not have passed me in Kensington Gardens without speaking to me."

"But I did speak to you. It was then I learned where to find you."

"That was the second time. If I had remained away, as I ought to have done, I suppose you never would have found me."

Ayala was then taken round to see all those magnificent groups and figures which Sir Thomas would have disposed of at so many shillings apiece under the auctioneer's hammer. "It was cruel,—was it not?" said Lucy.

"He never saw them, you know," said Ayala, putting in a goodnatured word for her uncle.

"If he had," said the sculptor, "he would have doubted the auctioneer's getting anything. I have turned it all in my mind very often since, and I think that Sir Thomas was right."

"I am sure he was wrong," said Lucy. "He is very goodnatured, and nobody can be more grateful to another person than I am to him;—but I don't agree that he was right about that."

"He never would have said it if he had seen them," again pleaded Ayala.

"They will never fetch anything as they are," continued the sculptor, "and I don't suppose that when I made them I thought they would. They have served their purpose, and I sometimes feel inclined to break them up and have them carted away."

"Isadore!" exclaimed Lucy.

"For what purpose?" asked Ayala.

"They were the lessons which I had to teach myself, and the play which I gave to my imagination. Who wants a great figure of Beelzebub like that in his house?"

"I call it magnificent," said Ayala.

"His name is Lucifer,—not Beelzebub," said Lucy. "You call him Beelzebub merely to make little of him."

"It is difficult to do that, because he is nearly ten feet high. And who wants a figure of Bacchus? The thing is, whether, having done a figure of Bacchus, I may not be better able to do a likeness of Mr. Jones, when he comes to sit for his bust at the request of his admiring friends. For any further purpose that it will answer, Bacchus might just as well be broken up and carted away in the dust-cart." To this, however, the two girls expressed their vehement opposition, and were of opinion that the time would come when Beelzebub and Bacchus, transferred to marble, would occupy places of honour in some well-proportioned hall built for the purpose of receiving them. "I shall be quite content," said Hamel, "if the whole family of the Jones's will have their busts done about the size of life, and stand them up over their bookshelves. My period for Beelzebubs has gone by." The visit, on the whole, was delightful. Lucy was contented with the almost more than divine beauty of her lover, and the two sisters, as they made their return journey to Kingsbury Crescent in another Hansom, discussed questions of art in a spirit that would have been delightful to any aspiring artist who might have heard them.

Then came the wedding, of which some details were given at the close of the last chapter, at which two brides who were very unlike to each other were joined in matrimony to two bridegrooms as dissimilar. But the Captain made himself gracious to the sculptor who was now to be connected with him, and declared that he would always look upon Lucy as a second sister to his dear Gertrude. And Gertrude was equally gracious, protesting, when she was marshalled to walk up to the altar first, that she did not like to go before her darling Lucy. But the dimensions of the church admitted but of one couple at a time, and Gertrude was compelled to go in advance. Colonel Stubbs was there acting as best man to Hamel, while Lord John Battledore performed the same service for Captain Batsby. Lord John was nearly broken-hearted by the apostacy of a second chum, having heard that the girl whom Frank Houston had not succeeded in marrying was now being taken by Batsby without a shilling. "Somebody had to bottle-hold for him," said Lord John, defending himself at the club afterwards, "and I didn't like to throw the fellow over, though he is such a fool! And there was Stubbs, too," continued his Lordship, "going to take the other girl without a shilling! There's Stubbs, and

Houston, and Batsby, all gone and drowned themselves. It's just the same as though they'd drowned themselves!" Lord John was horrified,—nay, disgusted,—by the folly of the world. Nevertheless, before the end of the year, he was engaged to marry a very pretty girl as devoid of fortune as our Ayala.

CHAPTER XXI.

AYALA'S MARRIAGE.

Now we have come to our last chapter, and it may be doubted whether any reader,—unless he be some one specially gifted with a genius for statistics, —will have perceived how very many people have been made happy by matrimony. If marriage be the proper ending for a novel,—the only ending, as this writer takes it to be, which is not discordant, —surely no tale was ever so properly ended, or with so full a concord, as this one. Infinite trouble has been taken not only in arranging these marriages but in joining like to like,—so that, if not happiness, at any rate sympathetic unhappiness, might be produced. Our two sisters will, it is trusted, be happy. They have chosen men from their hearts, and have been chosen after the same fashion. Those two other sisters have been so wedded that the one will follow the idiosyncrasies of her husband, and the other bring her husband to follow her idiosyncrasies, without much danger of mutiny or revolt. As to Miss Docimer there must be room for fear. It may be questioned whether she was not worthy of a better lot than has been achieved for her by joining her fortunes to those of Frank Houston. But I, speaking for myself, have my hopes of Frank Houston. It is hard to rescue a man from the slough of luxury and idleness combined. If anything can do it, it is a cradle filled annually. It may be that he will yet learn that a broad back with a heavy weight upon it gives the best chance of happiness here below. Of Lord John's married prospects I could not say much as he came so very lately on the scene; but even he may perhaps do something in the world when he finds that his nursery is filling.

For our special friend Tom Tringle, no wife has been found. In making his effort,—which he did manfully,—he certainly had not chosen the consort who would be fit for him. He had not seen clearly, as had done his sisters and cousins. He had fallen in love too young,—it being the nature of young men to be much younger than young ladies, and, not knowing himself, had been as might be a barn-door cock who had set his heart upon some azure-plumaged, high-soaring lady of the woods. The lady with the azure plumes had, too, her high-soaring tendencies, but she was enabled by true insight to find the male who would be fit for her. The barn-door cock, when we left him on board the steamer going to New York, had not yet learned the nature of his own requirements. The knowledge will come to him. There may be doubts as to Frank Houston, but we think that there need be none as to Tom Tringle. The proper wife will be forthcoming; and in future years, when he will probably have a Glenbogie and a Merle Park of his own, he will own that Fortune did well for him in making his cousin Ayala so stern to his prayers.

But Ayala herself,—Ayala our pet heroine,—had not been yet married when the last chapter was written, and now there remains a page or two in which the reader must bid adieu to her as she stands at the altar with her Angel of Light. She was at Stalham for a fortnight before her marriage, in order, as Lady Albury said, that the buxom ladysmaid might see that everything had been done rightly in reference to the trousseau. "My dear," said Lady Albury, "it is important, you know. I dare say you can bake and brew, because you say so; but you don't know anything about clothes." Ayala, who by this time was very intimate with her friend, pouted her lips, and said that if "Jonathan did not like her things as she chose to have them he might do the other thing." But Lady Albury had her way, inducing Sir Harry to add something even to Uncle Tom's liberality, and the buxom woman went about her task in such a fashion that if Colonel Stubbs were not satisfied he must have been a very unconscionable Colonel. He probably would know nothing about it,—except that his bride in her bridal array had not looked so well as in any other garments, which, I take it, is invariably the case,—till at the end of the first year a glimmer of the truth as to a lady's wardrobe would come upon him. "I told you there would be a many new dresses before two years were over, Miss," said the buxom female, as she spread all the frocks and all the worked petticoats and all the collars and all the silk stockings and all the lace handkerchiefs about the bedroom to be inspected by Lady Albury,

Mrs. Gosling, and one or two other friends, before they were finally packed up.

Then came the day on which the Colonel was to reach Stalham, that day being a Monday, whereas the wedding was to take place on Wednesday. It was considered to be within the bounds of propriety that the Colonel should sleep at Stalham on the Monday, under the same roof with his bride; but on the Tuesday it was arranged that he should satisfy the decorous feeling of the neighbourhood by removing himself to the parsonage, which was distant about half-a-mile across the park, and was contiguous to the church. Here lived Mr. Greene, the bachelor curate, the rector of the parish being an invalid and absent in Italy.

"I don't see why he is to be sent away after dinner to walk across the park in the dark," said Ayala, when the matter was discussed before the Colonel's coming.

"It is a law, my dear," said Lady Albury, "and has to be obeyed whether you understand it or not, like other laws. Mr. Greene will be with him, so that no one shall run away with him in the dark. Then he will be able to go into church without dirtying his dress boots."

"But I thought there would be half-a-dozen carriages at least."

"But there won't be room in one of them for him. He is to be nobody until he comes forth from the church as your husband. Then he is to be everybody. That is the very theory of marriage."

* * * * *

"I think we managed it all very well between us," said Lady Albury afterwards, "but you really cannot guess the trouble we took."

"Why should there have been trouble?"

"Because you were such a perverse creature, as the old lady said. I am not sure that you were not right, because a girl does so often raise herself in her lover's estimation by refusing him half-a-dozen times. But you were not up to that."

"Indeed I was not. I am sure I did not intend to give any trouble to anybody."

"But you did. Only think of my going up to London to meet him, and of him coming from Aldershot to meet me, simply that we might put our heads together how to overcome the perversity of such a young woman as you!" There then came a look almost of pain on Ayala's brow. "But I do believe it was for the best. In this way he came to understand how absolutely necessary you were to him."

"Am I necessary to him?"

"He thinks so."

"Oh, if I can only be necessary to him always! But there should have been no going up to London. I should have rushed into his arms at once."

"That would have been unusual."

"But so is he unusual," said Ayala.

It is probable that the Colonel did not enjoy his days at Stalham before his marriage, except during the hour or two in which he was allowed to take Ayala out for a last walk. Such days can hardly be agreeable to the man of whom it is known by all around him that he is on the eve of committing matrimony. There is always, on such occasions, a feeling of weakness, as though the man had been subdued, brought at length into a cage and tamed, so as to be made fit for domestic purposes, and deprived of his ancient freedom amongst the woods;—whereas the girl feels herself to be the triumphant conqueror, who has successfully performed this great act of taming. Such being the case, the man had perhaps better keep away till he is forced to appear at the church-door.

Nevertheless our Colonel did enjoy his last walk. "Oh, yes," she said, "of course we will go to the old wood. Where else? I am so glad that poor fox went through Gobblegoose;—otherwise we should never have gone there, and then who knows whether you and I would ever have been friends again any more?"

"If one wood hadn't been there, I think another would have been found."

"Ah, that's just it. You can know that you had a purpose, and perhaps were determined to carry it out."

"Well, rather."

"But I couldn't be sure of that. I couldn't carry out my purpose, even if I had one. I had to doubt, and to be unhappy, and to hate myself, because I had been perverse. I declare, I do think you men have so much the best of it. How glorious would it have been to be able to walk straight up and say, Jonathan Stubbs, I love you better than all the world. Will you be my husband?"

"But suppose the Jonathan Stubbs of the occasion were to decline the honour. Where would you be then?"

"That would be disagreeable," said Ayala.

"It is disagreeable,—as you made me feel twice over."

"Oh, Jonathan, I am so sorry."

"Therefore it is possible that you may have the best of it."

* * * * *

"And so you never will take another walk with Ayala Dormer?" she said, as they were returning home.

"Never another," he replied.

"You cannot think how I regret it. Of course I am glad to become your wife. I do not at all want to have it postponed. But there is something so sweet in having a lover;—and you know that though I shall have a husband I shall never have a lover again,—and I never had one before, Jonathan. There has been very little of it. When a thing has been so sweet it is sad to think that it must be gone for ever!" Then she leaned upon him with both her hands, and looked up at him and smiled, with her lips a little open,—as she knew that he liked her to lean upon him and to look,—for she had caught by her instinct the very nature of the man, and knew how to witch him with her little charms. "Ah me! I wonder whether you'll like me to lean upon you when a dozen years have gone by."

"That depends on how heavy you may be."

"I shall be a fat old woman, perhaps. But I

shall lean upon you,—always, always. What else shall I ever have to lean upon now?"

"What else should you want?"

"Nothing,—nothing,—nothing! I want nothing else. I wonder whether there is anybody in all the world who has got so completely everything that she ever dreamed of wanting as I have. But if you could have been only my lover for a little longer——!" Then he assured her that he would be her lover just the same, even though they were husband and wife. Alas, no! There he had promised more than it is given to a man to perform. Faith, honesty, steadiness of purpose, joined to the warmest love and the truest heart, will not enable a husband to maintain the sweetness of that aroma which has filled with delight the senses of the girl who has leaned upon his arm as her permitted lover.

"What a happy fellow you are!" said Mr. Greene, as, in the intimacy of the moment, they walked across the park together.

"Why don't you get a wife for yourself?"

"Yes; with £120 a-year!"

"With a little money you might."

"I don't want to have to look for the money; and if I did I shouldn't get it. I often think how very unfairly things are divided in this world."

"That will all be made up in the next."

"Not if one covets one's neighbour's wife,—or even his ass," said Mr. Greene.

On the return of the two lovers to the house from their walk there were Mr. and Mrs. Dosett, who would much rather have stayed away had they not been unwilling not to show their mark of affection to their niece. I doubt whether they were very happy, but they were at any rate received with every distinction. Sir Thomas and Aunt Emmeline were asked, but they made some excuse. Sir Thomas knew very well that he had nothing in common with Sir Harry Albury; and, as for Aunt Emmeline, her one journey to Stalham had been enough for her. But Sir Thomas was again very liberal, and sent down as his contribution to the wedding presents the very necklace which Ayala had refused from her cousin Tom. "Upon my word, your uncle is magnificent," said Lady Albury, upon which the whole story was told to her. Lucy and her husband were away on their tour, as were Gertrude and hers on theirs. This was rather a comfort, as Captain Batsby's presence at the house would have been a nuisance. But there was quite enough of guests to make the wedding, as being a country wedding, very brilliant. Among others, old Tony Tappett was there, mindful of the manner in which Cranbury Brook had been ridden, and of Croppy's presence when the hounds ran their fox into Dillsborough Wood. "I hope she be to ride with us, off and on, Colonel," said Tony, when the ceremony had been completed.

"Now and then, Tony, when we can get hold of Croppy."

"Because, when they come out like that, Colonel, it's a pity to lose 'em, just because they's got their husbands to attend to."

And Lord Rufford was there, with his wife, who on this occasion was very pressing with her invitations. She had heard that Colonel Stubbs was likely to rise high in his profession, and there were symptoms, of which she was an excellent judge, that Mrs. Colonel Stubbs would become known as a professional beauty. And Larry Twentyman was there, who, being in the neighbourhood, was, to his great delight, invited to the breakfast.

Thus, to her own intense satisfaction, Ayala was handed over to her

ANGEL OF LIGHT.

THE END.

Made in the USA
Lexington, KY
19 March 2014